PRAISE FOR VALERIE WOLZIEN AND HER NOVELS

"Valerie Wolzien is a consummate crime writer. Her heroines sparkle as they sift through clues and stir up evidence in the darker, deadly side of suburbia."

—MARY DAHEIM

"Wit is Wolzien's strong suit. . . . Her portrayal of small-town life will prompt those of us in similar situations to agree that we too have been there and done that."

—*The Mystery Review*

"Domestic mysteries, with their emphasis on everyday people and everyday events, are very popular and the Susan Henshaw stories are some of the best in this subgenre."

—*Romantic Times*

By Valerie Wolzien
Published by Ballantine Books

DEATH
IN
DUPLICATE

A NOVEL

VALERIE WOLZIEN

FAWCETT

BALLANTINE BOOKS • NEW YORK

A Fawcett Books Mass Market Original

Copyright © 2005 by Valerie Wolzien

Published in the United States by Fawcett Books, an imprint of The Random House Publishing Group, a division of Random House, Inc., New York.

Fawcett is a registered trademark and the Fawcett colophon is a trademark of Random House, Inc.

ISBN 0-345-46808-2

Printed in the United States of America

Ballantine Books website address: www.ballantinebooks.com

OPM   9   8   7   6   5   4   3   2   1

DEATH
IN
DUPLICATE

PROLOGUE

Hartford Daily News
July 14, 2003
Perry Island, Connecticut
This small community was shaken over the weekend by the news that three residents of the Perry Island Care Center, the only nursing facility located on the island, have died "in a suspicious manner" over the past few months.

When questioned, a spokesman for the local police department admitted that there has been official interest in the deaths, but declined to discuss further details until their investigation is complete.

The owners of the facility were unwilling to comment other than to say that their family had provided the best care anywhere for almost nine decades and they planned to continue doing so to the best of their abilities.

TWO PEOPLE STARED AT THE FRONT-PAGE STORY. THEY WERE both frowning. The young woman whose red braids were wrapped around her head in an attractive but decidedly unfashionable style spoke first. "This is terrible."

She had spoken quietly, but her companion didn't follow her lead.

"Yeah. More for me than you though." His hair, spiky and

black, contrasted dramatically with his pale skin and light azure eyes.

Her eyes flicked to his face. "Why? Why should this affect you more than anyone else in the family?"

"Don't look at me like that. I didn't kill anybody. Not that anyone is going to believe me."

"Why not?" Her voice rose and her anxiety was unmistakable. "You're clean. You're going to meetings. You've gotten your life together. Why should anyone suspect you of anything?"

He brushed his hair off his forehead with a tattooed hand. "Yeah. Right. Reformed junkie—just what the police are looking for. You're nuts if you think I'm hanging around to take the rap for this crap—"

"But you can't leave! They'll think you're running away, that you're guilty."

He shrugged his thin shoulders. "They'll think it anyway."

"But where are you going to go? How are you going to earn a living?"

"Who knows? I'll manage." A smile appeared on his face, transforming his dour expression, and his companion couldn't help but smile in return. "You know me. Babe magnet. There's lots of babes out there and one of them is gonna be lucky enough to take care of me. Maybe I'll find a rich old woman looking for a thrill."

"But you'll keep in touch? You'll let me know you're okay?"

"Let you know I'm clean, you mean."

"That's not what I said." But her denial came too quickly and they both knew it was exactly what she meant.

ONE

THE DAY SUSAN HENSHAW BECAME A GRANDMOTHER STARTED out badly.

"My cell phone is broken," she announced, giving the little silver disk one last shake.

"Susan, it's barely six AM. It's much, much too early to be calling anyone. Besides, there's a perfectly good phone on your nightstand. What do you need your cell phone for?" Her husband rolled over and pulled his head out from under a large down pillow.

"Jed, it's April eighth! The baby is due! Any minute now Stephen could be calling to tell us that Chrissy is in the hospital giving birth!" Susan jumped out of bed. Her long cotton nightgown billowed behind her as she stalked across the Aubusson carpet, smacking her phone with the palm of her hand and frowning.

"Aren't you the attractive woman who was telling me just last night that first babies are rarely born on time so we shouldn't get excited too early?"

"Rarely born on time does not mean never born on time! And I don't want to miss the call!" Susan yelled from the large walk-in closet she and her husband shared.

"You're not going to miss anything. There's a phone right

by the bed!" he pointed out again, abandoning the idea of getting any more sleep and sitting up.

Susan reappeared wearing a navy sweat suit, a huge stuffed dog clasped in her arms. "Do you think this might be a mistake? Is it scary? Do you think the baby will like it?" she asked, ignoring his statement.

"Clue certainly doesn't." The Henshaws' golden retriever had climbed into bed the second Susan left, settling down into a warm spot. One of the mildest of dogs, Clue was staring at the toy and growling softly. "And to be honest, I don't understand why a baby who is going to live with two huge, breathing bullmastiffs would want a dog made of fake fur."

Susan sighed. "I'm hoping Chrissy and Stephen will decide that a baby is more than enough work and find new homes for Rock and Roll," she explained, referring to the humongous dogs that had been a wedding present from her daughter's in-laws.

"Chrissy and Stephen love those dogs."

"I know. But they're a lot of work. And Chrissy is going to be so busy with the baby and Stephen's going to have a new job soon and they're really going to have to find a bigger apartment once the baby begins crawling around, and . . ."

"And you and Clue would prefer those dogs to vanish."

"Without a doubt. Anyway," Susan said, "Rock and Roll aren't what's worrying me right now. I'm worried that Stephen won't be able to get through to my cell. I suppose I could stay home by the phone all day, but I did have plans."

"So take my cell phone and do what you have to do. I'll be at the office and Stephen can call there and then I can call you."

But Susan was still involved in her own thoughts. "Or maybe he could e-mail me on my Clié," she muttered, picking a small rectangle off her dresser and flipping it open. "Do you think he'll have access to an online computer in the maternity ward?"

"It's always possible, but—"

"And he could certainly leave a voice mail message." Susan sat down in a window seat and pulled on her running shoes.

"Yes, but—"

"I suppose I shouldn't worry so much. The baby probably won't be born today anyway. I'll buy a new cell phone at the mall this afternoon."

"You might just remember to plug your old one in tonight." Jed was staring at the small screen on Susan's phone.

"I plugged it in!"

"Yes, you did." Now Jed was kneeling on the floor beside their king-size bed. "You plugged your phone into the charger. But tonight you might try plugging the charger into the wall outlet." He waved her unconnected charger in the air.

"Oh, I thought I had. Well, at least I won't have to buy another phone. I have enough to do today."

"What are you planning?"

"Well, I'm going to walk Clue and then meet Kathleen for breakfast after she drops her kids off at school. Then we're going shopping. We have a long list of things to buy. We're going to the bookstore first because it's really never too early to begin caring about reading. And I'm dying to buy some books for the baby. And I might pick up a few mysteries for myself at the same time. Then we're heading to Born Yesterday to look at their baby quilts. I just wish I knew whether to buy blue or pink." She stopped talking and looked up at her husband.

"Don't you think it's a little odd that Chrissy and Stephen

don't want to know the sex of their baby? I mean, they're usually such a modern couple and the technology is available and it would be much easier to shop for the baby if we knew its sex. Besides picking out names—"

"I can't say I disagree with you, but it's their decision, not ours."

"Well, because we don't know what sex the baby is, Kathleen and I are going to pick out two quilts—one blue, one pink. Then we can call the store when the baby is born and they'll have the appropriate one personalized once we know the baby's name. And they have the sweetest mobiles. I was thinking of picking out two . . . to match the quilts, of course. And the dry cleaner is just around the corner from there and I have to pick up the baby afghan that I made for Chrissy—it's being cleaned so that I can take it down for her to use for her own baby—it's yellow so it's fine for a girl or a boy. And the jewelry store is a few blocks away from the cleaners. I'll pick up the earrings I ordered for Chrissy and talk to the owners about a charm to add to Mother's bracelet—although we'll have to know the baby's name to finalize that, too. . . ." She took a deep breath. "And then we're going to go to Healthy Home, that new ecological housewares store that everyone has been talking about, and see what sort of cleansers they have for the baby's room. And for our rugs. They need cleaning soon, Jed, and I don't want the rug cleaner using anything that might make the baby ill when he—or she—starts to crawl. And then—"

"By the time you finish telling me what you're going to do, I'll late for work. Why don't we meet at the inn for dinner tonight and you can tell me over a glass of wine all that you accomplished."

"I guess. I'll come home and pick up my cell phone before

meeting you there. That way I'll be sure to have a fully charged phone with me at all times." Susan carefully plugged both ends of the charger into the correct outlets.

"Good thinking."

"See you tonight then," Susan said, starting for the door.

"Aren't you forgetting something?"

"No. I have your cell phone and my Clié. Turn the answering machine on when you leave and I'll check when I come home. I think I'm fine."

"I thought you were going to walk Clue first thing." Jed was grinning.

Susan stopped and looked at the dog, now lying in the middle of the bed, eyes closed. "I almost forgot!" She laughed. "Come on, Clue. Let's hit the road."

The restaurant was out of her favorite orange popovers. "I guess I'll have the buckwheat waffle with fresh fruit," Susan told the waiter.

"And I'll have the feta and spinach omelet with grapefruit juice," Kathleen said. As soon as they were alone again, she leaned across the table to continue their discussion. "So, why do you think the baby is a girl?"

"I was talking with Chrissy on the phone recently . . . a few days ago . . . well, yesterday afternoon actually—"

"I know. Jed told Jerry that you were calling daily . . . and I would too, if I was about to become a grandmother at any minute," Kathleen assured her friend. "Did you have some sort of premonition or did Chrissy say something that convinced you she knows the sex of her baby?"

"It was something Chrissy said. I was talking about the blanket that I knit for her when she was born—you know, telling her that I was having it cleaned and would bring it along when we went down there—and she asked if it was pink."

"And?"

"That's it. She asked if it was pink. Now why would she do that if she didn't want a pink blanket for a baby girl?"

"Because she didn't want pink for a baby boy?" Kathleen suggested.

Susan frowned. "I suppose that could be it."

"Are you going to be terribly disappointed if it's a boy?'

"No! Of course not! I'd just like to know. It was impossible to find out the sex of the baby when I was pregnant, but now things are different. You knew the sex of both your kids before they were born. It didn't make the birth one bit less important, did it?"

"No, but I really wanted to know. If Chrissy and Stephen don't—"

"I know. I know. I'm just obsessing about all this because . . . well, I'm not really sure why in fact."

"Are you concerned about being a grandmother? You know, getting old?"

"Hey, are you a grandmother?" their waiter asked, reappearing with their juice.

"Almost. Do I look like one?" Susan asked modestly.

He shrugged. "You don't look like my grandmother. She's really young. Do you ladies want more coffee?"

"I think we're fine. But perhaps you could check on our meals? We have a lot to do today," Kathleen said.

"And some of us don't get around as quickly as we did when we were younger," Susan added.

Despite Susan's comment, she and Kathleen got around just fine. Susan arrived home with the back of her Cherokee completely filled with various items for the baby. The two pairs of shoes and six mystery novels she had bought for herself were lying on the seat beside her purse. As she pulled into the driveway, Jed appeared at the front door, a wide smile on his face. She slammed on the brake and, heart beating rapidly, ran up the walkway to her house.

TWO

THEY WERE BEAUTIFUL.

"They're the most beautiful babies in the nursery." The speaker was male.

"They're the most beautiful babies in the world," replied a female voice.

Susan and Jed pulled themselves away from their enchanting view into the newborn nursery and turned to see who was reading their minds. They found themselves face-to-face with their daughter's in-laws.

"Blues!"

"Susan!"

"Rhythm!"

"Jed!"

The four grandparents hugged, turned back to admire their gorgeous grandchildren, and then, laughing, hugged again.

"Isn't it amazing how much more alert they seem than the other babies?" Susan said.

"And they have much more hair," Robert Canfield said. Better known as Rhythm, he had not quite recovered from growing up in the Sixties and was, Susan thought, inordinately proud of his own shoulder-length hair.

"Look at those pretty pink cheeks!" Susan said.

"Yes, their color is excellent," Blues (also known as Barbara) agreed. "I sent Chrissy some of my special compounded vitamins. They're entirely herbal—nothing unnatural and not yet available commercially—and they do seem to have made such a difference. The other babies are absolutely peaked."

Susan, who knew that Chrissy had tossed Blues's vitamins into the garbage and continued to take what her obstetrician had prescribed, didn't argue about the twins' appearance. "They certainly seem to be healthy."

"And Chrissy looks wonderful!" Blues added.

"Oh, when did you see her?" Susan asked immediately.

"This morning," Rhythm answered. "One thing about the red-eye from California—you get in early. We made it to the hospital by seven. Chrissy was still asleep—"

"And we were careful not to wake her up. We left a small present and a note on the table beside her bed and tiptoed right out of the room," Blues added. "But she did look wonderful. Stephen says she came through the birth like a real trouper. I don't know about you, but I can't imagine having two babies at once."

"How did you get in? We tried to see her and the nurse at the front desk in the maternity ward said visiting hours didn't start until eleven," Susan said, ignoring Blues's comment.

"Oh, Rhythm and I didn't stop at the desk. We just walked in as though we knew what we were doing and no one bothered us. We find that usually works in hospitals," Stephen's mother replied.

Susan turned to her husband. "We should have tried that."

But Jed wasn't paying attention. He was tapping on the glass and wiggling his fingers at his grandson. "Look, he's waving back at me."

"And he's smiling," Rhythm added, imitating Jed's moves.

Susan and Blues exchanged amused glances. "Gas," Susan whispered.

Blues nodded, grinning. "Not that he's not a remarkable child. You know, he looks just like Stephen when he was born. He was so happy. We called him our little beam of sunshine."

Susan, who had been about to express her belief that this baby was the spitting image of her own son when he was a newborn, smiled.

"Susan's been looking at old baby photos for the past few months and it seems to me that the girl looks like Chrissy when she was a baby," Jed said, still waving and tapping.

"Excuse me. Are you incapable of reading the sign, sir? It is printed in clear English. But perhaps you need someone to interpret it for you." A short, overweight woman wearing flowery scrubs stood behind them, her hands on her ample hips and an angry expression on her florid face.

"I'm sorry. Are you speaking to me?" Jed asked, apparently stunned by being addressed in this manner.

"If you are the person banging loudly on the glass and upsetting our babies, then, yes, I am speaking to you! Can't you read?" This time she pointed to a sign taped to the wall nearby.

BABIES SLEEPING!! DO NOT BANG ON THE GLASS!!

"I'm sorry but I didn't see the sign and I thought I was tapping gently," Jed said. "I had no intention of disturbing anyone."

Susan, glancing through the glass and observing that her grandson was the only baby not sleeping soundly, was about to protest when she noticed the clock on the wall. "It's eleven o'clock! We can go see Chrissy! Come on, Jed," she urged. Her husband was still trying to apologize to the woman who was standing in front of the quartet as though prepared to fling herself between them and the window if they displayed any more antisocial inclinations.

"Great! Let's—" Rhythm began.

"You and I will go get a cup of tea or something in the cafeteria," Blues said. "Susan and Jed might want some time alone with their daughter."

"But—"

"Come on, Rhythm." Pulling her husband by his arm, Blues led him down the hallway. But Susan and Jed didn't notice; they were hurrying off in the opposite direction to see their daughter.

Chrissy was sitting up in the bed nearest the door, writing notes on computer-generated birth announcements. She put down the pen and beamed when her parents walked in the doorway.

"You certainly don't look like a young woman who gave birth to two beautiful babies less than twenty-four hours ago," her father said, leaning over to kiss his daughter's forehead.

"Did you see them? Aren't they gorgeous? Are you mad at me?"

"We saw them. They're gorgeous. Why in heaven's name would we be mad at you?" Jed asked.

"You knew you were having twins and you didn't tell us," Susan said, getting the point. She kissed her daughter despite this fact.

"I just didn't want everyone to fuss . . ."

"You mean you didn't want your family to fuss more than they—we—were doing already," Susan corrected gently.

"Yes. I guess. I mean, Stephen and I thought we were timing this so well."

"And you did," her father assured her, sitting down on the

foot of the bed. "Getting pregnant nine months before Stephen got his degree, what could be better?"

"Stephen having a job, knowing where you're going to live. Little things like that, right?" Susan asked her daughter.

"Exactly! But now—well, I guess you haven't seen Stephen . . . or his parents."

"We ran into Rhythm and Blues outside of the nursery."

"And they didn't tell you?"

"Tell us what?" Jed asked.

"That Stephen has a job! He got the job he wanted!"

"Well, good for him," Jed said.

"Where?" Susan asked immediately. "Where is it?" She took a breath and held it, waiting for the answer. She hadn't even rocked her new grandchildren in her arms. If Chrissy and Stephen were moving to the West Coast . . .

"Mom, please don't get that expression on your face. You're going to like this. The job is in New York. New York City."

"You're coming home!" Susan cried, flinging her arms around her daughter's neck and beginning to tear up.

"We're going to New York City. We're not moving to Connecticut. We want to live in the city, Mom—"

"In the city! Have you and Stephen thought this through? Do you know how much you'll spend on private school tuition for two children?"

"They're only thirteen hours old, Mother. They're not ready for school yet. Besides, Stephen and I have enjoyed living in Philadelphia and you know I've always wanted to live in New York."

"What about the dogs?" Susan asked, thinking quickly. "You always say you'd never consider getting rid of them. You can't possibly have two bullmastiffs in a small apartment in New York City. Connecticut has lawns where dogs can run and the children can have a swing set and a sandbox and go to really excellent schools for free . . ."

"And live at home when they attend Yale," Chrissy finished, beginning to sound a little sarcastic.

"And when does Stephen start work?" Jed asked.

"That's the problem. They want him to begin in two weeks."

"You'll never find any place to live in two weeks . . ."

"I know, Mother. The company offered to put us up in a hotel for a few weeks, but with the dogs and the babies and . . . and all . . . Well, I was hoping we might be able to move in with you and Dad."

"Of course you can!" Susan's world changed. It was a dream come true.

"Just until we find an apartment in the city. And this isn't going to be easy. The house will be overflowing with Stephen and me and two babies and two dogs, and—"

"You are all welcome to come and stay as long as you like," her father assured his daughter. "We will love having you."

"Yes, but . . . Stephen!" Chrissy beamed as her husband walked in the door, his arms full. A couple dozen roses were squashed beneath two large fluffy teddy bears, two tiny Yankees caps, a five-pound box of Neuchatel chocolates, a bottle of champagne, and the latest issues of the *New Yorker, New York, Time Out New York,* and the day's *New York Times.*

"Hi, everyone. I think I have everything you asked for," Stephen said to his wife. "How are Ethan and Rosie doing?"

"Ethan and Rosie? You named them? They're Ethan and Rosie?" Susan asked.

"Yes. What do you think?" Chrissy sounded worried.

"Wonderful! Is Rosie a Rosemary or—?"

"Just Rosie," Chrissy said. "And Ethan is Ethan. We don't want anyone to put horrible nicknames on them."

Susan, who knew that parents didn't have as much power over their children's nicknames as her daughter (christened Christine) seemed to think, just smiled. "They're wonderful names. How did you come up with them?'

"I've always wanted a daughter named Rosie," Chrissy said, surprising her parents with this insight into her life. "And Stephen picked Ethan."

"My parents think it's a bit old-fashioned, but I've always liked the name," Stephen admitted as he struggled to open the champagne. "Speaking of my parents, did Chrissy tell you . . . ?"

Before he could finish, his parents entered the room, followed by a redheaded young woman holding what appeared to be the hospital gift shop's entire stock of "It's a Girl!" and "It's a Boy!" Mylar balloons. "Chrissy, you dear, dear thing!" Blues cried. "And so efficient—imagine having two children at the same time. So smart of you! And Stephen—champagne. What a treat!"

"Mother . . . Dad . . ." Stephen didn't seem to know how to continue. "When did you get in?" he asked after a short pause.

"Absolutely hours ago," Rhythm replied. "You know us. We don't like to let any grass grow under our feet."

"And it's not every day we add to our family. Look what I bought the babies!" Blues pulled two tie-dyed infant sleepers from her massive straw purse. "I found them at a craft shop up the coast. Isn't it lucky I bought two? They'll look adorable in them, don't you think?"

What Susan thought was that they'd look like miniature deadheads, but she just smiled. This was Chrissy's problem, not hers. Besides, Stephen had managed to open the champagne and was trying to keep a half dozen little white Styrofoam cups upright while he filled them. Susan helped to pass them around, serving her daughter first.

"A toast!" Rhythm said rather loudly, raising his glass in the air. Some champagne sloshed out onto the floor just as the same nurse who had chastised Jed in the hallway appeared.

"The babies will be brought into the room in fifteen minutes. Perhaps you might want to tone down this party before then. . . . You certainly will have your work cut out for you," she added to the woman holding the balloons before sweeping out the door.

Susan looked at the woman. "I can take those, if you need to get to work," she suggested.

"No, the babies are fine."

"The babies? Don't you work in the gift shop?" Susan asked, confused.

"No. That's what I was going to tell you. You see, my parents—," Stephen began, but Chrissy interrupted.

"Mother, this is Shannon Tapley. Rhythm and Blues hired her. She's going to be our baby nurse for six months. She'll be coming with us to your house," Chrissy announced.

THREE

CHRISSY, STEPHEN, AND THE BABIES WERE TO ARRIVE around dinnertime. Susan had spent the past three weeks re-organizing, cleaning, and childproofing her home and she was showing the results of this hard work to Nadine Baines, her new next-door neighbor.

". . . Chrissy and Stephen will stay in her old room as they always do. I had it redecorated right after they were married, so all I had to do in there was empty the closet. I've been using it to store clothing that I . . . well, that I wasn't wearing." Susan decided not to explain that she wouldn't be wearing those clothes again until she lost the ten pounds she had gained in the past two years. She didn't want that particular information spread all over town and Nadine Baines did love to gossip.

"I turned our guest room into a nursery." Susan opened a door farther down the hallway and stood back so the other woman could peer in. "Fortunately it's large enough for two babies and all their stuff."

"This is absolutely adorable!"

"Do you think so?" Actually, Susan thought so, too. After many hours of indecision, she had chosen a fairy-tale theme. Wanting lots of bright colors and animals, she had found a local artist to paint a room-sized mural depicting her favorites. Little Red Riding Hood was strolling through the woods, carrying an impossibly large straw basket to the right of the doorway. After a few feet, the mossy forest path to grandmother's house became a cobblestone road leading up a flowery peak to Cinderella's castle. Knights leaving that castle continued down the path on the other side, their horses clad in chamfrons and poitrels, and their banners spread out across a lapis blue sky as they paraded toward a gleaming sword embedded in a large gray stone. Right behind the stone, three houses, each with a pig lounging nearby, lined the dirt path that led to a thatched roof dwelling. A lovely young woman leaned out of the top of the dwelling's Dutch door, waving to seven dwarfs as they marched off to greet two children on their way to a house fashioned from candy and cookies. At the far side of the witch's house of sweets, the path turned into a stream where a scruffy looking baby bird tailed a flock of geese. A little mermaid watched from a rock nearby.

The room's two windows had been hung with white muslin which Susan herself had stenciled with a fantasy collection of animals, flowers, stars, suns, and moons. Two white cribs were covered with quilts, now appropriately personalized, as well as matching sheets, blankets, and see-through crib bumpers. A pair of changing tables stood nearby. Deep wall-to-wall mossy green carpeting covered the floor. The alcove between the windows was Susan's favorite spot in the room. A carefully chosen selection of children's books shared a floor-to-ceiling bookshelf with a new CD player and a collection of CDs appropriate for children's listening. Two rocking chairs, lined with plush pillows, were ready for late night feedings. Susan couldn't wait.

"You have so many closets," Nadine said, looking at the three doors.

"Only two. The other door leads to a bathroom. And the bathroom is connected to what used to be my sewing room. I turned it into a place for the baby nurse to sleep . . . just temporarily," Susan added, leading her guest into that room.

Susan's sewing machine had been pushed into the far corner of the room and covered with a flowered sheet. A narrow single bed was made up with matching sheets. Susan had emptied the top two drawers of the dresser and half of the small closet. She didn't understand why Rosie and Ethan needed a baby nurse when they were going to have a grandmother available twenty-four hours a day and this room showed it.

"This should be comfortable," Nadine said.

"I'd better get back downstairs. I have to take the leg of lamb out of the refrigerator. . . ."

"Yum. Leg of lamb. My favorite." Nadine followed Susan out into the hallway. "Are you going to roast it with garlic and rosemary?"

"Not this time. It's marinating in a mixture of raspberry vinegar, whole grain mustard, and herbs. Chrissy loves it. I'll give you the recipe if you would like," Susan offered.

"Oh, I don't have time to fuss with fancy meals. You can just ask us over for dinner the next time you make it."

Susan laughed, although she wasn't absolutely sure Nadine was kidding. "I suppose I'd better get started in the kitchen," she said, hoping Nadine would take the hint and leave.

"I'll keep you company."

"Oh . . . great." Susan was too polite to say anything else. Maybe Nadine would get bored and go home. Nadine, however, discovered the real estate section of the local paper occupying the middle of Susan's large pine kitchen table and sat down to enjoy herself.

"Are you planning on moving?" Nadine asked, flipping through the pages.

"No, I thought that Chrissy and her husband might want to look at what's available locally."

"Oh. . . . We looked at this house. Gorgeous outside, but a real dump inside. You should have seen the bathrooms. Tacky linoleum on the floor, old square tiles on the walls and the original fixtures." She shuddered as though describing the bleakest buildings in an urban slum rather than a spacious ranch built in the late 1950s and standing on land now worth more than a million dollars without improvements. "And you wouldn't believe what they wanted for it."

"I would," Susan said. She had been shocked to find herself on the other side of the real estate game Connecticut style. After decades of being thrilled by the growing worth of her own home, she had come face-to-face with the reality of young couples looking for their first home—prices way beyond their budgets.

"Well, remember Donald if you're seriously looking in the area. No one knows more about real estate in Connecticut than Donald. He's got a lot of inside info and I'm sure he'd be happy to find a real deal for your daughter."

"If we start looking seriously, I'm sure having a real estate broker living next door will come in handy," Susan agreed.

Nadine continued to comment on the homes for sale and the real estate market in general while Susan prepared dinner. She was making a leek tart and garlic mashed potatoes to go with the lamb and she was rummaging through the cabinet where she stored her baking pans when Clue began to bark.

"I wonder who . . . ?" It was a question Susan didn't have to complete. Two large bullmastiffs plunged into the kitchen, followed by a hysterical golden retriever. Nadine's startled scream then joined the wails of an exhausted baby—or two—from the hallway. Susan rushed to open the door into her backyard so the dogs could become reacquainted without destroying the house just as Chrissy and Stephen, each with a baby tucked into a baby carrier, entered the room. They looked so tired. The baby nurse, whose name Susan could not remember at the moment, brought up the rear. Bags and boxes were slipping from her arms and Susan hurried over to clean off a spot on the counter—and realized that the lamb roast had disappeared.

"Shit!"

"Mother!" Chrissy was clearly outraged. "We don't talk like that in front of our children."

Susan, stunned by the mayhem of the past few minutes as well as the fact that her daughter had just corrected her language, explained. "One of your dogs seems to have stolen our main course."

"No. It was about to fall on the floor when they ran past, so I grabbed it," Nadine explained. She was standing in the corner, holding the ceramic bowl in the air and frowning.

"Oh, thank you, Nadine. Let me introduce you to the rest of my family," Susan began.

"Is there someplace I can put these things?" The baby nurse spoke up.

"Of course," Susan said, not looking away from her grandchildren. "The babies are sleeping in the nursery—I redid our old guest room."

"The third door on the left at the top of the stairs," Chrissy explained.

Susan was still staring at the twins. "They've grown! In just two weeks, they've grown!"

"The pediatrician says they're the healthiest twins she's

ever seen." Chrissy leaned over her children with a proud smile.

"I think Ethan has more hair, too," his grandmother continued.

"But Rosie's blonder," Chrissy pointed out.

"Yes—"

"I think it's time for me to leave," Nadine said. "Susan, will you be home later?"

"I . . . I guess so." The question surprised her.

"I'll call you then . . . a bit later. Okay?"

"Sure. Whenever you want."

"Who was that?" Stephen asked, as the door closed behind Nadine.

"Nadine Baines. She and her husband Donald moved in next door a few months ago," Susan explained. "I meant to introduce you, but in the confusion—"

"You're going to have to learn to ignore the confusion. There seems to be a lot of it wherever we go," Stephen said, bending down to pick up the bootie that Ethan had just managed to pull off his foot.

"Oh, look, he can undress himself already," said the proud grandmother.

"I don't think he actually intended to do that," Stephen, a literal young man, explained earnestly.

Susan, remembering one of the reasons she loved her son-in-law, smiled. "Why don't we take the babies upstairs and I can show you their room?"

"Good idea. I'm sure Ethan needs changing. It's been over an hour since we stopped on the turnpike and his diaper was dry then so it won't be now. Did you call a diaper service, Mom?"

"I thought you'd be using disposables—"

"No way! We'd be broke in a week. Besides, disposable diapers aren't at all ecological. You know there's very little room left in most landfills."

"Oh. Why don't I show you the nursery and then we can get the phone book and make some calls? You won't mind using Pampers for a few days until we can get a service organized, will you?"

"Of course not. We're using disposables now. We didn't want to carry dirty diapers with us." Chrissy turned to her husband. "Maybe you should start unloading the car. Mother and I better get the babies changed or we'll never eat."

"Where do you want everything to go?" he asked.

"Bring our suitcases and the baby things upstairs and . . ." Chrissy looked at her mother.

"If you have household stuff with you, we can store it in the garage or the basement," she offered.

"I was thinking about our computers . . . ," Chrissy began.

"Put them in your father's study. I'm sure he won't mind."

"And I brought along some art supplies. I've gotten very interested in watercolor since my pregnancy. I've been trying to paint some while the twins nap, but it can be sort of messy."

Susan was a firm believer in mothers pursuing their own interests. "Do you think you could work in your brother's room? He won't be home from Cornell for five weeks."

"I'll set up an easel on his desk. There's even good light from his window," Chrissy said enthusiastically. "Take my stuff up there," she told Stephen. "Come on, Mom. Shannon can help Stephen with the baby stuff."

Susan started to undo the strap holding Rosie in her carrier.

"What are you doing?" Chrissy cried.

"I thought we should carry them upstairs and leave these down here."

"We can, but this is a safe way of carrying them both at once. And it will get the carriers out of your way."

"Oh, I don't mind having their things around," Susan assured Chrissy, lifting Rosie up to snuggle against her chest. "I'd forgotten how small babies are," she said to herself.

"By the end of the day they sometimes seem pretty heavy," Chrissy said, picking up her son.

Susan looked at her daughter. "You look tired. Are you taking care of yourself?"

"I'm fine. It's just that having twins and then packing up the apartment in two weeks and then driving up here—it's tiring."

"Isn't Shannon working out?" Susan asked.

"We can't imagine going through this without her. She's a godsend." Chrissy hefted Ethan's carrier up on her hip. "We'd better remember to get water for Rock and Roll when we come back down."

"They'll be fine. I already filled three large bowls and placed them outside on the patio," Susan explained, feeling very organized.

"Then let's go see the nursery."

"I—" The phone's ring interrupted Susan before she could say more. Rosie began to wail again, but Ethan dozed on. "I'll get that and be right up."

"Great." Chrissy continued on upstairs as Susan grabbed the receiver off the phone on the hall table. When she joined her daughter and grandchildren, a frown was on her face.

FOUR

CHRISSY'S WELCOME-HOME DINNER WAS NOT THE COZY, restful event Susan had planned. Unnerved by Nadine's phone call, she had been unable to concentrate on her cooking. As a result, the roast was overcooked, the tart burned, and the potatoes lumpy. The twins didn't help the situation either: when Rosie stopped crying, Ethan would begin. They also seemed to get hungry at the same time, needed to be burped together, and their diapers had to be changed simultaneously. They managed to keep their grandparents, parents, and the baby nurse from relaxing and getting any enjoyment from the meal. The only benefit came to the dogs that were nearly delirious with joy at the number of half-filled plates returning to the kitchen.

"Wow, those are two active little babies. Thank God, Stephen's parents thought to hire a baby nurse. I can't imagine how Chrissy and Stephen would manage without Shannon's help," Jed commented, putting glasses into the dishwasher.

"I suppose." Susan paused. "What do you think about Shannon, Jed?"

"She seems to be competent, energetic, and well trained. To tell the truth, I'm surprised Rhythm and Blues hired someone so . . . so normal. I expected a modern-day hippie."

"She does look normal, doesn't she?"

26

"Of course. Why? Did she do something that worried you?"

"No. Nothing like that. Let's talk about it later. When we know no one will overhear us," Susan suggested. She was reaching into the dishwasher to rearrange her husband's work when her son-in-law walked into the room.

"Chrissy and Shannon are going to bathe the babies and when she's done, I thought we could take the dogs around the block. I think we all need a bit of fresh air."

"Oh, let me help with the babies and you two can take some time off," Susan said.

Stephen grinned. "To tell the truth, I was hoping you'd say that."

"If you trust me to finish this job without your help, you could go upstairs now, Susan. Then Stephen and Chrissy can leave immediately," Jed suggested.

"Good idea!" Susan was dying to help with the babies, but she had another reason to be enthusiastic—she wanted to get to know Shannon. Leaving the kitchen to the men, she hurried up to the nursery.

It was a mess. Bags of baby supplies were stacked inside the door, still unpacked. The diaper pail was lying on its side on the floor. Both babies were crying in their individual cribs. Shannon was removing a damp romper from Ethan and Chrissy was patting Rosie on her back and singing quietly. Shannon looked up when Susan entered the room.

"Hello, Mrs. Henshaw—"

"Susan," Susan corrected automatically. "Chrissy, why don't you go downstairs and take the dogs for a walk with Stephen and I'll help with bath time?" she suggested.

"Mother, it's not easy to bathe the twins. Shannon and I have set up a routine."

"Chrissy, I'd really love to do it, and I bathed you and Chad without any problems," her mother reminded her.

"But taking care of two babies at the same time is not the same as taking care of one—"

"I can show your mother what we do," Shannon said.

"And Rock and Roll are dying for a walk," Susan lied. The dogs had spent the last few hours dashing in and out of the house making life miserable for Clue and, the last time Susan looked, had been lying together on the brick patio by the back door, enjoying the cool evening air. "You don't want them to think they're not getting enough attention now that the babies have arrived," she reminded her daughter.

Chrissy walked slowly toward the door. "I won't be long," she said, looking back over her shoulder at Shannon.

"Take your time. We'll be fine," Shannon answered.

"The linen closet is at the end of the hallway," Chrissy added.

"I'm sure your mother can help me find anything I need."

"Yes, and I bought an herbal baby wash . . . ," Susan began.

"We brought our own," Chrissy said, stopping in her tracks. "We're not introducing anything new. Ethan had a slight rash on his stomach yesterday."

"We'll use your wash. Go on, honey, you can use the fresh air too, you know," Susan urged.

"Well . . . You'll want to feed them once more before they go to sleep, Shannon."

"Of course."

Chrissy finally left the room. Susan looked at the cribs. Ethan was calm now, lying in his diaper, studying the knights on the wall above him. Rosie was in her crib, lying on her stomach, still whimpering.

"Do we give them their baths together or separately?"

Susan asked, putting first things first. "I bought two baby tubs, but I'm not quite sure how to arrange things. The bathroom next door is small, but the master bath is huge with lots of counter space and two sinks."

"We had to bathe them one at a time in the apartment, but if we could manage them both together, it would sure speed things up. And it would be nice if we could find some time before Chrissy returns to put things away in here. It would give your daughter a break. She's a wonderful mother and these are great babies, but she needs to get more sleep, to take better care of herself." Shannon looked at Susan and smiled. "But you know all that. That's why you're here."

Susan stared at Shannon for a moment and then turned around and grabbed the pink and blue tubs from the floor of the closet. "Okay. Give me two minutes and I'll get the bathroom ready."

She was true to her promise and, with Shannon's help, the two babies were splashing happily in their tubs on top of the Deer Isle granite counter in the master bath when Jed entered the room.

"Kitchen clean?" Susan asked. She had been pleased to discover that holding a wet baby in one hand and washing with the other was a skill she had not lost.

"Not quite. But I didn't want to miss a great photo op." Jed had celebrated the twins' birth by buying the most high-tech electronic camera on the market and he brandished it now.

"Oh, do you think you could wait until tomorrow morning? They're just settling down and the . . . the flash might get them all excited again," Shannon said quickly. "Or maybe you could take pictures of them when they're asleep tonight. And Chrissy and I will give them their usual baths tomorrow morning and you'll be able to get Chrissy in the pictures, too. It's been a long day."

Jed frowned, but he lowered the camera and didn't argue. "I understand. We had a saying when our kids were little. 'If you wake the baby, you play with the baby,' " he explained. "And, frankly, it's been a long day around here too, and I'm not sure I have a whole lot of energy left. I'll finish the kitchen and take Clue for a walk."

"Keep Chrissy and Stephen downstairs as long as you can," Susan suggested. "They need the break and we're doing fine up here." She picked up a plastic cup and rinsed Ethan's hair one last time before lifting him out of the water and placing him gently on the towel-lined counter. Shannon was already drying Rosie, but Susan could see her face in the mirror-covered wall. She looked unhappy. "You don't like your picture taken?" she asked quietly, when Jed was no longer with them.

"I . . . No, I don't," Shannon admitted.

Now that Susan had started asking questions, she didn't quite know how to go about it. "Have you been doing this type of thing long?" she began, but before Shannon could answer, Ethan began to gasp for air. "What? I . . ." Before Susan realized what was happening, Shannon had grabbed the baby, put her fingers in his mouth and pulled out a small lump of fluff the color of Susan's new towels. Ethan, seeming as stunned as his grandmother, was silent for a minute before beginning to scream. His sister, lying comfortably in the towel-lined sink where Shannon had placed her after her bath, joined in.

"You saved his life," Susan said, her heart slamming in her chest. "I . . . I couldn't move."

"I'm trained to respond quickly. You would have done it yourself if I hadn't taken over." Shannon spoke over the loud wails of the frightened baby.

"Not in time. I wouldn't have known what to do in time.

He might have suffocated. You saved his life," Susan repeated. Then she had another thought. "What will Chrissy say when she hears about this? She'll think I can't take care of her children."

"I don't want to speak out of turn, but would you feel comfortable not telling your daughter about this?"

Ethan seemed to be calming down a bit and Susan began to relax. "Not tell Chrissy?"

Shannon nodded. "She's a wonderful mother, concerned and competent. But she does tend to hover. Probably all new mothers do. And it doesn't matter much if you have only one baby. But your daughter is wearing herself out fussing over these two and organizing this move at the same time. If she thinks something might happen if she leaves them alone, she won't leave them for a second. And new mothers need time off, too."

Susan nodded. "You're right. We'll just tell her everything went well."

"And you might want to run your luxurious thick towels through the washer and dryer a few times before we use them again," Shannon suggested, handing Ethan over to his grandmother.

Susan looked down at her grandson—he smiled up at her as though nothing had happened—and over to his sister, who was rubbing drool into her chin as though it was a beauty cream. "Yes, I will. Definitely."

"Let's take them back to the nursery and get them dressed in their jammies and settled down. Then you can stay with them while I go downstairs and warm their formula. I can clean up in here later."

"Don't worry about that. I'll take care of the bathroom . . . and the laundry. Oh, did you see the laundry chute in the hallway? It's just outside the door of your room. You

can just dump their clothing down and it lands right next to
the washer in the basement," Susan said.

Shannon looked over at her and smiled. "That will be a lot
easier for me than running to where the Laundromat was in
Philadelphia. The babies go through a lot of clothing in a
twenty-four hour period."

"No problem. And do you use regular detergent? I used
Ivory Snow for Chrissy's things, but I don't remember if I
did for Chad. . . ."

The two women walked back to the nursery, each holding
a baby, quietly going over the babies' domestic requirements.
By the time Chrissy and Stephen returned from their stroll,
Susan and Shannon were settled in the rocking chairs, feeding the twins. The lights in the nursery were dimmed and
there was a CD playing tunes guaranteed to send a baby to
sleep. It was a peaceful picture if the viewer disregarded the
three black plastic bags stuffed full of dirty diapers on the
floor by the door.

"We're almost done here if you want to take a shower or
something," Susan suggested to her daughter.

Chrissy rubbed her back and glanced over at her husband.
"I think I . . ."

"Why don't you go ahead and get to bed early for once?"
Stephen picked up his mother-in-law's cue immediately.
"You know Ethan or Rosie will be waking up in just a few
hours."

"I'm not sure I'll hear them crying from our room."
Chrissy sounded worried.

"I'll keep the door open to my room and I'll let you know
if you're needed," Shannon said quickly.

"And I put a baby monitor in your room," Susan said.
"You can just turn it on and listen in to them if . . ." She
stopped. She had been about to say *if you don't trust Shan-*

non to get up, but Shannon had proved her worth in an emergency. How could she doubt her now? "If you want to," she concluded. Then she got up and put Rosie into her crib. "I'll be in the basement doing some laundry if anyone needs me." Taking one last fond look at the room, she grabbed the plastic bags of garbage and headed downstairs.

She was sitting on a tall stool, staring at the piles of dirty clothing when she realized someone was walking down the basement stairs. "I'm here, Jed. In the laundry room," she called out.

"It's not Jed. It's me." Kathleen Gordon appeared in the doorway. "I was jogging and thought I'd stop in to see the babies."

"They're sleeping."

"I know. Jed told me. So I thought I'd see how the new grannie is doing." She looked at the piles on the floor. "Laundry. So I guess being a grandmother is a lot like being a mother. My kids seem to create at least as much laundry as this every week."

"This is twenty-four hours' worth, I'm told."

"Susan, what's wrong? You look . . . well, you don't look happy."

"It's Shannon—"

"Well, I suppose you can't expect Rhythm and Blues to hire a normal baby nurse."

"It's not that she's not normal. Not exactly," Susan said. "It's that she was the primary suspect in the murder of three people."

" 'Primary suspect.' That means . . ."

"It means the cases were never solved. There wasn't enough evidence to indict anyone. No one knows who did it. It means my grandchildren's baby nurse could be a murderer."

FIVE

KATHLEEN STARED BRIEFLY AT HER FRIEND BEFORE REACH-
ing down to pick up one of the bags of laundry. "I'll sort.
You'll tell me what you know."

Susan grabbed another bag and dumped the contents into
a nearby rolling hamper. "We'll do the laundry together. If I
don't keep moving I may start screaming. I've been going
nuts inside ever since Nadine called."

"Nadine?"

"Nadine Baines. You know, my new next-door neighbor.
You met her at the Valentine's Day party we gave."

"That's right, I remember. So she called you today."

"Yes, but, you see, she was here this afternoon and saw
Shannon." Susan stopped speaking and held up a tiny little
tie-dyed T-shirt. "Well, at least the pattern hides the traces of
spit up."

"Susan . . ."

"Okay." She tossed the shirt on top of one of the piles
Kathleen was making on the fold-out table. "Nadine was here
when the kids arrived today—they were a few hours early.
Anyway, she didn't say anything then—well, she couldn't have.
It was mayhem with the twins and all their stuff and the
dogs. Anyway, she went home and pondered the problem—

her words—and then she called me." Susan frowned and picked up a white cotton blanket stained with baby vitamins.

"So she called. What did she say besides that she had been thinking about something?"

"Well, what she said is that she was chilled to the bone when Shannon walked in the door. Nadine tends to be a little dramatic," Susan explained, tossing the blanket onto a growing pile of white laundry.

"So she knows her."

"Yes. Well, I don't think they've ever met. You see, Nadine and Donald have a summer house on Perry Island."

"That's in Maine?"

"No, it's right off the Connecticut coast. It's large enough to have a public ferry running to it a few times a day, but so small that most people haven't heard of it. I think it's mostly a summer resort with a small year-round community made up mostly of retired people. I think Nadine may have once told me that Donald grew up there. She talks so much that I don't always listen. Anyway, they have a house. I don't know how much they go there. There's not a lot to do on the island unless you sail and they've never mentioned sailing. There aren't even a lot of businesses on the island—a small grocery, a post office, a few gift shops, and a hair salon—as well as a nursing home."

"A strange place for a nursing home, isn't it?"

Susan paused. "I don't know. I mean, I don't know very much about where nursing homes are located—or why they're located there. But the nursing home on the island is the point here. You see, a year or so ago, three people died in that home. And Nadine claims that Shannon was a nurse there at the time. . . . And a suspect in the murders."

"Which are still unsolved?" Kathleen guessed.

"Apparently so. I mean, that's what Nadine said."

"And you're worried that a homicidal maniac is taking care of your grandchildren."

"Yes."

"So why don't you just fire Shannon and find someone else?"

"She saved Ethan's life this evening."

"What?"

"She saved Ethan's life." Susan explained what had happened earlier.

Kathleen took a moment to drench five stained receiving blankets with Spray 'n Wash before tossing them into the washer and asking another question. "And you don't think you could just ask her about what happened at the nursing home on Perry Island? I mean, it's not an accusation."

"I'm afraid she'll leave. She's a wonderful baby nurse and she's concerned about Chrissy and . . . and what if she hadn't been here when Ethan started choking? He could have died! Kathleen, I just can't risk it!"

"But you don't want a killer taking care of your grandchildren."

"No, of course not. I just don't know what to do. If only I could find out more. I don't know Nadine all that well, but I know she tends to be a bit emotional. Maybe she's wrong about all this. What if Shannon just looks like the nurse who was a suspect or has a similar name or something?"

"You know, I might be able to help you out. One of the men I worked with in the city retired to an island somewhere around here. I suppose it might be Perry Island."

"It could be! There aren't many islands nearby. I mean, there's Fisher's Island, but I doubt if a retired cop could afford anything there."

"Well, we still exchange Christmas cards and I could check to see what the return address on the last one was."

"And you could call him and ask about the nursing home deaths."

"Susan, he probably doesn't know anything, but I'll try."

"Right away?"

"I suppose anything is better than dealing with this mess," Kathleen said, holding up a one-piece knitted suit covered with something that looked vaguely toxic.

"This may be the only time in my life when I've turned down an offer to help with the laundry," Susan said, removing the garment from Kathleen's hand and tossing it into a pan of sudsy water to soak. "But I'm so worried about all this. If you find out anything, call tonight—"

"What about the babies? Won't the ringing phone wake them?"

"Call me on my cell phone. I'll just turn it on to vibrate and keep it with me."

"Fine. I'll get going then." Kathleen started for the stairs and then paused. "Are they gorgeous?"

Susan knew exactly whom she was talking about. "They are! Completely, absolutely, totally gorgeous!"

"No matter what I find out or don't find out tonight, I'll be over to see them first thing in the morning," Kathleen promised, trotting up the stairs.

Alone again, Susan reached for the unopened box of Ivory Snow and poured the required amount into the machine. She turned a few knobs and leaned against its smooth enameled side as the wash cycle commenced.

The laundry took over an hour, but, despite her worries about Shannon, Susan found herself smiling as she folded immaculate tiny garments and placed them in little piles.

Perhaps, she thought, examining her work, she should order one of those handwoven, gingham-lined laundry baskets from Martha Stewart's Web site. It would look so much better than her old, ratty basket that still displayed the results of Clue's teething many years ago.

Susan sighed and picked up the basket. Balancing it on her hip, she started up the stairs. She would leave it in the hallway outside of the nursery so as not to disturb the twins and then take a quick shower.

But she couldn't even walk across her bathroom without moving the twins' bath stuff. And how could she have forgotten about those towels with their dangerous fluff! She picked up the baby baths, dumped them in the Jacuzzi, sprayed them with lavender scented cleanser, rinsed them, and turned them over to drain. She put away the Johnson's baby shampoo and Aveeno baby wash that Chrissy had brought and then grabbed her gorgeous new towels, rushed into the hall and dumped them down the laundry chute before returning to the bathroom and locating a set of older towels in the linen closet. Although not exactly threadbare, it had been years since they had shed loose fibers. She was hanging them on the brass towel bars when Jed came into the room, her cell phone in his hand.

"Kath's on the line," he said, a puzzled expression on his face. "Why did she call your cell?"

"She didn't want to wake up the babies," she explained, taking it. "Hi, Kath. Did you find out anything? Well, did you ask him to check around and let you know if he does find anything out?" Susan listened to the answer and Jed returned to their bedroom. A few minutes later, Susan found him sitting on the edge of their bed, playing with his new camera.

"Look at this. I think I got some great shots of Rosie.

Ethan had his back to me and I was afraid he'd wake up if we turned him over." He held out the camera. "Go ahead. Just press the button on the back. The arrows indicate the direction you want to go."

Susan took the camera from him and stared at the screen that displayed the enchanting image of her granddaughter. "We have a problem," she said quietly, going through the photos. Since Rosie couldn't roll over yet, they were pretty much identical and didn't take long to review.

"Could it wait until the morning? I hate to admit it, but those kids wore me out. I'm exhausted."

Susan didn't answer immediately. She knew she should share what she had learned about Shannon with her husband, but he had just said he was exhausted, and, to be honest, she would rather tell him after she had figured out what they should do. Of course, she owed it to him to be honest. Their marriage was based on honesty, on decisions made jointly. She opened her mouth to explain, but the screams from next door prevented anything further.

"My God! Listen to the lungs on those kids," Jed exclaimed, pulling his pajamas out of his dresser drawer. He tossed them onto the bed, then headed toward the bathroom.

"Jed, don't you think—?"

"If you're going to suggest that we volunteer to take care of the babies, the answer is no, I don't think we need to. They have a nurse. They have two parents. We're the grandparents. We're supposed to play with them and spoil them, not spend the middle of the night taking care of them. Not unless we have to."

"But—"

"Susan, you do what you want, but unless a miracle happens and Chrissy and Stephen find an apartment they love at a price they can afford that is available immediately, my guess is that they're going to be with us for a while—"

"Which will be wonderful!"

"Which will have its wonderful aspects. It will also be demanding and exhausting and difficult and I, for one, don't want to lose any more sleep than is absolutely necessary."

"I guess the kids will yell if they need us."

"I'm sure they will." Jed walked into the bathroom. "And they have Shannon to depend on too, remember" were his last words before the door swung closed behind him.

Susan put her cell phone down on the nightstand and retrieved her nightgown from beneath her pillow. It was one of her favorites, made from soft white lawn. She had bought it at Liberty's on her last trip to London. She looked at it, sighed, and headed for her dresser. She really didn't want to get up to help with the twins, but, if necessary, she would and she'd be properly dressed. She rummaged around in her dresser until she found the tailored taupe cotton pajamas her mother-in-law had sent on her last birthday. She looked a little like a prisoner in a penal colony wearing them, but the twins were too young to notice the resemblance.

By the time Susan was ready for bed, the house was calm. Kathleen's call had done nothing to still her worries about Shannon and she expected to have trouble falling asleep. She was wrong. The problem was staying asleep.

Susan was fairly sure she hadn't been asleep for more than an hour when the twins began to cry again. Jed rolled over, groaned, and put a pillow over his head. She was about to do the same when she heard something hit the wall in the hallway outside of their bedroom. It sounded as though someone had dropped something . . . or someone! She jumped out of bed and ran to the hall.

Stephen was kneeling on the floor, rubbing the rug with one of the receiving blankets she had just washed, dried, and folded.

"Stephen?"

"I knocked Rosie's bottle against the wall and the top fell off," he explained, looking up. "And I think her patience is wearing a little thin," he added as the crying became even louder.

"Where's Chrissy?" Susan asked.

"She's feeding Ethan, and Shannon is downstairs cleaning up the kitchen. I meant to put the pan I used to warm the formula in the sink, but I dropped it, too." He looked sheepish. "You must think I'm trying to destroy your house in just one night."

"I think you're exhausted." Susan swooped down and grabbed the cloth from his hand. "I'll take care of this later. You go tell Chrissy that there will be another bottle of formula coming up right away. Then you go to bed. You're supposed to be at work tomorrow, right?"

"Yes, but Chrissy is tired, too."

Susan smiled. What a wonderful son-in-law! "Don't worry about Chrissy. I'll make sure she has a long nap tomorrow, or I should say today. You go on." She hurried downstairs, not giving him time to argue with her plan.

Years ago, when her kitchen had been remodeled, Susan had reserved a corner of the room for a small built-in desk. She did a lot of the household paperwork here, using the space to pay bills as well as look up recipes in her large cookbook collection that was shelved nearby. Shannon was standing in front of the desk as Susan entered the room.

"We need another bottle of formula," Susan announced.

The nurse started, dropping whatever it was she held in

her hand. "I . . . I'll get it done right away." Shannon hurried toward the stove.

Susan glanced at her desk. What had Shannon been examining in private? There were a half dozen cookbooks on her desk, but only two books lay open on the pile: *Mastering the Art of French Cooking, Volume One,* and Susan's address book.

SIX

No ONE IN THE HOUSE GOT MORE THAN A COUPLE OF HOURS of uninterrupted sleep that night. As daylight finally penetrated the slit between the curtains, Susan gave up and got up. Jed and Clue were still snoring when, dressed in the warm clothing required to spend any time outside during spring in Connecticut, she slipped from the room. She noted the stain on the carpet and the splash on the wall as she walked around two bulging plastic bags that seemed to have sprouted in the hallway overnight. She was too tired to deal with any of this without a large mug of coffee. She needed it so much that she imagined she could smell the tantalizing brew wafting up the stairs.

But she wasn't imaging the full pot of coffee steaming in the coffeemaker—or the enticing pan of what looked like homemade cinnamon rolls cooling on the counter. Or the young woman sitting at the table reading the *New York Times* who jumped to her feet when Susan entered the room.

"Shannon?"

"Mrs . . . Susan, I hope you don't mind. I was just waiting for the rolls to cool a bit before I frosted them."

"No . . . I . . . Do you always get up early in the morning and bake?"

"Well, I always get up early in the morning. One of the

reasons I'm a good baby nurse is that I have insomnia. It's easier to take care of newborns if you don't need a lot of sleep," she added, smiling ruefully. "I hope you don't mind me taking over your kitchen like this. I've been cooking breakfast for Stephen and Chrissy since the twins came home from the hospital. She's so tired and cooking is one of my hobbies. It relaxes me." She glanced over at the floor-to-ceiling bookshelf. "And I couldn't resist your cookbook collection. You have so many books on baking. I hope you don't mind me going through them."

"Of course not," Susan replied. "If you're interested, there's a complete collection of bound *Gourmet* magazines on the shelves behind the door in Jed's study. I bought them at an estate sale a few months ago."

"Oh, that sounds like fun. Thank you." Shannon stood up and walked over to the counter where the rolls were waiting. "I usually put a bit of vanilla in the frosting."

"So do I." Susan poured herself a cup of coffee. "Have you always been a baby nurse?"

"I—"

"Shannon, could you come upstairs?" Stephen appeared in the doorway, a towel wrapped around his waist. "The babies are both yelling and I have to get ready to leave for the city and the dogs need to be let out."

The nurse reacted instantly. "Right away," she said on her way out the door.

"I'll frost the rolls," Susan called after her. Was Shannon hurrying toward the twins or was she anxious to get away before she had to answer Susan's question? "Would you like some coffee, Stephen?" she asked.

"I think I'd better pass. My train leaves in less than half an hour and I sure don't want to be late my first day on the job.

Will it be okay if I put Rock and Roll out in the backyard until Chrissy can take care of them?"

"Of course. And if you need coffee, you can always stop at one of the coffee places at Grand Central after you get into the city."

"Yeah. I guess." Stephen grabbed his towel as Rock and Roll dashed by, let them into the yard, and then hurried up the stairs after Shannon. Susan looked at the rolls and the bowl of frosting, gulped down half her coffee and, despite the early hour, reached for the phone and called Kathleen Gordon.

"Hi Kath. It's me. Did you hear anything else?" She picked a corner off a cinnamon roll and popped it in her mouth as she listened to the answer to her question. "You told him to call if he learns anything, right?" She pulled a second, larger piece from the bun. "Anytime. We've all been up most of the night. Okay. See you soon then." She hung up and grabbed a knife. Sometimes it was easier to think on a full stomach, she told herself as she pried the largest cinnamon roll from the pan and dipped it into the frosting.

Like most people living in the affluent suburbs north of New York City, the Henshaws had many people working for them in and around their home—cleaning women, window washers, caterers when they gave a large party, carpenters for small remodeling jobs, plumbers, roofers, painters, landscapers, and swimming pool cleaners to name a few. The list was long as they kept their large colonial style home in tiptop shape. But this, Susan realized, was the first time anyone other than family or house guests had actually lived with them.

She didn't like it. She knew Shannon had been looking at things on—or near—her desk last night. What if this burst of enthusiasm over baking was all a cover-up for her snooping?

Susan bit into the bun and frowned. Shannon did, however, know how to bake. The cinnamon roll was excellent. And the kitchen was remarkably clean. Shannon would have to be in her kitchen frequently if she was fixing the babies' formula as well as meals for Stephen and Chrissy. But if Shannon stuck to the nursery and the basement and the kitchen . . . Except that she wouldn't. Susan had just given Shannon an excellent excuse to spend time in Jed's study—which is where all the family's financial records were kept. And she would also be taking care of the dogs, which meant she'd be following them into every corner of the house and yard.

Susan stopped eating and stared at her coffee cup. They didn't know anything about Shannon—except that she might have been a suspect in an unsolved murder investigation—but Shannon was in an excellent position to discover a lot about the Henshaws. Unless Susan gave up sleeping at night and going out during the day, Shannon could easily look around at her leisure. She stood up. Maybe Kathleen hadn't been able to discover what happened at the nursing home yet, but Susan might have another source of information about Shannon. All she needed to do was find a corner of the house where she could make a private phone call.

It turned out that Jed's study wasn't all that private after all. First Jed appeared to kiss her good-bye on his way to the train and tell her that he had put Clue in the backyard with the mastiffs. Then he reappeared with the news that the dogs needed to be fed when she got a chance and that he might be late for dinner tonight. Chrissy came in to rummage through the large pile of suitcases, boat bags, and equipment that had been piled in the corner when they arrived yesterday and had yet to be unpacked. After finding what she wanted, she disappeared back upstairs only to reappear almost immediately searching for a phone book. Shannon had walked by the open doorway a few times carrying bottles, clean blankets, and the like but did not enter the room. It was fortunate that Susan's end of the conversation was limited.

The call took every bit as long as Susan had anticipated and she was just hanging up when Kathleen appeared in the doorway, a half-eaten cinnamon roll in one hand, a mug of coffee in the other.

"Susan, I can't believe you. With everything that's going on around here, you get up early and bake."

"Not me. Shannon made those."

Kathleen raised her eyebrows. "Really? They're as good as yours." She closed the door behind her and flopped down in one of the pair of wing chairs beside Jed's large mahogany partner's desk. "I haven't learned anything new," she announced. "But it's possible we'll hear something after my friend makes a few phone calls."

"I've just gotten off the phone with Blues—"

"Who? Oh, Chrissy's mother-in-law! Did you call her or did she call you?"

"I called her. I'd already dialed the number when I realized what time it is in California and I was afraid I was going to wake her, but it turns out that she was up studying the stars."

"I didn't know she was interested in astronomy."

"I think it's more astrology that interests Rhythm and Blues. But that's not important." Susan glanced at the closed door. "I called her to ask about Shannon. After all, they hired her for the kids so I figured they must know a lot about her. But—"

"Don't tell me. They found her through some sort of Zen spiritual adviser they met on a retreat somewhere."

"Nope. They heard about her through a mutual friend whose daughter gave birth to a baby with some sort of serious health problem. Apparently this friend couldn't say enough about how wonderful Shannon was and Blues got the idea of hiring her when the kids had their babies."

"Did they check into her background?" Kathleen asked, leaning forward.

Susan frowned. "I don't want Blues or anyone to know that we're worried about Shannon. She's not terribly discreet and Chrissy and Stephen might find out and it would upset them and—"

"You're telling me that you didn't ask any direct questions about Shannon."

"Exactly. Fortunately Blues loves to talk so all I had to do was mention Shannon and she was off and running."

"And?"

"They had only heard about Shannon when they found out that Chrissy and Stephen were going to have twins."

"How did they know that?"

"Indirectly. Stephen told an old friend who also has twins and that old friend told his mother and she ran into Blues and mentioned it. I felt a bit hurt that they knew and we didn't, but fortunately they were smart enough to see that the kids would need help when the babies were born. Blues said that she's heard that some baby nurses won't work with twins. Can you believe that?"

"Every few weeks I pick up the newspaper and I read something else about the nursing shortage so I suppose nurses can pick and choose the jobs they want."

"Apparently that's true. Blues said it wasn't easy to convince Shannon to work for the kids. And not because they were twins. Blues said Shannon didn't like the idea of moving when the babies were only a few weeks old. I can't blame her for that. The last twenty-four hours have been mayhem, and everyone around here has been run off their feet."

"How did Blues convince Shannon to take the job?"

"I have no idea. Blues said that she sent positive messages out into the universe directed at the problem and the cosmos answered in a positive manner. Frankly, I have no idea what she was talking about, but apparently whatever she did worked. Shannon's last job ended three days before Ethan and Rosie were born . . ." Susan yawned. "And she called the Canfields and said she would be happy to take the job."

"So she was already working in Philadelphia?" Kathleen asked.

"No, she wasn't. The job with the ill baby was in D.C. so she didn't have far to travel." Susan's second yawn made her eyes water.

"Where does she live? I mean, when she isn't working?"

"I have no idea. I didn't even think about it. Just because she lives in on her jobs doesn't mean she doesn't have a home, does it?"

"I doubt it. She must have someplace that she goes between jobs—or on her days off. She does have days off, doesn't she?"

"Lord, I never thought of that." And Susan already couldn't imagine how they would manage without her.

"Is she a registered nurse, an RN?"

"I think so."

"Was she hired through an agency? I mean are Rhythm and Blues paying her directly or are they paying an agency that then pays her?"

"I have no idea. If she worked for an agency, they would know about her work history, wouldn't they?" Susan asked.

"Yes, but they might not be willing to tell just anybody. You know," Kathleen added, "you could just ask her."

"I suppose, but I don't want her to feel as though I'm interrogating her or worried about her."

"But you are!"

"I know, but I didn't hire her, and the kids—and my grandchildren—are depending on her. Kathleen, I don't want to wait for your friend. I think we should drive up to that island and ask some questions . . . Although I don't want to leave Chrissy and Shannon alone today."

"Look, why don't we do some online research? Murders at a nursing home must have gotten mention in more than a few newspapers."

"And there's even a Web site that rates nursing homes. I remember someone at the club, who was looking for a place for her parents, telling me about it," Susan suggested.

"If you can check that out, I'll go home and see what I can find out from newspaper archives," Kathleen said. "At least I'll try. We had parental controls put on the computer so we wouldn't have to worry about Alex running into something a ten-year-old shouldn't see. Unfortunately they seem to control the oddest things. Jerry's niece is graduating from Beaver College next month and we wanted to find out when the ceremony is—"

"And the computer wouldn't let you."

"You got it! But I'll keep track of any dead ends and you can research them. You know, Susan, maybe you could bring these things up in casual conversation. It's not suspicious to ask someone you don't know where they live—or where they worked."

"Kathleen, don't think I haven't tried. But you can't imagine how impossible it is to have a casual conversation around here! In the past . . ." She paused and glanced down at her watch to check the time. "In the past nineteen hours since the kids arrived, I've hardly managed to finish my thoughts, never mind communicating them—"

As if to prove what she was saying the doorbell rang.

Kathleen swiveled in her chair and glanced out the window at the street. "United Parcel truck," she announced.

"Oh, that must be the stroller I ordered. I guess I'll have to send it back and find one for two babies," she said, getting up and going to the door.

"Oh, my lord!"

"What's wrong?" Kathleen asked, following her out into the hallway.

The tall man in a dark brown uniform was pushing a loaded dolly up the driveway. And, from the pile next to the door, Susan got the impression that he had waited until his third or fourth trip to ring the bell.

"You having another wedding here?" the deliveryman asked as he added to the mound of packages. Susan recognized him as being the same man who drove this route the year her daughter was married.

"No." Susan glanced at the label on the top package. It was addressed to Chrissy and Stephen. "My daughter and her husband and their babies are staying with us for a while though."

"Mr. and Mrs. Stephen Canfield?" he asked.

"Yes. Are these all for them?"

"All these and about twenty more in the truck. I'll get the rest of 'em and then someone's got a lot of signing to do."

A loud wail floated down the stairway.

"I'll sign," Susan said. She had a feeling Chrissy was going to be busy for a while.

SEVEN

IT TOOK SUSAN ALMOST HALF AN HOUR TO CARRY ALL THE boxes inside and put them in place. She stacked them in the living room, up until now the only room in the house spared a lashing of baby paraphernalia. And then, after tossing another load of baby clothing into the washer, she went back to Jed's study and turned on the computer.

Susan found the Internet both fascinating and time consuming. She would start looking for a new recipe for chicken for dinner and end up spending hours checking out weekend rates at luxury ski lodges in the Italian Alps—before going out to dinner. Over the past few years, she had planned hundreds of vacations they had never—and would never—go on, learned how to do dozens of projects she would never even begin, and contemplated the personal musings of strangers who seemed convinced their every thought worth her time. They rarely were.

Today she was determined to maintain her focus and in less than five minutes she had found what she was looking for: the Perry Island Care Center's Web site. After checking out photos of the grounds, representative resident rooms, and a highly self-congratulatory description of the services it offered, she had the name and phone number of the admissions director, the center's street address, and a map. A few minutes more and she had discovered the ferry schedule to the island. She exited the program, turned off the computer, sat back, finished the last half inch of cold coffee in her mug, reached for the phone and dialed the Perry Island Care Center's admitting office.

In a few minutes, she had set up an appointment to tour the nursing home and to discuss her mother's possible admission. She grabbed the papers she had printed and hurried into the hallway. Shannon was coming up from the basement with a basketful of clean laundry. Susan looked into the open doorway to the kitchen and saw her daughter sitting at the kitchen table, eating a cinnamon roll and thumbing through the newspaper.

"Chrissy, I've got to go out for a few hours," she said, entering the room.

"Oh, are you going by a drugstore? We're out of A and D ointment. I know I packed an extra tube, but Shannon and I can't find it."

"No problem. I'll stop in town on my way home. Anything else?"

Chrissy used both hands to push her thick blond hair off her shoulders and took a deep breath. "I don't think so," she answered uncertainly.

"Tell you what, I'll get my errands done and call you before I go to the drugstore and you can let me know if you've thought of anything else . . . unless you need the ointment right away?"

"No, we'll be fine. We need a diaper service, but—"

"I thought you were going to call some."

"I'm going to, but they're expensive and they all want a monthlong contract and I don't know which one is best. And Ethan has such delicate skin."

"Why don't you call Kathleen and see if she has ever used

a service. Or Erika. You know she and Brett have a six-month-old."

"Good idea," Chrissy said without a lot of enthusiasm.

"You're exhausted, aren't you?" Susan asked, instantly back in mother mode. "Having the twins and then moving . . . Maybe you should see a doctor. The gynecologist you used to go to is still in town and—"

"I'm fine, Mom. Just tired. I planned on going into the city this afternoon and start looking for a place to live, but I really don't think I'm up to it."

"Chrissy, you don't want to do too much yet. You'll make yourself ill. Take a nap today."

"I don't sleep well during the day. I lie down and think I hear Ethan or Rosie crying and then I have to get up and see—"

"Look, you have a baby nurse. Let Shannon worry about the babies and at least lie down for a bit. You really look pale."

Chrissy took a deep breath and sat up straight. She had never enjoyed being fussed over and Susan recognized the stubborn expression on her daughter's face. "I'm fine."

Susan knew it was time to stifle her concern. "Then you might want to start opening the pile of packages in the living room."

"Packages? Oh, I sent baby announcements last week and gave this address. Do you think they're presents for the babies?"

"I'd be surprised if they were anything else. I noticed more than one from Tiffany's."

Chrissy cheered up. "Really? Maybe I'll just take a peek."

Susan left her daughter to check out the goodies and went upstairs to get ready for her trip to the nursing home.

*   *   *

The Perry Island Care Center looked a bit less elegant than the photos on their Web site had led Susan to expect. A large brick building with an excessive amount of white wood trim, a new paint job and some tuck-pointing would have improved its appearance immensely. In the publicity photos, the building had been surrounded by blazing red azalea bushes. But today only a few crocuses, so close to the sidewalk that they had been trampled repeatedly, were blooming. Susan pulled her purse up on her shoulder and entered through the wide handicapped accessible doors.

The interior was cheerful and well maintained. There was a wicker desk in the foyer and the young woman sitting behind it looked up from her *Vogue* magazine when Susan entered. "May I help you?"

"I'm here to see Astrid Marlow," Susan explained.

"Do you have an appointment?"

"Yes. For noon." Susan looked at the clock hanging on the wall behind the desk. "I'm a bit early."

"You must have come over on the ten-thirty ferry."

"Yes, I did."

"There isn't a lot of traffic off-season so it doesn't take any time to unload. During the summer, our noon appointments are always late. Astrid's office is right down the hallway on the left. I think she's in."

"Thank you." Susan started off in the direction indicated. An elderly man slowly making his way toward her leaned on his walker with an expression of intense concentration. Susan smiled in what she hoped was an encouraging manner, but as he got closer, a loud bell startled her and caused her to jump back. "What was that?"

A short heavyset woman popped out of the doorway Susan was making for and gently took hold of the man's arm. "Mr. O'Neill, you know you're not supposed to be off the ward alone." She glanced over at Susan. "If you're Mrs. Henshaw, why don't you go on into my office? You don't mind waiting while I sort out Mr. O'Neill, do you?"

"Of course not." In fact, she would welcome the opportunity to look around a bit. Susan walked in the doorway.

Astrid Marlow's office was large and well organized. One wall was dedicated to photographs taken at the care center. Birthday parties, Christmas parties, anniversaries . . . all were apparently celebrated with enthusiasm by staff and residents alike. Susan looked carefully, hoping to identify Shannon in the pictures. It was impossible to date the events; the residents, mostly women, had apparently preferred wash-and-wear clothing in floral prints for many decades. The staff, dressed in brightly printed scrubs, was always smiling. Failing to pick out a familiar face, Susan turned her attention to the rest of the room.

Two chairs faced a large walnut desk, where a multipaged application form was laid out. There were also piles of slick brochures. Susan picked one up and was perusing it when Astrid Marlow returned.

"I'm sorry about that. We must keep careful track of some of our memory-impaired residents. They do tend to wander. Mr. O'Neill has been with us for some time but, unfortunately, he has become more and more confused in the past six months or so.

"So, tell me about your mother," Astrid Marlow continued.

Susan was unprepared for the change of topic. She had assumed that this woman would start out by telling her about the nursing home, not ask questions about her mother, who was, thankfully, healthy and vital and would almost certainly be angered by the idea that her daughter thought she was ready for this particular change of residence. "Ah . . ."

"Perhaps I misunderstood you on the phone. Is it your mother-in-law whom you're looking to place somewhere?"

"Oh, no . . . I . . . It's my mother. She's getting old, you see." Susan realized the inadequacy of her explanation.

"Is she mobile?"

Susan thought of the large, silver Lexus sedan her mother used to zip around town and nodded yes. "But she doesn't get out as much as she used to," Susan lied. As she spoke, her mother and father were on a monthlong walking tour of the British Isles.

"Does she have memory issues?"

Susan's mother was unfortunately inclined to mention things she considered mistakes in Susan's life that dated back over forty years. "No, her memory is just fine. She just needs help. You know, she's getting old," Susan repeated.

"Well, you understand that we can't accept new residents without medical records."

"Of course, I understand. Tell me about the Perry Island Care Center," Susan said. "This is such an unusual location for a nursing home, isn't it?"

Astrid passed a pile of papers across the desk to Susan. "We have an interesting history. We're a full-care nursing facility, one of the oldest in the state. We've been around since the turn of the century. Of course, things were quite different then. The care center was started by the Perrys, descendants of the family the island was named after. They were an unusual couple. Childless and wealthy enough not to have to earn a living. Mary Perry had some limited training as a nurse and her husband, a Methodist minister, felt a need to be of service in the community on days other than Sunday. They owned much of the island as well as the largest house.

They took in some of the older residents on the island, or relatives of residents, and cared for them as best as they could. Of course, the new addition hadn't been built then and they could only accommodate about twelve people. But they did an excellent job. When they retired, a distant relative inherited the care center and everyone was relieved that they would continue the center and its services."

"It was lucky that there was someone available who wanted to do this sort of thing." Susan felt obliged to say something. Astrid Martin had obviously repeated this story many times.

"Well, there is a black spot in the story of the care center," Astrid Martin admitted, but smiling to show that it wasn't very important. "The young man who inherited was, perhaps, more interested in the land included in the inheritance than in running a nursing facility—or 'old folks home' as some people called them in those days. He moved here from New York City, bringing along a wife and infant son. They cared for the residents for a while, but then, discovering that terms of the will mandated that the inheritance had to be kept intact and he couldn't sell off any of the land, that young man left for an extended visit to Europe, planning to write the Great American Novel. He didn't write it nor did he ever return. His wife picked up the reins and added residents by the simple expedient of putting ads on the walls of nearby Connecticut hospitals.

"The story is that she had been a socialite in New York City. I don't know about that, but this place is the result of her excellent business sense and her dedication to the center. Her insistence on high standards of care built our reputation and, by the time she died, we were as well known off the island as on."

"And her son?" Susan asked.

"He graduated from Yale Medical School where he specialized in geriatric medicine. He became the head of our Board of Directors and married a nurse. And ever since then, we have continued to have family members on staff and involved in our future. We are quite proud of our history."

"I can see why you would be," Susan said.

"You see, we are unique. We remain—and hope to remain—unconnected with any of the many large, impersonal for-profit companies that are building nursing homes faster than they can staff them. We are very proud of our staff-to-resident ratio. It is the highest in the state."

Susan noticed the reference to the future, but decided to wait to bring it up. "How do you find staff here on the island?" she asked.

"Oh, most of our staff lives on the mainland and commutes by ferry." Astrid Martin glanced down at her watch. "Perhaps I can show you around as we chat," she suggested, standing.

Susan got up immediately. "Of course!"

"You might want to take along our admission forms as well as the rest of our information. You might not know it but we are the only nursing facility of which I'm aware that gives its prospective residents and their families the Medicare comparison form."

Susan looked down at the pile of papers she had just grabbed from the desk. "Thank you," she muttered. She had no idea what a Medicare comparison form was. "I'll study them when I get home."

"Then we had better get going if you're going to catch the early afternoon ferry. We're a fifty-bed facility, not counting our small Memory Impaired Unit—and obviously your mother has no need for that—so there's quite a bit to see."

Susan, who had made no plans of any sort, merely smiled and followed the other woman from the room.

The Perry Island Care Center was bright and clean. Nice smells emanated from its stainless steel clad kitchen. There were flowers (plastic, but it was early in the season, Susan realized) on the tables in the spacious dining room. Attractive paintings lined the walls of the hallways. Bulletin boards announced upcoming events, trips to the Museum of British Art at Yale, and shopping expeditions to the Once in a Blue Moon Outlet Mall right outside of Hancock as well as weekly Friday afternoon musicales in the Art Therapy Room. The nursing stations were staffed by cheerful young people who seemed to be working rather than chatting among themselves. The residents looked well cared for and, those who weren't asleep, appeared happy and content.

There was no mention of the murders.

Perhaps she would have learned more if she had been allowed to wander about on her own, talking with both employees and residents, but Astrid Martin was not about to let that happen. She led Susan from place to place, drawing her attention to the many advantages of the Perry Island Care Center and comparing it to other unnamed institutions that placed profit before resident care.

Forty-five minutes later, Susan thanked Astrid Martin for the tour and walked out of the front door into the chilly daylight feeling discouraged. She had learned nothing and wasted time that would have been better spent helping her daughter take care of the twins. Thinking of Ethan and Rosie, she perked up immediately. She would catch the next ferry and, after stopping at the drugstore, head home. She'd pull some of the cilantro-spiked chicken chili—Chrissy's favorite—from the freezer, bake a pan of cornbread, and then help out with the twins. The relaxing family evening she had hoped for last night might only have been delayed. Stuffing the papers Astrid Martin had given her in her purse, she hurried back to the car.

She was surprised to find a young man leaning on her trunk and smoking a cigarette as he studied the macadam with the sullen expression that so many young people seemed to adopt these days.

"Pardon me," Susan started.

He raised his eyes from the ground, but his expression didn't change.

"You're leaning on my car," she explained.

"I wasn't hurting it," he said.

"But I'm afraid I might hurt you when I back up. I want to make the next ferry," she explained, wondering why he didn't just move.

"Oh." He looked over his shoulder at her car and then back at her. "I'm waiting for someone."

"Well, if you could just wait someplace else," she suggested, concerned about how long this might take.

"I . . .Yeah, there she is." A smile transformed him. "My girl," he said, looking over Susan's shoulder as he moved away. "She works here."

Susan turned and realized that the young woman who had been sitting at the desk in the entrance was walking toward them. "Do you need a ride?" she offered, seeing another opportunity to learn about the care center.

"No. We're fine," the young man assured her, without turning around.

Well, she had tried her best, Susan thought, getting into her car.

EIGHT

If it hadn't been for Clue's enthusiastic greeting, Susan would have thought her house abandoned when she arrived home. The kitchen sink was full of dirty dishes and she stopped long enough to fill the dishwasher and turn it on before she started upstairs.

Except for the wicker laundry basket full of clean, folded, and sweet smelling baby clothes, the hallway was deserted. Susan thought she heard wind chimes and peeked in the open nursery door. The sight that greeted her was so close to what she had envisioned when she created this room that, for a moment, she thought she had imagined it.

Ethan lay on his back, feet flying in the air, staring up at the nearest knight marching toward the castle, apparently fascinated, and certainly content. Shannon was sitting in the rocking chair giving Rosie her bottle as a CD of the Sonos Handbell Ensemble played. Shannon looked up at Susan and smiled.

"Is Chrissy lying down?" Susan whispered.

Shannon shook her head no. "Out after the dogs."

"What?"

They both looked down at the babies, who seemed to be completely disinterested in their conversation. "She ran after her dogs," Shannon explained, turning up the volume a bit.

"Someone left the gate to the backyard open and they ran away."

"Oh no!"

At Susan's cry, both babies stirred but settled back down almost immediately. Ethan's eyelids began to close and Rosie sighed deeply before getting back to the serious business of eating.

"When?" Susan asked. "How long has she been gone?"

Shannon looked up at the Cow Jumping Over the Moon clock which hung over the door. "About half an hour."

"She could be anywhere. I'd better go help her . . . unless you need me?"

"I'll be fine here."

Susan didn't wait around to hear more. She charged down the stairs and out the back door, pausing only long enough to fill the pockets of her jacket with dog biscuits. Clue trotted behind her and Susan was careful to latch the gate, trapping her dog in the backyard. Susan then ran down the driveway and stopped. There was no sign of either her daughter or Rock and Roll. Which way had they gone? She decided to jog around the block. If she didn't run into them, or someone who had seen them, she would come home and call the police. The mastiffs had visited Hancock on a few occasions, but they didn't really know their way around. They could be anywhere.

The afternoon was waning and the warmth of the day disappearing. Susan pulled her jacket tight across her chest and began to speed walk. Early bulbs poked up in gardens, their cheerful color relieving the dull brown that predominates in New England in the spring, but she didn't stop to admire them. Up ahead, a neighbor appeared, walking a large Irish wolfhound. Susan, who knew the dog's name was Sage but wasn't as familiar with its human walker, waved and hurried toward her.

"Hi! Where's Clue?"

"At home. Did you see two bullmastiffs? They're brindle and they're my daughter's and they've run away."

"No! But if I do . . ." The woman paused, apparently not sure what to offer.

"If you do, would you call the police and ask for Brett Fortesque and tell him where they are?" Susan asked.

"Of course." A chipmunk, popping its head out of a crack in a high stone wall, attracted Sage's attention and he and his mistress took off down the street.

Susan continued her search, but fifteen minutes later she was rounding the corner back to her street and had seen no sign of either the dogs or her daughter. With a sigh, she decided to go home and call Brett. She probably should have called him in the first place.

As soon as she made this decision, he appeared. Susan almost couldn't believe it as the police chief's car roared around the corner, lights flashing, and pulled up to the curb. She ran over to the driver's window.

"Brett! How did you know we needed you?"

"Chrissy called," he answered.

Susan smiled. Her daughter had everything under control.

"There's a rig overturned on 95, but we'll have more officers on the scene in a few minutes," he said, getting out of the car and starting up the sidewalk.

"That will help. They don't know the neighborhood very well. I mean, we walk them when they're here, but not a lot. You know how it is with two large dogs and—"

Brett turned and stared at her. "What are you talking about?"

"Rock and Roll. Didn't Chrissy call the police to report missing dogs?"

"Susan . . . Chrissy called us, yes. But she was reporting a body."

"A what?"

"A body. Apparently your new next-door neighbor is dead."

"Nadine or Donald?"

"I don't know who. I didn't take the call."

But Susan was already running up the sidewalk to the Baineses' house. A not-too-accurate replica of a turn-of-the-century Queen Anne Victorian, the house had four different doorways as well as three porches. Susan dashed to the front door and hammered on the brass knocker shaped like a mermaid. Large panes of engraved glass were set in the door and Susan could see Chrissy as she hurried across the wide foyer. By the time Chrissy had the door open, Brett was at Susan's side.

"Chrissy! What happened? Why are you here? Who's dead?"

Brett placed his hands on Susan's shoulders and gently pushed her aside. "Where's the body?" he asked.

"The kitchen." Chrissy sounded calm, but Susan realized her face was unnaturally pale. "She's lying on the kitchen floor."

"An ambulance should be here in a few minutes. Would you stay here and direct them to the kitchen when they arrive?" Brett asked. "Your mother can show me the way. Can't you?" He looked at Susan for confirmation.

"Yes. Of course."

"My dogs. Rock and Roll. They're in the basement. I didn't know where else to put them. They'll scratch up the door," Chrissy added.

"How did they get in? They didn't kill . . ." Susan couldn't even finish the question, it was so horrible.

"Mother!" Chrissy sounded so much like her adolescent self that Susan almost smiled despite the seriousness of the situation. "They didn't hurt her. They found her. She . . . she . . . she was stabbed. A lot." Chrissy took a deep breath and turned away.

"Susan, maybe you should stay with your daughter. I can find my way—"

"I'll be fine," Chrissy said. "You go with Brett, Mother. It's been a shock. That's all."

Susan hesitated. "You're sure?"

Chrissy's shoulders stiffened. "Yes. I'm fine. Really. Fine. You don't have to treat me like a child."

This was not the time to assure her daughter that many grown-ups would fall apart if they discovered a body, and Susan led Brett from the foyer as sirens sounded in the distance.

Nadine Baines's elegant "chef's kitchen" was usually spotless, everything in its place, granite countertops immaculate, Italian hand-glazed floor tiles shining. Now it was covered with blood. Nadine herself was lying beside the dark red Wolf stove, the $200 Sabatier chef's knife she had bought in France stuck in her chest. Susan suspected it was the first time the knife had actually been used for anything other than status conferral.

"Can you identify her?"

"Of course. It's Nadine Baines. You and Erika probably met her at my Valentine's Day dessert party. She and Donald moved here in January."

"How well do you know her?"

Susan hesitated. "I see her a lot, but I don't really know her all that well."

Brett, who had been leaning over the body, looked up at her. "You don't like her."

"No, not really. It's not that she's a bad person or anything, but she's sort of self-centered. And she has too much time on her hands . . . and . . . and someone must have hated her an awful lot," Susan concluded.

"It certainly looks that way," Brett agreed, walking around the body, being careful not to tread in the blood. The dogs hadn't been so careful; their paw prints were everywhere.

"Not exactly a pristine crime scene, is it?" Susan commented.

"Not exactly. Oh well, it's amazing what forensics can come up with." Brett furrowed his brow. "I vaguely remember meeting her—hair a bit too blond, very loud voice—but I can't come up with a face for the husband."

"Donald. His name is Donald. He's a big deal real estate broker in town and he's usually talking about it when you see him."

"Can't say that rings a bell."

"Are you going to call him and tell him about this? Or just wait until he arrives home?"

"Where does he work? Do you know what time he usually gets home in the evening?"

"He has an office in Hancock—Donald Baines Executive Homes. But he doesn't have a regular schedule as such. Well, most real estate agents don't, do they? I mean, he shows houses at all hours. And then there are open houses and things."

"Is he connected with Blaine Baines Executive Homes and Estates?"

"Yes. His mother owns that agency. His agency is connected to it. At least, I think it is," she added.

"We'll find out all those things."

"I can't imagine Donald killing anyone." She looked over

at Brett. "I know. You're going to tell me that people always say that about any murderer."

"No, I'm going to ask you if that door is the only way out of the basement. I'd like to get the dogs out of there without them passing through here again."

Susan thought for a moment. "I don't think so. I mean, the house looks old, but it's fairly new so it does have all the amenities that you expect in a new home. I think there's an exit on the side."

Brett looked out the window toward the fence around the Henshaws' backyard. "That side?"

"No, the other one. There's a garage over there and a small garden shed. And I think there is another door—one of those metal things—that leads to the basement. Do you want me to go around to get the dogs and take them home?"

"No, I think we'll wait to see if forensics wants to look at them first . . . Susan, I'll let them go as soon as possible. That's all I can promise."

"I was just wondering how much damage they can do down there in the meantime."

"Can't be helped," Brett said.

"Brett." Susan grabbed his arm. "Chrissy gave birth to twins a few weeks ago and they only arrived yesterday and she's looking so pale."

He nodded. "I know, and I'll make this as easy for her as possible. We'll need a statement, but after that, she can go on home." He smiled for the first time since entering the house. "It's not as though she'll be difficult to find."

The door to the foyer opened as he finished speaking and Chrissy herself appeared. "They're here," she said simply as a large group of uniformed officers followed her into the kitchen.

Brett stood up and the murder investigation began.

NINE

THE PHONE WAS RINGING WHEN SUSAN ARRIVED HOME. Kathleen was on the other end of the line.

"Oh, Kathleen, you won't believe what's happened. Nadine was murdered and Chrissy—well, not Chrissy, the dogs really—found her."

"What were they doing at the nursing home? Or even on the island? Was Nadine at her summer home? Did you take them there?"

For one moment Susan thought that the confusion of the past twenty-four hours had affected her brain, but then she understood Kathleen's assumptions. "I'm not talking about the Perry Island Care Center. Nothing happened there—at least not today. Nadine was murdered next door. In her house. Chrissy and the dogs found her."

"They found her inside her house? How did they get in?"

"I have no idea."

"Did you call the police?"

"Chrissy did. Brett's there now. Chrissy has to make a statement and then she'll be home. Kathleen, I'm worried about her. She looks completely wiped out. I'm afraid this is all just too much for her."

"She's young and resilient. But having a doctor check her out might not be a bad idea."

"If I can convince her to see one. You know, I should start dinner. Stephen and Jed will be arriving home any minute now. And Chrissy will feel better if she eats something."

"Is there anything I can do to help? Our dinner tonight is mac and cheese, carrot sticks, and applesauce. I can get it on the table in minutes if you need me. I could pick up some take-out and bring it over there if that would make things easier."

"Thanks, but I think we're okay."

"Then I'll say good-bye and go see why the kids are so quiet. I always think they're doing something they shouldn't be doing when I don't hear them for a bit," Kathleen said and hung up.

Susan put down the receiver and turned around. Shannon was standing in the open doorway, a bulging plastic bag in each hand. "I'm sorry. I didn't mean to startle you. But the garbage cans out back are full and I don't know where to put the overflow."

"Oh." Susan thought for a moment. "Why don't you just pile them up in a corner of the garage? We'll have to remember to put them on the curb early tomorrow morning so they get picked up."

"I'll take them out after the babies' first feeding. Ethan and Rosie probably have their breakfast before the garbagemen are even thinking of getting out of bed," Shannon offered. "Do the cans go on the left or the right side of the driveway?"

"The left," Susan said, frowning. "Shannon, do you have a minute?"

"I . . . Do you want me to put these outside first?"

"Just toss them out the back door for now."

"I don't like to leave the twins alone for too long."

Susan reached across the counter and flipped the switch

on a small plastic box. "We'll hear them on the baby monitor if they start to yell. Sit down. Do you want a cup of tea or anything?"

"No. I'm fine." Shannon remained standing, shifting her weight from one foot to the other and staring down at a spot in the middle of the tile floor.

Susan plunged right in. "There's been a murder in the neighborhood. Right next door, in fact." She watched Shannon's face carefully. Did the nurse seem startled? Wouldn't anyone be startled by her statement?

But Shannon remained composed. "Who died?" she asked.

"Nadine Baines. She was over here yesterday when you arrived." Susan wondered about Shannon's lack of reaction to this news. Perhaps nurses were more familiar with death than people in other fields? Especially nurses who had worked in nursing homes?

"How was she killed?"

"She was stabbed . . ." Susan remembered the blood-spattered kitchen. "Many times," she added.

Shannon shifted her attention to the wrought iron lamp suspended over the table, but she didn't ask any more questions.

"The police will probably be over here sometime this evening," Susan continued. "They may want to ask you if you heard anything or saw anyone . . . since you were the only person home here when the murder happened."

"No, I wasn't."

"What do you mean?"

"I wasn't the only person here when the murder occurred. Chrissy was also home. You told your friend on the phone that Chrissy found the body. So the murder must have happened earlier. While she and I were here taking care of the babies."

"I . . . You're right!" Susan wondered if Shannon heard the relief in her voice. "Well, then Brett probably has already realized that and he might not want to bother you."

"Who's Brett?"

"Brett Fortesque. Hancock's chief of police. We're old friends."

"The chief of police is one of your friends?"

"Yes. I've helped him solve a murder or two in the past," Susan added modestly.

"This doesn't seem to be the type of place where people would be murdered."

"You might think that, but—"

"That sounds like Ethan," Shannon interrupted as the baby monitor emitted a loud wail.

Susan hurried over to turn down the volume. "You can tell them apart? Just by hearing them?"

"Ethan's voice is a bit higher than Rosie's. I'd better go get him. He's going to wake up his sister."

Shannon left the garbage bags on the floor and hurried back to her charges as Brett Fortesque walked in the back door.

"Sounds like my house," he said, a smile on his handsome face. Fatherhood had brought nothing but joy to his life. Of course, he was here and, if his infant daughter was unhappy, his wife was coping with her.

"Where's Chrissy?" Susan asked, reaching into a cupboard for a pair of mugs.

"Chrissy left a few minutes ago. Isn't she here?"

"She probably came in the front door. I was talking to Shannon and didn't hear her." She waved the mugs in the air. "Coffee? Or maybe a glass of wine?" It was well past five PM she realized.

"The wine sounds great, but coffee will have to do. It's going to be a long night."

"Have you told Donald about his wife's death?"

"No. We called him at his office, but his secretary—or someone—said he was out with a client and not expected back at work today."

Susan nodded. "Apparently real estate is like that. Nadine was always complaining that she couldn't reach him."

"He doesn't have a cell phone?"

"That's what I asked. But she said Donald had been interrupted once too often when he had just about made a sale. So now he just turns it off whenever he's with clients."

Brett nodded.

"Do you think it's significant? Do you think Donald killed his wife?"

"I have no idea. There is no sign that the house had been burgled—at least nothing I could see in my brief look around. But she might have surprised someone breaking in and been killed."

"But you just said nothing was taken."

"I said it didn't look as though anything had been taken. It's too early to tell. Donald will know if anything is missing."

Susan wasn't so sure about that. In her experience, husbands didn't necessarily know where things went around the house and quite possibly weren't all that likely to discover anything missing. A thief could take the silver and a fortune in jewels, but as long as the television, DVD player, TiVo, CD player, and his computer were left behind, Jed certainly might not notice. But Susan was a loyal wife and didn't disagree.

"I—What's that?" Brett interrupted himself as loud shrieks drowned out anything else he might have been about to say.

"Twins." Susan once again turned down the baby monitor.

"They certainly sound unhappy. Do you need to go to them?"

"No, Chrissy and Shannon will be able to deal with them. Why?"

"If you have the time, I'd like to hear what you know about Nadine."

"Of course," Susan answered and then paused.

"Susan, no matter what you thought about her, I need information."

Susan grimaced. "I know, but I didn't really know her all that well. At least, not enough to like her. Maybe if I had known her better I would have discovered many redeeming characteristics."

"Why don't you just tell me about the characteristics that you didn't like, as well as anything you know about her background, relatives, marriage—you know the drill."

"Well, Donald and Nadine moved in next door just a few months ago. And about a week later, Nadine moved into my kitchen."

"What?"

Susan sighed. "Nadine had too much free time and was just a bit too self-involved. I had offered to help them out when they moved in—tell them the name of the best dry cleaner, stuff like that. You know how you do with a new neighbor."

Brett smiled at her. "I know how nice people like you and Jed do, yes. Go on."

"Well, in their case none of that was really necessary. Donald's mother has lived in town for years. In fact, Nadine told me about a wonderful dressmaker downtown who I'd never heard of. . . ."

"So she knew her way around Hancock."

"Yes. The problem was, I think, that she didn't have enough to do and she needed a lot of attention. So she began to stop over here once a day or so—just to chat. That's how she put it."

"Bugged the hell out of you, didn't it?" Brett's smile broadened into a grin.

"Yes. It did. There was no getting rid of her. She didn't take hints. I don't think she even heard hints. I would say things like I've got to get this done and she would tell me to go ahead and she'd keep me company. But it wasn't only her presence that was so irritating; it was that she was so sure I wanted to hear every detail of her life, everything she thought . . ." Susan stopped. "But that doesn't mean I know everything about her life."

"You didn't listen," Brett guessed.

"Most of the time, no. Oh, I did at first. I heard about every place she had lived and how Hancock compared. And her problems with decorators and deliverymen when she was getting settled. And how hard it was on her that she had to be home to answer the door for all these people and how they didn't show up on time. And the store that sent the wrong curtain fabric . . . Things that happen to everyone. Minor things that happen to everyone. But Nadine thought that when they happened to her, they were a crisis. And she made a big deal about them. She was always writing letters to the heads of huge international conglomerates to complain about an employee or some small thing that had happened to her. And she got responses, too—polite ones. I was amazed."

"Employees? Did she ever get anyone fired?"

"Not that I know of, but she sure tried. She used to rant and rage over the simplest mistake. Like if she ordered a salad and asked for the dressing on the side but then it came drenched in blue cheese, she wouldn't just send it back and ask for a substitution; she would insist on speaking to the owner of the restaurant and then go on and on—in public—about what had happened. And it happened a lot because she never just ordered what was on the menu. She always had to have something special. We ate dinner with them once at the Hancock Inn, but Jed said never again. Do you think that could be the answer? Maybe she was killed by an angry . . . uh . . . an angry unemployed person," she said, realizing just how silly she sounded.

But Brett took her suggestion seriously. "People have been killed for less than that. The loss of a job can change a person's life. And not for the better."

"But I don't know anyone who was actually fired."

"It's still something to keep in mind. Tell me more about her. If she's been sitting in your house daily for the past few months talking, you must have learned a lot."

"Besides that she liked to listen to herself."

"Besides that she liked to listen to herself," he agreed. "How about some background. Where she grew up. Does she have any family living nearby? What sort of shape was her marriage in?"

"Actually she grew up in Connecticut, up near Hartford. She was an only child. You know, I always wondered if that's why she expected so much attention. It can be lonely being an only child. Anyway, she seemed to have a fairly normal childhood. She complained that her mother was a feminist and didn't allow her to get involved in activities she considered sexist—like the Girl Scouts—which is not at all a sexist organization as far as I'm concerned. . . ." Susan realized she was about to go off on a tangent and returned to the topic. "She was encouraged to play sports on the boys' teams. But other than that, it sounded like she lived a traditional suburban life. I don't remember her mentioning her father too much. He was an expert in bridge engineering and was away from home a lot.

"I do know she met Donald in college. She went to Trinity and I think he went to Fairfield. They met her junior year and got married right after graduation."

"What was her major? What sort of work did she do?"

"Interestingly enough, while she listened to her mother and prepared for a career—she had a degree in marketing— she never worked. She always claimed that Donald wanted a traditional stay-at-home wife and so that's what she did."

"So she didn't listen to her mother after all."

"I guess not. As far as I know, she's never worked. In fact I always thought that was a bit odd. I mean, she doesn't have any children and not a whole lot of interest in domestic things. She hated to cook although she has a wonderful kitchen. Her house is immaculate, but she has a cleaning woman who comes twice a week so I don't suppose she spends any time on her hands and knees scrubbing the floors."

"What does she do with her time? Does she have any hobbies?"

"Not unless you consider shopping and taking care of yourself a hobby."

"What sort of care?"

"Oh, you know. Working out. Getting your hair done. Manicures, pedicures."

"The usual."

"And the not so usual as well. She went to a specialist in some sort of stone massage, and an Alexander Technique teacher, a Rolfer, two or three herbalists, a practitioner of Chinese medicine . . ."

"Any reason why she took such good care of herself?"

"Nothing else to do?" Susan realized she was being seriously bitchy. "I shouldn't say that. She had a cancer scare a few years ago—irregular cells in a Pap smear—and she always said it changed her life. It probably did. I've been lucky enough to have good health. I don't know how I would react to something like that."

"After the initial shock was over, you would be mature and sensible, just like you always are."

"I hope so," she said, less assured than he was on this subject. "Anyway, Nadine put an enormous amount of time and effort into taking care of herself."

"And money. I assume these services aren't cheap."

"No, but they have a lot of money."

"How do you know that?"

"Well, Donald has sold a lot of houses around here in the past few years. And there aren't many that would sell for under a million and most go for a lot more than that. I don't know exactly what percentage of the sale goes into his pocket, but more than enough for Nadine to indulge, I'd imagine."

"Six percent."

"What?"

"The agent's fee—it can run as high as six percent of the sale price. Erika thinks we need more room now that the baby's here so we've just begun looking at houses in the area— not that a policeman's income buys much around here." He frowned. "So you said Donald works for his mother."

"Well, he's certainly connected to her agency. If you're in the market for a house, you would have heard of Blaine Baines."

"If you've picked up any newspaper in southern Connecticut or the Real Estate section of the Sunday *New York Times,* you've heard of Blaine Baines Executive Homes and Estates. The ads are everywhere. And they all have her photograph prominently displayed. Is she old enough to have grown children?"

"I think she's using a photograph that was taken more than a few years ago," Susan explained. "Although she looks pretty good for a woman in her early sixties. But I did hear that one of her husbands was a plastic surgeon."

"Just how many husbands has she had?"

"I think five—or maybe six. I do know that Donald's father was her first and Travis Dean—you know him; he works down at the Field Club—was her last."

"The only Travis I know at the club is the bartender."

"That's him."

"He couldn't be more than twenty-five."

"I think closer to thirty, but yes, he's a lot younger than she is. Anyway, they're divorced." Susan wasn't sure what she thought about any of this. On one hand, it seemed very liberal and up-to-date for a woman to be involved with a younger man. On the other hand, she had a twenty-one-year-old son and she sure hoped he would fall in love with someone his own age. The last thing in the world she wanted was a daughter-in-law as old as she was!

"You said they moved to town recently. Did Donald just start working for his mother?"

"No, he ran her office over in New Canaan for years and years. I got the impression that he moved here to help out his mother. . . ." She hesitated.

"But you're not so sure."

"Not really. I'm not sure where I heard it or how I got the impression, but for some reason I think Donald's mother wasn't too thrilled with the situation. But she owned the firm so she could certainly have him work wherever she wanted."

"Interesting. How did Nadine get along with her high-powered mother-in-law?"

"I think just fine. I know Blaine liked her. She was always saying that the best thing Donald ever did was marry Nadine. And if Nadine didn't reciprocate those feelings, she was smart enough to shut up about it."

Brett nodded. "It's important for relatives to get along."

While Susan agreed with him, that wasn't exactly what she had been saying.

"If there's nothing else important, I'd better get back to the crime scene," Brett said, standing up.

"No, there's nothing else that I can think of," Susan lied.

TEN

THERE WAS A DINER ON A SIDE STREET IN HANCOCK THAT few residents patronized. Frequented by workmen, contractors, landscapers, and groups of disenfranchised high school students, the booths were nearly as greasy as the food, but that didn't matter as much to the clientele as the fact that they were unlikely to run into their employers—or their parents.

A young man slouched in the rear booth, looking much the worse for wear. His silky blond roots betrayed an inept dye job on hair that drooped into his eyes. The way he fell on the food his waitress brought was a sign of recent hard times.

It was a slow night and the waitress propped one hip against his table, ready to chat. "I don't think I recognize you. You a student at the high school?" she asked amiably.

"No."

"Do you work here in town?"

"No."

"Just passing through?"

He looked up from his burger and fries. "Yeah. That's it. Just passing through." And he was gonna keep passing. What a mistake to pause in this town. Here he was trying to avoid the police, and the house next door to the place Shannon was working was swarming with them. God, she sure could attract trouble. But she was generous. He'd say that for her. He stopped eating long enough to pat the bulging wallet in his jacket pocket. But he wasn't going to hang around here for long, that was for sure. Staying here could bring him nothing but trouble.

Susan sat up in bed and turned on the light hanging over her nightstand. "Jed, are you asleep?"

They had been married for over three decades; he knew answering "yes" wouldn't help him. "It's after midnight," he replied.

She ignored his statement and continued. "I'm worried about Chrissy. She has hardly even glanced at her baby presents."

"I was going to talk to you about that," he said, sitting up. "Do you think we could move them out of my library? I was going to pay some bills after dinner tonight and couldn't even find them in that mess."

"Oh, don't worry about that. I hid them. But about Chrissy, Jed . . ."

He was completely awake now. "Why did you hide the bills?"

"Shannon." She saw the surprise on his face and continued. "We don't really know her and she's going to be alone in the house sometimes—well, not counting the twins. Anyway she has a lot of opportunity to go through our things and . . . well, I just felt more comfortable with everything put away."

"How is she different from the dozens of people we've hired to clean or fix appliances over the years?"

"It's a different situation completely. In the first place she's here all the time. Because she was sort of dumped in our laps—or in our house, I guess is more accurate."

"You're saying that we don't know anything about her—

and I'm not arguing with you—but that's also true of lots of people we hire."

"But those people aren't here overnight while everyone is asleep. Shannon could be downstairs right now going through everything we own and we would never know it."

"Or she could have dashed next door this afternoon and killed Nadine?"

Susan gasped. "What do you know?"

"Nothing at all, but that's what's worrying you, isn't it?"

"It is true that Shannon arrived here and then Nadine was killed."

"And what's the connection between the two of them?"

Susan hesitated. "I don't really know if there is one."

"So you suspect her of killing for no reason?"

"Jed, you're making me sound like an idiot."

"If you believe the woman who is taking care of our grandchildren is a murderer and you've decided to do nothing about it, you just might be."

"I don't really believe that. In fact, I know she isn't. She and Chrissy were here together all afternoon."

"So why in heaven's name did you wake me up?"

"Because I'm worried about Chrissy. You were the one who changed the subject."

Jed sighed. "Okay. You're right and, to tell the truth, so am I. She looks horrible. Do you think she should see a doctor?"

"I suggested it and she almost bit off my head. It's probably just fatigue. But some women do suffer from depression after giving birth and she has so much to do, so many changes going on in her life. I was wondering if perhaps we should duplicate the Canfield's gift and hire another baby nurse. The babies need a lot of care. Maybe they're just too much for two people."

"Then you'd be worried about two strangers in the house."

"Maybe not! Maybe we could find someone that someone knows . . . If you know what I mean."

"It's almost one in the morning. I don't know what I mean. Hon, let's leave this till tomorrow." Without waiting for a response, he slid back down under the sheets and rolled over.

Susan frowned at his broad back and reached out to turn off the light.

She fell asleep almost immediately and, if more people were wandering up and down the stairs and in and out of rooms than was usual in the middle of the night, she wasn't aware of it. But Clue, lying on an old Burberry blanket at the end of the bed, didn't get as much sleep as usual and, if the Henshaws had been listening, they would have heard uncharacteristic growls coming from their dog.

The next day followed the lead of the one before, with the mayhem beginning very early. The twins were still asleep, Shannon was dozing in the rocking chair between their cribs, Jed and Stephen were driving to the train station, Chrissy was in the shower, all three dogs were exploring the backyard as though they had never been there before, and Susan was standing in the middle of her basement wondering if the big puddle on the floor of her laundry room had emerged from the hot water heater or her less-than-a-year-old washing machine, when the doorbell rang.

Pulling her flannel robe across her chest and yanking its sash tight, she ran upstairs, hoping she got to her visitor before the babies woke up. She was too late. Rosie—at least she thought it was Rosie—began to wail as she pulled open the door. Donald Baines stood on her doorstep, the very image of a shattered widower.

"Susan." He seemed unable to go on.

"Donald. Come in. I was just going to make some coffee and . . . and something to go with it."

"I really don't think I could eat anything—as good as your cooking is—but perhaps a cup of coffee."

"Of course. Why don't you go on into the living room—we'll be more comfortable there—and I'll bring it out? It will only take a few minutes."

"That would be nice."

"You know the way," she added as he paused in the hallway.

"Yes, I was just afraid of knocking over some of these boxes . . ."

"Good Lord! I . . . I guess Jed moved some things out of his library last night. Baby presents," she explained, staring at the large pile stacked on the floor near the door.

"Of course. I had forgotten. You're new grandparents. Congratulations. I didn't realize gifts were appropriate."

"Oh, they're not for us. They're for the babies. My daughter and her family are living with us while they look for a place to live. My son-in-law just started a new job," she said, naming a prestigious brokerage house.

Donald perked up immediately. "And they'll be looking for a home in Hancock?"

"They're talking about an apartment in the city, but I'm thinking that once they look around and see what they can afford, they might change their minds."

"Well, don't forget your new neighbor if they need a real estate broker," Donald said, the possibility of a new client apparently wiping all thoughts of his loss from his mind.

"So you think you'll stay in the house . . . instead of moving somewhere smaller?" Susan instantly regretted the question. How could she be so insensitive?

But Donald didn't seem to notice. "Oh, I'll stay here. That

house is a great investment. I got a bargain on it and it's going to do nothing but appreciate in this market." He took a deep breath and returned to his depressed mode. "Of course, it won't be the same without Nadine. She really knew how to turn a house into a home."

That was the last thing Susan would have said about Nadine, but she wasn't going to argue with a bereaved husband. "I . . . I'll get our coffee."

She was gone from the room for only a few minutes. When she returned, she discovered Donald standing in front of the bookshelves that lined one wall, examining a current best seller as though it was a rare first edition. "Have you read that one?" she asked, moving aside a large box from Hanna Anderson to make room for the tray she carried.

"No. I don't have much time to read. Well, not as much as I would like. I have so many obligations for my work. Rotary, Elks, Kiwanis, Lions' Club, golf. Networking is very important to a real estate agent," he added, perhaps noticing Susan's startled expression.

"Yes . . . Why are you here? I mean, is there anything I can do for you?" She passed him a cup of coffee.

"Your daughter found my wife's body. Is there any cream?"

"I . . . she . . . yes . . . Well, it's milk, not cream, but I could get some cream if—"

"No, this is fine." He poured milk to the top of his cup, sipped, and grimaced. "Fine. Really fine."

"Chrissy did find Nadine. She was looking for her dogs."

"That's what someone—one of the police officers, I think—told me. But I don't understand how she got into the house."

That had been one of the first questions discussed over dinner last night. "Chrissy was looking for her dogs and she heard one of them barking. She assumed they were in your yard, but, when she went to look, she discovered the back door already open. Rock and Roll, the dogs, are bullmastiffs and they can pretty much push open any door, but only if it isn't latched."

"Yes. That makes sense." He nodded as though the simple thing she had just told him was important. "I'd like to see your daughter sometime."

"She's still asleep. But we talked a lot last night. Maybe I can help you?" She didn't add that their conversation had been constantly interrupted by the babies' demands and she probably knew more about the twins' routine—or lack of such—than the situation surrounding Nadine's discovery.

"You saw her body." It was a statement, not a question.

"Yes. You must have been shocked."

"Nadine would have hated people seeing her like that."

"Uh . . . well, yes." What a strange comment. It wasn't as though Nadine had been discovered with her hair a mess or wearing old jeans. She had been covered with her own blood, for heaven's sake. She looked at Donald carefully. Was he drugged? In shock? "When are you going to have the funeral?" she asked, not knowing what else to say.

"There will be an autopsy. The police insist, although it's a complete waste of time. It was obvious to anyone who saw her yesterday what the cause of death was. And then her body will be released to me. I suppose we'll hold a memorial service sometime after that. I must remember to say something about that in the obituary." He reached in his pants pocket and pulled out a small, elegant leather bound notebook with a tiny silver pen attached. He spent a moment writing and then looked up at Susan. "Would you like to hear the obituary or would you prefer to see it in the newspaper this evening?"

"I . . . Yes, I'd like to hear it. Did you write it yourself?"

"Mother and I got together over it late last night. I couldn't sleep, see."

"Of course. I understand."

"And Mother made me hot Ovaltine like she used to when I was a boy, and we worked and worked. She thought it would take my mind off my problems. And that we should do what needed to be done. 'Let's get on with it' is what she said. Mother is very big on getting on with it."

Definitely drugged, Susan decided. "Do you want to read it to me?" she asked.

"Yes, I would like that. It may be a bit unconventional. It is unconventional, but I think unconventional times call for unconventional responses, don't you?"

"Yes. Of course." She picked up her cup, sipped, and hoped the expression on her face looked sympathetic as well as encouraging. "Go ahead."

Donald took a deep breath and began reading in a voice about half an octave deeper than his normal speaking voice.

" 'Mrs. Nadine Baines, née Mortimer, died unexpectedly in her home yesterday afternoon.' I thought that was probably more than enough detail. What do you think?"

Since Susan was sure the front page of the paper where this would be published would be covered with details of the murder itself she could only agree.

" 'Born in Connecticut, she graduated with honors from Trinity College. She was married to Donald Baines, owner of Donald Baines Executive Homes. The couple moved to Hancock this year. Mrs. Baines was a deacon at the Hancock Presbyterian Church as well as active in their Women's Circle. She played on the mixed doubles tennis team at the Hancock Field Club.' Well, she would have this summer. We had signed up," he explained to Susan.

She nodded.

" 'She was also a member of the Women's auxiliary of the Lions' Club, the Kiwanis Club, the Elks, and the Rotary. A founding member of the Hancock Women's Reading Circle, she also did volunteer work for the public library. A famous hostess, she will be sadly missed by her loving family and her friends.' "

"What do you think?"

"I . . . I think it's very nice." Susan stumbled over her words. This was the woman who had been wasting so much time in her kitchen for the past few months?

Shannon entered the room, a baby in each arm, and a frown on her face. "I think I've broken the babies' bottle warmer."

There was a crash and a splash and Donald Baines looked down at the Samarkand carpet. "I think I've broken your lovely coffee cup," he explained needlessly, not taking his eyes off Shannon.

ELEVEN

SUSAN DIDN'T KNOW WHO WAS PALER—SHANNON OR DONald. But she knew where her priorities lay; she got up to take Ethan and Rosie from their nurse's arms.

"I . . . Oh, I . . ." Shannon seemed unable to express herself.

Donald was not having that problem. "You! You're that nurse!" He pointed at her dramatically. "What are you doing here?"

"I work here," Shannon whispered, hugging the babies close to her chest. She turned to Susan. "If you could just check on the warmer for me and put a pan of water on a burner to warm? I don't trust microwaves to heat evenly and these little guys will realize how hungry they are any minute now. I'm going to go back upstairs. I was trying to let Chrissy sleep. But . . ." She glanced over at Donald Baines. "I . . ." She left without finishing her sentence.

Donald Baines wasn't so discreet. "You know who that is, don't you?" he asked. "That's the person who killed my wife! Call the police immediately!"

"I won't and she isn't," Susan protested loudly, hoping Shannon was still close enough to overhear. "She was with Chrissy and the twins yesterday—all day. She couldn't possibly have murdered your wife!"

Donald Baines got up, oblivious to the fact that he was grinding the handle of Susan's antique Herend cup into her carpet. "If you won't call, I'll go home and do it myself!" he announced and stormed out.

Susan sat quietly for a moment, gazing at the mess on her carpet. She didn't have long to wait. Shannon walked back into the room, bouncing the now whimpering twins in her arms. "Let's go into the kitchen and warm up those bottles. We can talk while we do it," Susan suggested.

"What he said . . . I can explain . . . but you . . . It didn't surprise you, did it?" Shannon asked, following Susan.

"No. Nadine told me about the Perry Island Care Center deaths."

"And that I was working there at the time."

"Yes."

"And that's why you know I was here with Chrissy when the murder occurred. You checked."

"Yes." Susan grabbed a heavy copper pan, filled it with water, and plopped it on the stove. She turned back to Shannon. "You know what?"

"No. What?"

"I think we need two baby seats in here. We could put them on the table and then the babies would be nice and safe when you're working at the stove or getting things from the refrigerator or whatever."

"Chrissy is trying to keep their stuff from taking over the house."

Susan smiled. "Fat chance."

Shannon didn't return her smile. "Why are you letting me stay here if you knew about P.I.C.C.?"

"You're such a good nurse. And I don't believe you're the murderer."

"Yesterday you said you have discovered the identity of murderers in the past."

"Yes," Susan answered modestly.

"So you can tell who is a killer and who isn't—that's why you trust me?"

"No. I'm not psychic or anything. I just . . . I can figure things out. It started years ago—there was a murder in the PTA. The police began an investigation immediately, of course. But they didn't know anyone involved or the various groups or how things work in town. You could say I had inside information."

"Like you have now. I mean, you knew Nadine and she told you about me."

"Yes, I knew Nadine but not all that well. She only moved to town a few months ago."

"And you've really found murderers."

Susan nodded.

"It's too bad you don't live out on Perry. My life would be different if someone had figured out who killed our residents. And not just my life, the lives of others as well," she added sadly.

The water began to simmer and Susan put the bottles in to warm. Ethan started to grizzle so she took him from Shannon's arms. Tucking his head underneath her chin, she began to walk about the room. Just as this movement had consoled her babies decades ago, Ethan settled down immediately. "What exactly happened on Perry Island? I remember hearing about some deaths in the nursing home there, but not many of the details." She decided it was not the time to tell her that she had visited Perry Island only yesterday.

Shannon gently wiped a line of drool off Rosie's chin before answering. "It's hard to know where to begin."

"At the beginning." Susan was always willing to use a cliché if the circumstances required it.

"That's just it. I'm not sure when the murders began or who was the first person to be killed."

"I don't understand."

"Nursing homes aren't like other places. The residents of nursing homes are old and many of them will die there, so when there is a death, no one thinks of murder. Death is just not all that unusual."

Susan tried out the formula on her wrist before handing one bottle to Shannon and sitting down to offer the other to Ethan. "I understood that three people were killed."

"Well, there were deaths that the coroner called murder, but there was one death right after I began working there that struck me as odd—well, not when it happened, but later when we knew about the other three. You see, the murders were all different. More than one method was used. That's the reason no one knew what was happening at first. There was no pattern."

Susan smiled down at the baby in her arms and thought how nice it was that he was too young to understand even one word of their conversation. "What do you remember about each death?"

"Everything!"

"Could you tell me about them?"

"I suppose . . . yes."

"Why don't you begin with the one that you didn't realize was a murder at the time?" Susan said.

"Okay. It was Mr. Roper; we used to call him Mr. Reporter. That's what he had been. He worked on a paper in California—I don't remember which one—and he loved to talk about it. The good old days. You know, lots of the residents felt that way about the past and we tried to humor them."

"Like calling him Mr. Reporter."

"Exactly."

"How did he die?"

"He was diabetic and his blood sugar got out of control and he went into shock. After he died, empty bourbon bottles were found in his locked drawer. Each resident had a locked dresser drawer although we never had any problems with theft, at least not while I was working there. Anyway, after they found the bottles, everyone assumed that he had drunk himself to death—not a terribly difficult thing to do if you have diabetes, a serious heart condition, and you're almost a hundred years old."

"But you didn't believe that was the cause of his death?"

"I . . . it didn't make sense. See, one night we—some of the younger staff—were having a little celebration for another nurse who had just gotten engaged. We had champagne and little cakes, but we weren't getting drunk or anything. It was just a toast and a bite to eat and back to work. Anyway, Mr. Reporter was having trouble sleeping and he wandered down the hallway so we asked him to join us. And he did, but he refused any champagne or anything to eat. He said he hadn't gotten to be as old as he was by ignoring doctor's orders."

"So you don't think he drank?"

"Oh, it's possible. I know that some alcoholics refuse to indulge in public and will drink only when they're alone. But . . . well, everyone was surprised when the bottles were found. And we took good care of our residents. I don't think something like that could have gone unnoticed."

"How could he have died then?"

"It would have been possible for someone on the staff to

either give him the wrong medication or withhold the proper meds and cause a serious imbalance in his blood sugar levels."

"And then plant the bottles in his locked drawer?"

"Yes."

"What about the lock?"

"There was a master key. It was kept in the office. Almost anyone could have gotten hold of it if they had wanted to."

"Anyone on the staff or anyone at all?"

"Oh, I think just the staff . . ." She paused and rearranged Rosie's arms, much to the baby's dismay. "I guess . . . I mean, no one ever thought it might be a resident."

"Why not? Were they so incapacitated that they couldn't have killed someone, or taken the key and stashed empty bottles in that drawer?"

"No. We had residents who were quite . . ." She paused as if searching for the correct word.

"Spry?" Susan suggested.

"Spry and more. Most of the residents were elderly and many were incapacitated, but a few were perfectly able to . . . to do what you just described."

"Were the residents ever considered suspects?"

"Not that I know of. Not seriously. The police questioned them of course, but one was the result of a lethal injection, one was suffocation, and . . . and another was pushed off the top of the building." She shuddered. "That was Mrs. Hershman. I found her."

"Was she the next person to die after Mr. Roper?" Susan asked.

"No, she was the last. The next person was Mr. Blake. He suffocated."

"So everyone knew it was murder right away."

"No, an accident. He was found tangled in his blankets. It

sounds odd, but it could have been just one of those things—an old man thrashing around in the night. Anyway, no one thought of murder until Miss Breen died the very next day. She was a lovely lady, a retired school teacher—Latin. She had lived all over the world teaching in unusual places and she knew so many interesting people. P.I.C.C. was pretty out of the way, but she had lots of visitors, people she had taught mainly. Two of her students are now professors at Yale and it was one of them who went to the police and insisted on an investigation. If he had done it earlier, it might have stopped the murderer."

"She was the one who died because of an injection?"

"Yes. . . . There was no reason for her to have been given it at all, so once it was found in the body, everyone knew something was wrong. But the results of the autopsy didn't get back until the afternoon of the day I found Mrs. Hershman."

"Tell me about that."

Shannon sighed. "She . . . She was . . . It was awful. It was late morning and I went outside to get some fresh air. P.I.C.C. was clean and it certainly didn't smell the way some nursing homes do, but it was hot. Many of our residents had circulation problems of some sort and they all got chilled easily so the thermostats were always turned up way too high. Anyway, I went out to cool off and I found her. She was lying on the ground. Her arms and legs were in a weird position, but I just thought she had fallen down. I called to her and touched her gently on the shoulder, but she didn't move. I thought maybe she was in shock so I took off my sweater and put it around her and ran back inside to get help. She was dead and . . . and it was obvious right away that she hadn't just tripped and fallen down."

"I'm surprised that residents were allowed to wander around outside on their own."

"They weren't. And I don't remember it ever happening before. There were only a few doors and all of them were alarmed except for the back door where supplies were delivered, and there was a door between that area and the living area that was kept closed as well as alarmed. And there was always someone working in the kitchen twenty-four/seven, so no one could have gone out there without being seen. I don't think anyone could have just wandered out, but I didn't think about that then. I mean, what's more likely—that someone had wandered out the back door where the alarm was turned off or someone had gone up on the roof and been thrown off?"

"Good point," Susan said. "But how did they know she had been thrown off and not gone up there alone and just fallen?"

"The police searched all over. They thought she might have jumped out of a window, but all the windows on that side of the building are semisealed. They only open a few inches. So they checked out the roof. They found a necklace up there that she always wore. It had been pulled off her neck and broken. The autopsy showed that as well as other signs of a struggle before her death. They also found heavy leather gloves. They had been used to strangle her before she was tossed off the wall."

"Was there any way to tell who had worn them?"

"No. Apparently the killer had put on surgical gloves before putting on the leather ones—there were boxes of gloves outside of each room; everyone had access to them—and dozens of pairs were tossed out every day, so searching the garbage didn't reveal anything."

Susan put down the almost empty bottle and moved Ethan

up onto her shoulder and patted his back gently. "But there was no doubt that she was murdered."

"None. And then they looked into the other two deaths and decided they were also suspicious . . ."

"But not Mr. Roper's death."

"No. I wonder why."

"Me, too. It doesn't make sense," Susan said. But she didn't mention the other thing that didn't make sense to her. Why someone who went outside to cool down would still be wearing a sweater.

TWELVE

SUSAN HAD NO IDEA WHAT TO DO SO SHE DID WHAT MANY
women would do in her situation: she called her best friend.
And, proving her worth as a best friend, Kathleen responded
immediately.

"We can talk on the phone, but I sure don't want to be
overheard by . . . by anyone." Susan looked at her closed bedroom door. She had come upstairs to make this call, but she
knew Shannon might interrupt at any time.

"You could come over here. Or we could meet someplace," Kathleen said.

Susan thought for a moment. "There are errands I should
run. The baby bottle warmer broke this morning. Do they
sell those things anyplace beside baby stores?"

"Sure. You can pick them up in any big drugstore. You can
buy almost anything in those places. I bought my new steam
iron at that gigantic place out on the highway."

"In the new mini mall? Isn't there a coffee shop there?"

"Yes, but it's a little late for breakfast and too early for
lunch. Are you hungry?"

"I'm starving. I haven't had anything to eat since last
night. Lord, I can't remember the last time I was too busy to
eat."

"So let's meet at that coffee shop in fifteen minutes."

"You're on! Paper and pens," Susan said. And they had been close friends long enough for both women to know what she was talking about.

Susan stopped at the drugstore on the way to the coffee shop so she arrived after Kathleen, a half dozen plastic bags in one hand and a huge stuffed rabbit in the other. "Isn't he adorable?" she asked, holding out the toy.

"Cute, but which baby are you giving it to?"

"I'm not sure. There was only one this big—or this cute—and I didn't want one twin to feel slighted so I didn't buy another. Maybe I'll stop at Toys 'R' Us on the way home and see what they have."

"Chrissy and Stephen are going to need an awfully big apartment just to house the baby toys."

"I know." Susan glanced down at the rabbit. "Maybe I'll take it back. The kids have so many baby presents that they haven't opened yet."

"Chrissy didn't open presents the second she laid eyes on them? That doesn't sound like her."

"You can't imagine how hectic things are. The babies keep all the adults so busy that Chrissy and Stephen haven't even finished unpacking. And I think Shannon has done more laundry in the past few days than I've done in the last month."

"Sounds like you're all running on overload."

"And then some." Susan picked up her menu as their waitress appeared. "What are you having?"

"Just some coffee and a blueberry muffin. I had a big breakfast less than two hours ago."

"Well, that's not enough for me. . . . I'll have the Western omelet and hash browns with rye toast and coffee," Susan ordered. "Now," she started, leaning on the table as their waitress hurried off, "Shannon told me about the murders out on Perry Island."

"Really?" Kathleen pulled a small leather-covered notebook and a slim gold Cross pen from her purse.

"Yes, and it was very interesting. She says death is different in a nursing home. . . ." Susan began the story.

By the time their breakfast arrived, Kathleen had covered two pages with notes and Susan really was starving. She stuck a fork into the pile of hash browns on her overflowing oval plate while Kathleen picked up her mug of coffee, a serious expression on her face.

"What do you think about the murders?" Susan asked.

"Actually, I was thinking about Nadine's death. Did you see the morning paper?"

"No, I've been so busy. Was there a story about it?"

"It covered the entire front page. The details of the murder itself, of course. A short interview with Brett in which he managed to say almost nothing, like the good cop he is. A fairly long interview with Donald who repeated over and over that he was distraught, miserable, and didn't know who could have wanted to harm a hair on the head of his perfect wife—you know the sort of thing."

Susan, her mouth full of omelet, only nodded.

"And an even longer interview with Blaine Baines."

Susan swallowed. "Really? What did she say?"

"After describing her son as the best husband in the world and explaining that she was shocked and horrified at the death of his beloved wife—"

"What did she say about Nadine?"

"All the normal things. How sweet she was, how she couldn't imagine why anyone would want to kill her, how they always got along perfectly."

"Working to make sure that neither she nor her son might become the primary suspects?"

"Definitely. And more than that. She was very careful to tell the reporter that not only did she and her son learn of the murder together, but they were together when it occurred."

"I'm not sure that's surprising. I think if I was in her— their—situation I would be tempted to do the same," Susan said.

"Do you think one of them might have killed her?"

"I have no idea. But I think you could describe Blaine Baines as ruthless, and ruthless people certainly might kill someone who stood in the way of what they wanted."

"Ruthless?" Kathleen mused. "Sounds like someone in one of those thrillers Jerry likes to read, not the local real estate agent."

Susan, her initial hunger sated, stared at her plate and thought a bit before answering. "Blaine's not your average housewife turned house seller. She owns and runs a multimillion-dollar business. But it's not her business self I'm talking about. It's her personality. She's completely egocentric. She quite literally sees things only from her own perspective."

"Don't we all?"

"Sure, to a point, but Blaine's egocentricity is extreme. I don't think she's capable of seeing the other person's—any other person's—point of view."

Kathleen put down her mug and stared across the table at her friend. "What happened?" she asked.

Susan put down her fork, took a sip of coffee, and tried to answer the question.

"We were once close . . . well, not close, but we spent time together. I didn't know a lot of people in town in those days. . . ." She stopped for a moment and then started again.

"I met Blaine . . . she introduced herself to me about two weeks after we moved to town. She was living just around the corner back then, in the big split-level the Sanders now live in."

Kathleen nodded to show she knew what house Susan was talking about and Susan continued. "She came by to be neighborly. That's what she said and I appreciated it although the house was a mess and—well, you know me. . . ."

"You want everything to be perfect when you have company."

"Yes. And I was new in town and didn't know much about the area. Anyway, I was thrilled to be meeting people. And Blaine explained that she was an important person in Hancock."

"What do you mean?"

"She was on the membership committee of the Field Club, a member of the town zoning board, and she was running for a seat on the town council—which she won that year with my help."

"Your help?"

"I volunteered to make phone calls for her."

"That day?"

"Yeah, that very day."

"I'm afraid you're not exactly filling me in on all the details."

"Sorry. To tell the truth, I still feel like a fool when I think about it."

"Why? Did you later learn that she was completely unqualified for the job?"

"No, I later learned that calling strangers is a horrible job that no one in their right mind would volunteer for . . . and that I was completely unprepared for. I called hundreds of homes and asked them to vote for someone I hardly knew and then, if they asked questions about Blaine's qualifications, I had a sheet of prepared answers to read to them. It took hours and hours, and I was made to feel like a fool more than once because I knew almost nothing about the town then and I wanted desperately to get involved, to feel as if I belonged. It was my own fault. I shouldn't have said I would do it."

"Exactly how did you end up doing it?"

"Well, Blaine said she was running and I asked how the campaign was going and she probably—this was years ago, remember—said she needed to find volunteers to make phone calls, that it was an easy job, could be done from home in spare time."

"And you leapt right in and volunteered to do it. I know you, Susan. That sounds just like you."

"Yes, I did. And, of course, it turned out to be a huge task. She gave me a list of three hundred households and said it was terribly important that I speak personally to at least one adult in each house. It took forever and, of course, I couldn't do it in my spare time—when the kids were napping, for instance—because no one was home then. I had to call during dinnertime or right after dinner and the people I called were irritated by me interrupting their family time and sounded like it. It was awful."

"And?"

"What do you mean?"

"You don't describe someone as ruthless because they manipulated you into making a few hundred phone calls," Kathleen said.

"Well, no. But, you see, Blaine didn't care about getting elected as much as she cared about her business. She used her elected office to become better known in the state. I wasn't helping create good government in Hancock. I was helping her become a real estate mogul. I should have refused to help."

"Why didn't you?"

"It sounds stupid—it's not like I don't have any will of my own, for goodness sake—but Blaine was so good at manipulating me. And I don't think she set out to do it. She's just so focused on herself and her goals and she can't imagine why anyone wouldn't be just the same. You know, she's a bit like Nadine, although with ambition. Nadine could spend hours talking about herself as though her life, opinions, you name it, were of compelling interest to anyone she happened to be talking to. Blaine is the same way. She just happens to be more goal oriented."

"And you ended up being taken advantage of."

"Like an idiot."

"Like a very nice person," Kathleen corrected her.

"Like an idiot," Susan repeated slowly. "I really thought I'd gotten a little backbone until right now. I can't believe Nadine used me the same way her mother-in-law did years ago and that I didn't even realize it. Damn."

"Look, you can either spend years and thousands of dollars on therapy or just figure it's in the past and forget about it. Besides, when you realized what Blaine was doing, you began to avoid her, right?" Kathleen asked, smiling.

Susan smiled back. "You know me—anything to get out of a confrontation. She moved to a bigger house on the other side of town.

"So what else did the paper say?" Susan added.

"Not too much else. The space was taken up by photographs of Nadine's home. There wasn't an obituary."

"There will be tonight. Donald brought it over early this morning for me to look at."

"Anything interesting?"

"Not really. Mostly an exaggerated telling of a pretty ordinary life."

"That could be said about a lot of obituaries."

"True."

"You know, there's really no reason—other than the unsolved murders on Perry Island—why Shannon should be considered a suspect in Nadine's murder," Kathleen said.

"Until some reporter or cop discovers the connection," Susan said.

Kathleen frowned. "You're probably right."

"So all we have to do is investigate Nadine's murder as well as three—or four—murders that took place on Perry Island over a year ago, while helping with the babies, not getting enough sleep, and doing all the extra things that houseguests demand."

"You're a modern woman. You can do it—with my help," Kathleen said encouragingly. "So what do we do first?"

"I think I'll go back to Perry Island and see if I can find out anything more."

"Great. What do you want me to do?"

Susan looked up from the remains of her meal. "Isn't it time you and Jerry thought about buying a bigger house?"

THIRTEEN

There was a bit of spring warmth in the sunlight and Susan got out of her car and stood by the rail as the ferry chugged across the Sound to Perry Island. The water was the steely gray of winter, but willows on both the mainland and the island were showing the sharp yellow of new growth and the salty air felt fresh against her face.

"Are you perhaps on your way to P.I.C.C.?"

Susan hadn't heard anyone approach over the roar of the boat's diesel engine and she turned to discover an elderly couple standing at the rail nearby. "I . . . yes, I am. My mother is getting old . . ." She brushed her hair off her forehead and didn't finish her explanation. Her mother, in fact, was probably younger than these people.

"It's a very nice place," he said to her.

The woman Susan assumed to be his wife reached out and placed one hand on Susan's arm. "It is, you know. We looked at most of the nursing homes in this part of Connecticut before deciding on P.I.C.C. for Frank's mother."

Susan hoped she didn't look as surprised by this statement as she felt. "Your mother?" she asked, and was immediately embarrassed by her rudeness.

But the gentleman only chuckled. "We live a long time in my family. My father passed a few months ago just six days short of his hundred and third birthday. Mother will be a hundred and one in June."

"How wonderful!" Susan said sincerely. "I . . . could I ask you a few questions about P.I.C.C.?"

"Ask away. Stupid not to check out the place as thoroughly as possible," he replied.

"Yes, dear, ask us anything," his wife urged.

"I've only been there once, but it looks like a very nice place."

"It is and the staff is quite caring and remarkably competent. You have to be very careful about that. Some of these places will hire just anybody. P.I.C.C. is still family owned, you know."

"But I heard . . . that is, there were stories in the newspapers near us. I live in Hancock. Well, I heard that some of the residents were . . . died under suspicious circumstances a few years ago."

"Oh, dear," the woman said, her pleasant expression changing into a frown. "That was so sad. Three of the residents did die."

"Three of the residents were murdered," her husband interrupted. "Gotta call a spade a spade when it's something as serious as murder. The police never found the culprit although some of us had our own ideas."

"I understood that it could have been someone on the staff," Susan said, getting right to what interested her.

"The staff members have the most access to the residents, of course. But I believe—and I think others who know the facility as well as my wife and I do would agree—that there are any number of people who could have killed those poor unfortunates."

"Really?" Susan didn't know if this was good news or bad news. On the one hand, it meant that Shannon was on a very long list of suspects rather than a short one. On the other hand, it probably made discovering the identity of the killer much less likely.

"Oh yes. You see, like all good nursing homes, P.I.C.C. encourages family members and friends to visit the residents as often as possible."

"And they just let you walk right in. There isn't a lot of standing around in the lobby waiting for them to get the resident ready for your visit," his wife added.

"You mean things are up to snuff all the time," Susan said.

The older woman nodded so vigorously that locks of gray hair slipped from her neat bun. "That's one of the things you want to look for when you're considering placement for a relative. Some of these places—well, they don't stand up to their promises on close inspection."

"But in reference to the murders"—her husband returned them to their initial subject—"visits are allowed at any time, day and night. I believe that almost anyone could have gotten into P.I.C.C. claiming to be a friend of a resident and then killed those people."

"So allowing unlimited visitations might not be a good idea," Susan mused.

"Well, you can't have it both ways, my dear. Either you give people the freedom to do bad things or you keep the residents from what little contact with the outside world is possible for them."

"I suppose. But this is an island. Wouldn't that limit the number of people who come here?"

"Not really. The ferry service is regular so people can come and go from the mainland six times a day. And there are year-round island residents as well as seasonal renters. No, I don't think the location of the nursing home limits the number of suspects in any way. . . . But here we are. We had better get back in our cars and prepare to leave the ferry. Perhaps we'll see you at P.I.C.C., my dear."

"Yes. I have to see something else on the island first, but maybe we will run into each other," Susan said, heading for her Cherokee. She didn't want anyone at P.I.C.C. to know she was interested in the unsolved murders just yet so she thought that she would try to arrive at the home after these people. And, now that the subject of life outside of the nursing home had come up, she decided to explore the rest of the island. Driving off the ferry, she turned down the road in the opposite direction of her former destination. She wasn't sure where she was going, but she was fairly sure that, on an island, she would ultimately end up where she began.

The road outlined the coast and Susan drove slowly, admiring the view and the enormous cottage style homes so popular a century ago when large staffs were common and heating costs minimal. Small wooden signs indicated the locations of public fishing docks and beaches, but she didn't turn off until an arrow pointed the way to Perry Town. Following directions, she found herself at the intersection of two streets devoted to various shops, a small grocery store, a large liquor store, a real estate agency, and the local branch of an international bank. She pulled her car over to the side of the road, parked, got out, and looked around.

She stopped in front of a tiny shop. ISLAND BOOKS AND GIFTS—SUSTENANCE FOR THE MIND AND THE EYE was printed on the display window and from the open doorway came the scent of fresh brewed coffee. A brass bell tinkled as Susan pushed the door open wider and walked inside.

A short, heavyset woman with curly blond hair greeted her enthusiastically. "Welcome. Welcome. I'm Mandy Duncan. I own this store and you're my first customer of the day! How can I help you? Thrillers? Mysteries? Romance novels?

Nonfiction? Biography? I'm small, but I carry them all as well as gifts."

But Susan had spied a large poster for *The Wizard of Oz* hanging over a shelf of children's books and she was drawn in that direction. "*The Big Snow* . . . that was one of my favorites when I was little." She plucked the book from the shelf.

"An early Caldecott award winner. Wonderful book. I believe I have a few other volumes by the Haders as well." Mandy Duncan knelt down beside the shelf and rummaged through the stacks, passing volume after volume to her customer.

"I'll take them all," Susan said. "And . . ."

"And?" .

"I thought I smelled coffee."

"I have a coffee bar up by the cash register. Can I get you a cup while you look?"

"That really would be wonderful." Susan stood up, her arms full.

"I hope it's to your liking. I began offering snacks a few weeks ago and I'm never quite sure if I use too many beans or too few."

"Just as long as it's hot," Susan said, sitting down on a stool and placing the books on the counter. "Have you owned the store long?"

"Almost a decade, but things have changed for bookstore owners in recent years. I used to be the only outlet for books on the island. And I still am if you don't count Amazon and Barnes & Noble online. Unfortunately they can have books delivered to their customers before I've even gotten them into my ordering system. The gifts and snacks are my attempt to keep my head above water and the store making a profit."

"It must be difficult to run any business on an island," Susan commiserated.

"Depends on the business. This is mainly a summer resort community and so the real estate office does quite well with rental properties; the bank and the grocery store deal with necessities and do just fine, too. But I'm afraid there are simply too many people in the world who don't consider books a necessity."

"Well, I'm not one of them," Susan assured her, eyeing a shelf of new biographies. "But I'm not really on the island to buy books. I came here because my mother is getting old and I'm looking for a nursing home."

"Perry Island Care Center. An excellent facility."

"Really?" Susan asked. The response had been abrupt and she thought a certain coldness had crept into their conversation. She decided to jump right in. "I've heard wonderful things about it, but there were those murders . . ." She left her thought unfinished.

The store owner nodded sadly. "Yes. One of my best friends and my best customer was killed. I mean she was my best customer . . ."

"And one of your best friends as well," Susan finished. "I understand." She paused. "Perhaps she was the teacher that I heard . . . read about," she corrected herself.

"Yes, I believe there was more mention of Carolyn Breen's life than the lives of the others who were murdered. She was a remarkable woman."

"How long was she at the nursing home?" Susan asked gently.

"Almost ten years."

Her answer came as a complete surprise to Susan. "Really? I thought most people . . . well, to tell the truth, I thought most people in nursing homes didn't live in them that long, that they would be in assisted living or something less . . ." She didn't finish, realizing that she really had very little idea of what she was talking about.

"I know what you mean. You think of becoming infirm, needing some help, as something that happens gradually. And it does for many people, maybe for most of us. But that wasn't true for Carolyn. You see, she had multiple sclerosis. And, in her case, it meant that she needed a lot of care at a fairly young age."

"Oh. So not everyone in a nursing home is old," Susan said.

"Heavens no. There are three residents at P.I.C.C. younger than thirty."

"Why are they there?"

"Two are in comas. It takes a lot of care to keep someone unconscious alive. And one is a young woman, Molly Reilly— she's quadriplegic. She just turned twenty-four last week. I was at her birthday party."

"So she's a friend." Susan spoke slowly, trying to digest this information.

"Sort of. She's been at P.I.C.C. for three years and I used to see her when I was there dropping off books and visiting Carolyn. The staff at P.I.C.C. is wonderful, but of course it is impossible for Molly to have any sort of normal life living there. They make a big deal out of her birthdays. Half the island was invited to the party."

"That's wonderful!"

"Actually it is. I don't think I've ever seen Molly so happy. But, of course, in her circumstances, I probably wouldn't be perky either."

"No, I guess not." Susan was silent for a minute, sipping her coffee and thinking. "Does she get many visitors?"

"Not enough. Some of the people around here do make a

point of stopping in to see her a few times a month, but that's about it."

"What about her family?"

"Her parents are divorced. Her father lives in California and manages to make a flying visit once or twice a year. Her mother lives in Groton and comes to see her about once a month. I gather those visits are very painful for both of them."

"Poor girl," Susan said.

"Yes."

"About the murders . . . ," Susan began.

Mandy Duncan's open, welcoming expression faded. "I don't like to think about them."

"But if Mother is going to live at P.I.C.C., well, I have to ask."

"They were an aberration. Nothing like that has ever happened on the island before. You don't have to worry about your mother's safety."

Susan was astounded. "Why? How could you possibly know that?"

"Because the murderer killed the person he—or she—wanted to kill and then killed everyone who knew who had done it, including Carolyn."

Susan didn't mind repeating herself. "How could you possibly know that?"

Mandy Duncan got up, locked the door, flipped over the OPEN sign, and proceeded to answer Susan's question.

FOURTEEN

"ABOUT TWO DAYS BEFORE SHE DIED . . . BEFORE SHE WAS killed . . . Carolyn called me at the store; she said she needed to talk to me and asked that I come over to P.I.C.C. that evening. I didn't suspect that anything was wrong, but I should have. She had never done that before."

"Never asked you to come to P.I.C.C.?"

"Not without a reason. She frequently ordered books and asked me to either have them delivered or to deliver them myself. I loved talking to Carolyn so, unless it was completely impossible, I always made the trip over there myself."

"And she knew that?"

"Yes, I'm sure she did. Anyway, she called around four-thirty—half an hour before I usually close the store—and asked me to come over sometime after six-thirty. I said yes and asked her if there was anything she needed. I often picked up things for her at the drugstore or the grocery when I was delivering books. She said no, nothing, so I ate dinner early and arrived at P.I.C.C. around six-thirty-five."

"Did she tell you what she wanted to talk with you about?"

"No. I didn't have a single hint what was coming."

"Which was?"

The bookstore owner didn't answer right away and when

she did it was with a question of her own. "Are you investigating the murders at P.I.C.C.?"

Susan didn't answer immediately and Mandy continued. "I don't only carry books. In the summer I carry newspapers for summer people who want to keep up with what's going on in their hometown. I recognized you from an article about the murder of the building inspector in Hancock a few years ago. There was a photo layout."

Susan nodded. She remembered both the article (inaccurate) and the photo (was it possible that she actually looked that awful today?). "Yes, I am."

"Why? Why not just put your mother in a different nursing home and forget about P.I.C.C.?"

"My mother is an excuse." Susan decided to trust this woman with her secret. "I just became a grandmother—twins—and the baby nurse was here at the time of the murders. She's wonderful, but I'm worried about what happened here."

"You think she might hurt your grandchildren?"

"No. I'm afraid she will be accused of murdering my next-door neighbor who was stabbed to death in her kitchen two days ago."

Mandy's eyes widened. "You do live an interesting life, don't you?"

"Too much so," Susan agreed.

"Well, I don't know about your nurse, but I'll tell you what I do know. I'm happy to do anything that might help capture Carolyn's killer."

"That's wonderful. You were telling me what happened when you went over to P.I.C.C. to see Carolyn."

"It was an odd visit. There was an after-supper program going on. Supper is very early at P.I.C.C. It begins around five and is usually over by six. After-supper programs begin at six-thirty and take an hour or so. Sometimes there's a late-night snack after the program—well, as late night as things get in a nursing home. Anyway, there was a pianist and a singer that night who were performing old Sinatra songs. I knew that sort of thing wouldn't appeal to Carolyn so I avoided the living room."

"There's a living room at P.I.C.C.?"

"Sort of. That's what they call the large room if you turn right when you enter the building. It's furnished with comfortable sofas and chairs and there's a fireplace that is sometimes turned on in the winter. It's about as close to a living room as you can find in an institution."

"But Carolyn wasn't there."

"I didn't even bother to look. She used to say that her musical taste ran more to the baroque than the banal." Mandy paused and took a sip of her coffee. "I'm making her sound like a snob and Carolyn was anything but. She read mystery novels as avidly as she reread Elizabeth Gaskell and Jane Austen. She adored going to art museums, but she collected Mickey Mouse watches. She played in a weekly poker game that the staff at P.I.C.C. has been holding for decades—completely outside of their officially sanctioned functions."

"She sounds like an interesting person."

"She was. And she had a Ph.D. in Victorian lit and had taught at one of the most respected private schools in the country for decades."

"Brilliant and practical?"

"Yes. And the MS hadn't affected her mind one bit. Not one bit!" Mandy repeated with emphasis.

"So when she said something, people—intelligent people who knew her—listened," Susan concluded.

"Exactly."

"What did she say?"

Mandy surprised her by jumping to her feet and hurrying over to the cash register. "I wrote it down. After she died, I wrote down what I could remember."

Susan, who knew that memory could be enhanced or diminished by shock, reached out to take the sheet of yellow-lined paper Mandy offered. She looked at the document, a frown appearing on her face while she read. "It seems . . ." She stopped and began again. "I don't know what to say. Did she mention any other names?"

"Not that I remember."

"How limited was she? Could she get around on her own?"

"The MS had pretty much paralyzed her limbs and she was incredibly weak."

"So anything she knew she had been told by someone who came to her, right?"

"Look, I've told you some things, but it's really hard for me to explain what an unusual woman we're talking about and what a moral person she was."

"Is it possible that her mind was impaired more than you knew?"

"She had just finished reviewing a new biography of Sir Walter Scott for the *New York Times*. I really think she was as sharp as ever."

Susan reread the note. It was more upsetting—and puzzling—the second time through.

"You haven't really told me about your meeting with her," Susan said, carefully placing the paper on the counter.

"Well, I couldn't find her at first. She wasn't in her room, which is what I was expecting. She usually spent her evenings in there, reading or sending e-mail."

"She was online?"

"Yes. Not many of the residents at P.I.C.C. are, but the facility is wired for modems and Carolyn was one of the first people to take advantage of that fact. But that night she wasn't at her computer. I figured she had decided to check out the concert and looked in the living room, and, when I didn't find her there, I went to the library."

"There's a library?" P.I.C.C. was sounding better and better.

"Not really. There are a few shelves in the craft room where residents can place books they either don't want or don't have space for in their own rooms. Carolyn sometimes left books there. She used to say that she was trying to improve the quality of the other residents' reading. There were usually a bunch of old Robert Ludlum books, some romances, crossword puzzle books with a few puzzles half filled out—mostly incorrectly—and a few out-of-date almanacs. I didn't expect her to be there. It was just the next place I thought to look for her."

"And?"

"No luck. So I did what I should have done in the beginning—I asked some of the staff if they had seen her recently. And an aide—I don't know her name, but I'd seen her around before—told me that Carolyn had been on her way to the kitchen for some hot water for tea the last time she saw her."

"And was she there?"

"Yes. Well, not in the kitchen. She was sitting in her wheelchair outside the kitchen door chatting with someone, a young man."

"Did she introduce him to you? Do you know his name?"

"No, I don't think so. At least, I don't remember his name. He was short, had hair dyed black. He was wearing turquoise scrubs. That's about all I remember."

Susan glanced down at the sheet of paper again before she asked the next question. "And how did she seem?"

"Just fine. Perfectly normal. She was trying to convince the young man that he should go back to school. She was passionate about education and she was always interested in young people." Mandy wiped a tear from her cheek, took a deep breath, and continued. "She was doing what she always did."

"And her mood? Did she appear upset or nervous or anything like that?"

"Not right then, but later she changed. You see, we never did have a chance to really sit down and talk."

"Why not? What happened?"

"The young man—I guess he was an aide. He was dressed like one at least. Well, he left to get her some water for tea and we waited in the hall and chatted."

"And what exactly did she say?"

"What I wrote down. She told me that she thought someone was killing the residents of P.I.C.C."

"And what did you say to that?"

"I was startled . . . well, shocked. To tell you the truth, I wondered, just for a moment, if perhaps Carolyn was losing her mind, but she was speaking calmly, explaining what she thought as she always did. It was just a passing thought. Carolyn was as sane and intelligent as you or me."

"So tell me exactly what you remember her saying."

"It's what I wrote down. She said that someone had killed a resident and she thought was going to kill again."

"And did she identify this someone?"

"She said I had to watch Mike Armstrong. That's the name I wrote down."

"But what you wrote down is that she told you to watch Mike Armstrong and everyone connected to him. But she didn't say he was the killer, did she? She might have been telling you that Mike Armstrong—"

"And people connected to him."

"Yes. And the people connected to him—that they were in danger. Is that possible?"

"I didn't interpret it like that, but I suppose you could be right."

"Did you tell anybody about this?"

"I told the police after Carolyn was killed." She looked down and Susan realized she was close to crying.

"What did they say?"

The bookstore owner took a deep breath and looked up. "The officer I spoke with told me that this Mike Armstrong had disappeared and that he was the main suspect."

"Did you realize that Mike was the young man she was speaking with when you found her?"

"No, I had no idea. Are you sure?"

"Not positive, but I think it's likely."

"Oh, but she liked that young man. And she wouldn't have if she thought he was a killer. I don't understand."

"I don't either," Susan said honestly. "Did he say anything when he came back with the hot water?"

"Oh, he didn't. There was some sort of problem with the alarm system. For some reason the fire alarm went off. You can probably imagine the resulting mayhem. The PA system began barking out orders: residents were to gather in the living room, the staff was to carry out a room check immediately—that sort of thing."

"And what did you do?"

"I pushed Carolyn to the living room where all the residents had gathered. Staff members were working to keep everyone calm, but some of the people were very upset. Some wanted to leave the building and some wanted to return to their rooms for photos and things like that. Fortunately, someone came in almost immediately and explained there was nothing to worry about—it was a false alarm."

"A false alarm or had the system malfunctioned?" Susan asked.

"I don't remember. Is there a difference?"

"Yes. A system malfunction is completely different from someone using a cigarette lighter to set off the alarm—and, of course, to force an end to the conversation you and Carolyn were having."

FIFTEEN

THE PERRY ISLAND CARE CENTER WAS GETTING READY FOR Easter. Cute cardboard cutouts of improbably attired bunnies had been taped up in the hallways. Plastic eggs hung from the budding branch of a quince tree standing by the front door and a gigantic basket of drooping tulips took up an unreasonable amount of space on the receptionist's desk. The young woman seated at that desk looked up, and around the plant, as Susan entered the building.

"May I help you? Oh, you've been here before, haven't you?"

"Yes, I met with Astrid Marlow a few days ago. She said I could return at any time and look around, and . . . and I have a few questions about . . . about security. My mother worries more and more as she gets older . . . about fire and things like that," she added, not sure exactly what was like fire.

"We have a state-of-the-art fire alarm system. It connects directly to the volunteer fire department as well as to the police station," the receptionist assured her. "The state inspected it just a few months ago and found everything completely satisfactory."

"Oh." Susan wasn't quite sure how to continue.

"Have you seen the results of the inspections?"

"No."

"They're printed up and are part of the prospective resident package. I'm surprised you weren't given one on your first visit."

Susan realized that she had been given one, but she hadn't bothered to look at it. "I did have one, but it was misplaced somehow."

"Let me get you another then. Perhaps two copies so you can share one with your mother?"

"That's a wonderful idea."

"I believe there are extra copies on a bookshelf in the living room. I'm not supposed to leave this desk unmanned, but—"

"I could go get them," Susan said quickly.

"That would be helpful. Do you know the way?"

She didn't, but she could bluff. "It's down that hallway, right?" She pointed to the left.

"I'm afraid you're turned around. It's that way." The receptionist pointed in the opposite direction.

"Of course. I'll just go get them. You did say on the bookshelf, didn't you?" Susan asked, hurrying off to the right.

She recognized the living room from Mandy's description. A few groups of residents congregated in the elegantly decorated space, sitting on the chintz-covered couches and chatting as they perused today's newspapers and current magazines. Three women sat around a card table, working on a large, nearly completed jigsaw puzzle. Susan removed two Perry Island Care Center brochures from a nearly empty bookshelf, then walked over and peered down at the table. "What is that?" The puzzle seemed to have been created from thousands of small brightly colored disks.

A woman with a gray bun on top of her head looked up. "Bottle caps of the world. My grandson sent it to me for Christmas. He's a hotshot student up at M.I.T.—probably thought it would stump a bunch of senior citizens. He's going to be up here for my birthday next week. We're determined to get it done before then."

"Yes, nothing is quite as motivating as proving to the young that we're not completely brain dead." This from a chubby woman with twinkling pale azure eyes and white curls bobbing on her head.

"It looks impossible," Susan said.

"Nothing's impossible when you have as much free time as we do," the last woman in the group assured Susan, getting up and wandering off to another group.

"I wonder if I could ask you some questions," Susan said to the remaining women.

"You can ask what you want, but you won't necessarily get any answers," the grandmother of the M.I.T. student answered, not even bothering to look up.

"Ignore her," said the woman with curls. "She's suffering from low blood sugar. Her endocrinologist can't seem to get her meds adjusted."

"That's what's wrong with this place—too much talk about doctors and medications," the woman being discussed growled, putting another piece of the puzzle in place.

"That's what I want to talk to you about—what's wrong with this place?"

"Which relative are you planning on sticking here? Your mother? Father? Mother-in-law?"

"How do you know I'm interested in putting someone here?" Susan realized that her cover story was being accepted as the truth.

"Well, you collected the publicity info from the shelf and you're wandering around looking uncomfortable. Those are two unmistakable signs that we're going to be joined by another unwilling inmate—"

"Sally!" Her white curls bobbed. "Please ignore my friend, Mrs . . ."

"Henshaw. Susan Henshaw."

"Mrs. Henshaw, nice to meet you. I'm Tally Consadine. This is my friend Sally Worth. We are all very happy here despite what Sally says. Believe me, this is the third nursing/rehab facility I've lived in and it's by far the best. P.I.C.C. is wonderful. Everyone knows it. If it hadn't been for the murders, there wouldn't be any openings here."

"Sure, tell her about the murders, Tally. That will encourage her to think highly of P.I.C.C." Sally looked up from the puzzle. "There were people killed here, you know. And the murderer—or murderers—has never been identified."

"I know," Susan said simply, sitting down in the empty chair. "That's what I was hoping to talk to someone about."

"Well you'd better talk to my fellow inmates then. The staff has orders to pretend they didn't happen."

"Sally is exaggerating—as usual," Tally said. "Management was concerned, quite legitimately, I believe, with maintaining the quality of care here. The police investigation was fairly discreet, but the influx of what I can only call gutter press was more than a little distressing to many of us. It's shameful to benefit from the unhappiness of others, but if that dreadful movie actor hadn't shot his mistress between the eyes at a restaurant down in Greenwich, we might never have gotten rid of those nosy parkers!"

"The murderer was never found, was he?" Susan asked.

"No, but you don't have to worry, dear. We all agree that the killer is long gone from Perry Island Care Center."

"How do you know that?"

"We don't know anything. Tally's just talking. She's like that."

"We know that a lot of problems ended when he left."

"You're confusing murder and petty theft, Tally."

"No, I'm not. There's a huge difference between taking someone's wristwatch and someone's life. *But* I do know that a lack of morals leads to both things and I don't believe even you will argue with that, Sally Worth." Tally stood up. "It's time for dinner, Mrs. Henshaw. We are allowed to have guests so if you would like to accompany me to the dining room you could sample our healthy—but slightly dull—cuisine."

"I think I'll stay here," Susan said. "It's a bit early for me."

"Then don't get old. You'll hate living in a nursing home. We have breakfast at eight, dinner at eleven, afternoon tea at three and supper at five-thirty. If the staff is lucky, we're all tucked into bed by nine at night," Sally said, still moving around puzzle pieces.

"Aren't you eating lunch . . . ah, dinner?" Susan asked now that they were alone together.

"No. I have a stash of fresh fruit and cookies in my room if I get peckish before teatime. Have a seat if you want to help me with the puzzle—or if you have more questions." She looked up and smiled, deep wrinkles almost obliterating her eyes.

"I came here wondering about the murders, but I didn't know anything about watches being stolen," Susan started.

"Tally is a sweet woman, but she lived a fairly sheltered life. She knows about crime—well, can anyone who turns on television these days not know the intimate details of the most horrendous events?—but she doesn't know the criminals."

"And you do?"

"My grandson is a cocaine addict—oh, not the one at M.I.T., although I'm not so naive as to believe there aren't a few addicts at every institution of higher learning. It's perfectly possible to be smart and an addict. Anyway, my grandson the addict has been in and out of jails, prisons, rehabs for the last twenty years of his life. He'd steal you blind—well, he has to feed his addiction—but he'd never kill anyone. He's been through a lot, but he's still a good person underneath all the evil drug crap."

"You think the person who stole things was—is—an addict, someone who worked here and has now left," Susan guessed.

"Got it in one. And so did I," she added, fitting another piece of the puzzle into its place.

"Do you know the identity of the person?"

"Yes. Mike Armstrong. Nice young kid. Not that we see many kids here, nice or not nice. But I liked Mike and he's sort of family here. He was in trouble with the law while he was in high school—graffiti. I don't approve of vandalism, of course, but he definitely has real artistic talent. Not that talent will make any difference if he gets involved in drugs."

"And was he?"

"I don't know. He might have been. I noticed that his eyes were red on more than one occasion. I do know that he was very, very upset the day before he vanished."

"And when was that? After the murders?"

"The day after the last one. I'm not telling this story very well, am I?"

Susan didn't want to criticize. "Well . . . ," she began reluctantly.

"You don't have to tell me. I know I'm not. My mind is not as sharp as it was, and there are days when I'm confused. Time goes so slowly here and, despite the inane decorations they're always taping up on the walls, it is not always easy to tell one season from another. But I remember this . . . I remember the day Mike Armstrong left. And the circumstances."

Susan sat and quietly waited for Sally to put her thoughts in order and begin her tale.

"We were all upset about the murders. Death is all too familiar to those of us who live with other elderly people. But unnatural death, death intentionally caused by another human being—well, that's different, isn't it? We were all on edge."

"Thinking you might be the next to die?" Susan asked.

"I don't know about everyone else, but that didn't concern me much. I wanted—I want now—to know who was killing the other residents, but murder is not the way I expect my life to end."

Susan thought that was probably true of most victims of murder, but she didn't interrupt.

"But some residents and staff were very upset, and Mike was among them. I was surprised by his reaction. I mean, a lot of old people get weird and paranoid and of course the murders upset them a lot. But Mike always impressed me as being a pretty tough kid—self-sufficient, streetwise. I didn't expect the murders to have quite such an effect on him."

"What had happened?"

"He was a wreck—nervous, on edge. I swear, he looked as though he was going to cry."

"What did he do here exactly? What was his job?"

"He was an aide, a health care assistant. He helped out in any way he was asked to—feeding residents, helping male residents get in and out of bed, things like that."

"Was he good at it?"

Sally smiled. "Sometimes. He was wonderful working with the people he liked, residents as well as staff. But he wore his heart on his sleeve and if he didn't like someone, they knew it. So he wasn't always the most popular of the staff, but he did what he was supposed to do even if he didn't always have a smile on his face.

"But as I said, the murders upset him. At first I thought he was shocked—this was his first job working in a nursing home and he just wasn't used to people dying. It sounds callous, but if every time a resident died the staff became distressed, things would be much more difficult around here."

"But murder . . ."

"Of course we were all upset by the thought that there was a killer among us, but Mike more so than normal—if there is a normal in an abnormal situation. . . ." She stopped speaking and frowned.

"You were going to tell me about the day before he vanished," Susan reminded her.

"Sorry. It's so easy to get lost—there is little logic to my train of thought these days, I find. I was telling you about Mike stealing things."

"He did? Are you sure?"

"Oh, yes. I'm sure. I actually saw him. He was cleaning up after one of our hideous art therapy sessions. The teacher who comes in to help us explore our artistic capabilities—that's what she calls it; I'd say make messes—had removed her watch while she demonstrated painting on silk. Mike was cleaning up the room after the class had ended. He just slipped it into his jeans pocket. I was walking by and happened to see him."

"Did you say anything to him?"

"I certainly did! I told him to put it right back and he said that he hadn't been going to keep it. Of course, he was lying, but I knew a lecture about the virtues of honesty wouldn't change him. I'm over ninety years old and I've never known anyone to change their life because someone lectured them about it."

"And did he give it back?"

"Yes, but that doesn't mean he didn't take other things and get away with it."

"No, of course not. But you were telling me about the day before he left," Susan said.

"He was upset—well, I told you that didn't I?—and he came into my room late in the afternoon and said that he was being accused of things that weren't true and he wasn't going to put up with it. He was angry and I thought for a moment that he was talking about me. I explained that I hadn't told anyone about what I'd seen and he laughed. He said that if I'd seen what he'd seen, I'd be dead from the shock."

"Did you ask him what he was talking about?"

"Yes, of course. And he answered with one word. Murder."

"And?"

"That's all—murder. And then he turned and left my room and I never saw him again. The next morning the police were around asking about him. They never found him, though. Two or three days later his cousin quit her job and left P.I.C.C. as well."

"His cousin?"

"Oh, yes, she worked here too. She's a nurse. Her name isn't Armstrong though. It's Tapley. Shannon Tapley."

SIXTEEN

SUSAN'S CELL PHONE RANG AS SHE CROSSED THE SOUND. Scrounging around in her large Coach bag, she managed to find the phone and answer before the caller hung up. It turned out to be Kathleen, who knew Susan's penchant for misplacing her phone in the massive purses she preferred.

"Kathleen, you'll never believe what I found out!" Susan said.

"I could say the same thing." Kathleen's answer was as clear as a bell.

Susan frowned. Just her luck—her new phone's reception was best in the middle of the water. "Mike Armstrong is Shannon Tapley's cousin."

"Who is Mike Armstrong?"

"A young man who worked at the nursing home and my guess is that right now he's a major suspect in the murders at P.I.C.C."

"And he hasn't been arrested?"

"Apparently no one knows where he is."

"Not even his cousin?"

"I don't know."

"Are you going to ask her about him?"

"I guess. . . . Why are you calling?"

"Because I have some information I thought you might be interested in."

"What?"

"Nadine and Donald were having marital problems—before his mother put him in charge of her company's branch office and he bought the house next door to you."

"You're kidding! Where did you hear that?"

"At the office of Blaine Baines Executive Homes and Estates right here in Hancock."

"Who told you? Who? Kath? Kathleen, I'm losing you. . . . Damn." Susan flipped her phone shut and reached out for the key in the ignition. As the ferry bumped gently into the dock, she started her car, and drove onto the mainland.

The days were getting longer, but it was dusk when Susan entered her house to the sound of babies screaming, dogs barking, and the phone ringing. Clue forgot all her obedience training and leapt all over Susan. "Down, Clue," she ordered, smiling and roughing up the fur around her dog's neck. "Let me get the phone." She decided to deal with the simplest problem first.

"Susan? Hon?"

"Hi, Jed," she said and waited for him to tell her that he was on his way to the train.

"I just spoke with Stephen. His new boss has asked him out for a drink. We both agreed that he should accept so I'm going to catch up on some work here at the office and meet him at Grand Central when he's finished. That way we can drive home together."

Susan realized that there was only one car waiting at the station. "That's fine. I'll . . . I'll keep dinner warm for the two of you," she promised—not that she had any idea what anyone in the house would get for dinner that evening.

"That would be great. Thanks, hon."

Susan hung up and looked down at Clue. "You haven't had a decent walk all week, have you, sweetie?"

Clue did her canine best to look neglected.

"I'm doing this because it's the only way I can find a quiet moment to think," Susan told her dog, reaching for the leash that usually hung over the end of the banister. Today it had been replaced by a pink knit baby blanket and one aqua crocheted bootie with a hole in the toe. A quick search revealed the leash lying on the floor nearby underneath an antique walnut console. Susan clipped it to Clue's collar and escaped from the house before anyone could ask her to do anything.

"It's not that I don't love my grandchildren to death," she explained to the dog as they trotted down the walk. "It's just that I need to decide whether or not to tell Shannon what I learned today before I see her."

Clue, in good golden retriever fashion, looked up with understanding eyes and Susan felt better although she knew the expression was genetic rather than emotional. She was feeling in her pocket for a plastic bag in case she needed to pick up after Clue, when Donald Baines appeared by her side.

"Susan! I was hoping to run into you!"

As he was wearing a sweat suit and running shoes, Susan thought perhaps he meant this literally. Donald was barely keeping up a slow jog, but sweating profusely. His outfit was brand new. What sort of man started an exercise program less than forty-eight hours after his wife was murdered, Susan wondered. "What can I do for you?" she asked automatically.

"The memorial service." Donald breathing was labored.

"What about the memorial service?" She hoped he wasn't going to ask her to bake for the reception afterward. As a good neighbor, she wouldn't refuse, but between the twins and the murders . . . well, she was much busier than usual.

"We haven't been in town for all that long . . ."

Susan began mentally reviewing her list of easy recipes fit for a funeral reception. She had just settled on tortellini salad when she realized that Donald was asking her for a more significant contribution.

"But I hardly knew her," Susan protested.

"Nadine always said she could tell you anything."

Nadine, in fact, had told Susan a lot, but that didn't mean Susan had actually listened. Nor, for that matter, had Nadine said much, if anything, that might be useful in preparing a eulogy. "Perhaps your mother might speak . . . ," Susan said, grasping for an answer.

"I already suggested that to Mother, but she was afraid that the people who attended Nadine's memorial service might think we were trying to get publicity for our company—which would be completely inappropriate."

So Blaine Baines Executive Homes and Estates and Donald Baines Executive Homes was the same company! Susan tried to think of another option. "What about the neighbors where you lived before this? Perhaps one of them?"

"That town was nothing like Hancock. We only chose to live there because we found a property we couldn't resist. And Nadine didn't really get along with our neighbors there."

Susan didn't know what to say. Too many things seemed to be happening at once. But she knew her primary focus should be the babies' safety and helping Chrissy. And that meant keeping Shannon out of jail. Which meant finding out who killed Nadine. And maybe, she realized, Donald had just offered her some help with doing just that.

"Perhaps if I could talk to other people who knew her better . . . longer. . . ."

"I suppose." Donald looked as though he didn't believe his own words. "But I don't see how you're going to contact them."

"Perhaps I could look in Nadine's address book."

"I can't imagine where I'd find it."

"Her desk? Pocketbook?"

"I'd rather not go through all that right now. Her purse is so personal. It doesn't seem like something I should do. This has all been very upsetting, you know."

Susan knew she was being insensitive, but really, he had asked her to do him a favor and seemed to be completely disinterested in helping her do it. If she hadn't been hoping to learn something from all this, she would have had no trouble turning him down. And she was about to do that anyway, figuring that she could just get on with her own life, when Donald offered a solution.

"I could probably have my secretary give you a copy of our Christmas card list."

"Your business list?"

"Oh, no. Mother kept that separately. I'm talking about our personal list. Nadine and I both believed that it was important to keep in touch with old friends and acquaintances and Christmas is surely the easiest time to do so, but my wife was always too busy during the holidays to send out cards so my secretary took over that chore. She—my secretary—is very efficient. I'm sure the list is up-to-date."

"It might be helpful if I could take a look at it," Susan said, trying not to sound too excited. She had investigated many murders, but no one had ever offered her a complete list of the deceased's acquaintances.

"Then perhaps I should go to the office and ask for a copy of that list for you." Donald paused and Susan had an idea.

"I could stop in and get it if that would be easier for you."

"Oh, it would be. Everyone is so upset about Nadine's death, of course, and they're worried about me. If I go into the office, I'll just have to waste time calming down my staff."

"If you call and tell your secretary that I'm coming . . ."

Donald beamed as though Susan had had an original thought. "Then you can just stop in and pick it up! Exactly!" The beam faded. "There is just one problem though."

"What?"

"If you should happen to run into Mother . . ." He took a deep breath. "She might ask about me."

"Of course she's concerned about you," Susan said, speaking as a mother rather than a neighbor.

"I hate for her to worry. It's a horrible shock, of course, but I'm going to be fine."

"I'll tell her that I just saw you and—"

"Oh, no! Don't say that! She thinks . . . well, I didn't want her to worry."

"What do you want me to tell her?" Susan asked.

"I told her I wanted to be alone today . . . tonight. I just don't want her to worry."

"But if I run into her what reason shall I give for being at your office?"

Donald, no longer the bereaved widower, smiled broadly. "You could just tell her that you're interested in selling your house," he said. "Mother would be more than happy if she thought she was getting such an important listing."

Susan and Clue returned home, both a little tired, one more than a little puzzled. Donald was not acting like a man who had lost his wife in a brutal attack. At least he was the first person she had known to drown grief in a new exercise routine. And his request that she take part in the memorial service . . . she was still thinking that one through when she walked into her living room.

And discovered Shannon sitting on the couch surrounded by baby presents. She was writing in a large notebook, but looked up when Susan entered the room.

"Hi."

"Where are the twins? Chrissy?"

"All three are upstairs asleep. In fact, I think this is the first time all three of them have been asleep at the same time since I started this job. We spent a few hours unwrapping baby gifts and it wore everyone out. I decided to take advantage of the calm to make sure the names of the givers and the gifts were recorded. Chrissy said she wanted to start writing thank-you notes as soon as possible."

"That's probably a good idea," Susan said, removing a few stuffed animals from Clue's reach.

"Your daughter must be very popular. I don't think I've ever known anyone to get so many baby presents."

"Well, of course, being twins there are two presents for every one." She glanced at the gifts. "What is that?" she asked, indicating a pile of patterned cotton that seemed familiar.

"Baby clothes. Apparently dressing up your baby as though he—or she—is going off to war is the latest thing in New York City." Shannon held up two tiny rompers made of camouflage-patterned fabric.

Susan wasn't quite sure what to say. "Well, at least they're not discriminating between the sexes."

"I suppose you could say that for them," Shannon agreed. "To tell the truth, it's about the only thing positive I can think of to say. I think children should be children as long as possible and not miniature military officers . . ."

"Or gangster rappers," Susan finished holding up a pair of baggy baby jeans.

Shannon grinned. "At least there's lots of room for diapers."

Susan laughed and then changed the subject. "I was over on Perry Island this afternoon."

Shannon's smile vanished and she looked down at the page she had filled with names and addresses. "And?"

"And I met a new woman, one of the residents. Her name's Sally Worth."

"Sally was one of my favorite residents, along with Carolyn Breen. And Carolyn was killed . . ."

"Well, Sally and I talked for a bit and she told me about this young man who a lot of people at the Center think might be the killer. . . ." She paused, waiting for Shannon's reaction.

The nurse didn't look up and said only one word. "Mike."

"Yes. Mike Armstrong. She also said he is your cousin."

Shannon nodded. "My favorite cousin." she said. Then she took a deep breath and began her explanation.

SEVENTEEN

KATHLEEN AND SUSAN WERE STANDING OUTSIDE OF DONald Baines Executive Homes, pretending to examine photographs of homes for sale as they exchanged information.

"Shannon didn't hesitate for a moment when I mentioned Mike Armstrong. She said he's her cousin . . . her favorite cousin . . . and she admitted that she's worried about him," Susan explained, as she peered at a huge stucco home with such a variety of sizes and shapes of windows it could have served as a display for the Pella Windows Company.

"Does she think he might be the murderer?" Kathleen asked.

"She claims to believe his story that while he did steal some of the residents' belongings, he never harmed anyone in any way. She described him as sweet, if somewhat confused."

"Back when I was a cop, I heard that type of thing said by relatives of mass murderers," Kathleen said.

"But Sally, the resident who told me about Mike, said the same thing about him—in different words, but the idea was the same. And she gave me the impression of being a very astute individual."

"Susan, she's in a nursing home."

"I know, but she really impressed me. In fact, she's not the only one. Her friend was funny and bright as well."

"Well, I hope you and I are like them when we get older," Kathleen said and then returned to the subject. "What exactly did Shannon say about her cousin?"

"She said he had been in trouble with the law a few years ago and left P.I.C.C. because he was afraid the police would see his record and not bother looking further for a suspect."

"What sort of trouble?"

"Well, Shannon mentioned graffiti, but Sally Worth suspects that he used drugs."

"Strange that a nursing home would hire someone with a police record."

"I wondered about that too, and I asked Shannon if her cousin was hired because he was related to her. I thought I was being subtle, but she knew exactly what I was thinking. She told me that Mike was considered because he was a relative, but that he had been completely honest about his past and that the administration at P.I.C.C. had felt that he deserved a second chance."

"Really? There aren't any laws about that sort of thing?"

"What sort of laws?" Susan asked.

"Well, you're not allowed to hire people with police records to work in schools, are you? All the employees are fingerprinted and have to go through a background check."

"Children aren't the same as the old people."

"No, but many of the elderly are at least as vulnerable as children. When I was working in the Bronx, I was shocked by the number of crimes against senior citizens. And a lot of incidents were never reported."

Susan looked over and saw a scowl marring her friend's beautiful face. "Bad memories?"

"Sort of. And a bit of guilt."

"Guilt? What do you have to feel guilty about?"

"I was helping people then. And I felt particularly good when I worked on cases of elder abuse. Sometimes I feel as though I've abandoned them."

"Kathleen . . ."

"You know my grandmother raised me. . . ."

Susan nodded. Friends for over a decade, the two women had spent many hours discussing their lives.

"And did a good job of it, if I do say so myself. She was old, but she was healthy and strong. Not everyone is lucky enough to age like she did," Kathleen added. "When I was working I saw a lot of old people who needed protecting. And I was helping do just that until . . . well, until I moved here, got married, and gave up police work." She shook her head and her long blond hair shimmered.

"You're raising two fine children."

"I'm not questioning the value of my life now. I'm just wondering if perhaps I should get more involved, be more hands-on or something." She paused and Susan waited patiently for her to continue. "Maybe do some volunteer work outside of the schools."

"That's a great idea. . . ."

"And we'll talk more about it after we figure out who killed Nadine," Kathleen finished, returning her focus to the problem at hand. "You said Shannon is worried about her cousin. Has she seen him since he left Perry Island?"

"That's just it." Susan looked over her shoulder to make sure no one overheard her. "She's seen him since she came here."

"In Hancock?"

"Yes, he actually appeared at my house."

"When?"

"The day Nadine was killed."

"How did he know Shannon was living with you?"

"She says he's been keeping in touch with her by phone. You know, he called her on her cell . . ."

"From where?"

"Well, from his cell . . ."

"And so she doesn't know where he is. Unless he told her."

"She said she didn't ask him. She said she was so relieved to hear from him that she didn't even think of asking anything other than how he was doing."

"And you believe her."

"I do. I wouldn't swear that she's telling me the complete truth about everything, but she does believe Mike is not involved in the murders. She told me that the next time he calls, she'll ask him to talk with me. After all, I'm trying to help her."

"And she's trying to help her cousin. But, Susan, while you may have decided to trust Shannon, Shannon may not have decided to trust you."

Susan thought that one over for a moment. "You could be right, of course, but . . ."

"But you've decided to believe what she's saying and you're sticking to it."

"I don't think I have any other choice while Chrissy is depending on her so much—Hi!" Susan interrupted herself to greet a young woman in a peacock blue designer suit and high heels—more than slightly overdressed for a small suburban town.

"You've been looking at our current listings for an awfully long while now. I was wondering if I might be of help to either of you." Perfectly groomed down to her long shocking-pink fingertips, she made the offer without bothering to smile.

"We're not—" Kathleen began.

"Actually I'm here because Donald Baines sent me. His secretary has something for me," Susan said.

"Are you Susan Henshaw?"

"Yes."

"I think I saw an envelope with your name on it on Mr. Baines's desk. Would you like to come in while I look?"

"That would be nice. It's getting a bit chilly," Susan said, tugging on Kathleen's sleeve.

"If you're interested, there are more listings posted inside," she added to Kathleen.

"Actually, I am," Kathleen said. "Do you have any more information on the house on the Sound? The third from the left in the top row," she added, pointing.

A smile appeared. "Yes, that's one of my listings. It's a wonderful home, has all the amenities and it's one of the largest properties in Hancock. Six bedrooms, eight and a half baths, huge living room connected to an equally large sunporch, library, den, media room, eat-in kitchen, full dining room, and a three-room maid's suite. It's been professionally landscaped, of course. There's an indoor swimming pool, a hot tub, and two clay tennis courts on the property if you're athletic—as well as a professionally designed putting green in the basement and an exercise room, of course. There's also a small pool house with a gorgeous bar—perfect for entertaining at summer pool parties. The garage has space for four cars. And the circular driveway is equipped with an embedded heating system to prevent snow and ice from sticking. The current owner shows championship keeshonds so there are kennels as well as a guesthouse with room for the dogs' handler right behind a charming knot herb garden that was featured in an issue of a very popular garden magazine last spring. "

"If you could just find the papers Mr. Baines left for me," Susan prompted. She wondered why Kathleen was pretending to be interested in a property far out of her price range. But Kathleen whispered her strategy as they followed the woman back into her office. "I'll keep her busy. Maybe you can find someone to ask about Nadine's relationship with Donald—or with his mother!"

It had been decades since Susan had been in a local real estate office and it was immediately obvious that there had been substantial upgrades over the years. Decorated less like a place of business than a living room, chintz-swathed sofas were grouped on Oriental carpets. Brilliant watercolors of historical and scenic spots in Connecticut hung on the walls. A top-of-the-line Italian espresso maker topped a cherry credenza that had been rigorously distressed in an attempt to make it appear antique. Spindle-legged desks supported discreet notebook computers, the only visible connection to the world of buying and selling.

The Realtor courteously directed Kathleen to the nearest love seat and gave her a small booklet that, Susan assumed, described the beachfront property in even more detail. Susan, relegated to the status of nonbuyer, was pointed to Donald's desk where she was expected to find on her own the information Donald had left for her.

She was happy to do so when she realized that lying next to the envelope, which did indeed have her name on it, was a list—a very long list—of telephone messages for Donald. Susan skimmed through it. There were, of course, many messages from clients and acquaintances expressing sympathy for Nadine's death. And more than a few messages from news reporters requesting an interview or "an opportunity to clarify some of the details of their story on Nadine's murder." Heading the list were three calls from his mother. They had urgent written next to them. How strange, Susan thought, that Donald's mother would call him at the office instead of at home or on his cell phone. She glanced up. Kathleen was pointing to something on a sheet of paper and the real estate agent was staring down at it. Susan opened the envelope with the names of Nadine's Christmas list on it, slipped the other list inside, and tucked it underneath her arm. Donald was a grieving widower; most people would understand if he didn't return their phone calls.

"I think I have everything I need here," Susan said brightly—and honestly.

Kathleen stood up immediately. "Then we'd better be going."

"But I have other properties that you might be interested in, and we could go see this one any time. I just have to call the owners first." The agent reached out and almost grabbed Kathleen's arm in her attempt to forestall their escape.

"If I could take a copy of this to show my husband and then get back to you . . . ," Kathleen said.

"That would be wonderful. And I have your phone number. If you don't call me in a day or two, I'll just call you."

Susan realized the smile on Kathleen's face was a bit strained. "We really have to go," she explained and pushed her friend out the door in front of her. "Thank you for all your help," she called back over her shoulder. "You'll never guess what I found," she whispered when she was sure they could no longer be overheard.

"It better be worth being put on a list of potential buyers of a seven-million-dollar estate," Kathleen whispered back,

"Seven million!" Susan was momentarily sidetracked. "Do you think you qualify for an adjustable rate mortgage?" she added, grinning.

EIGHTEEN

SUSAN HAD PLANNED TO GO OVER THE TWO LISTS—THE ONE she had been given and the one she had stolen—first thing in the morning. And she did, although "first thing" in this case described 3 AM rather than her usual wake-up time four hours later. She had arrived home to find a nervous Shannon, two babies with what experience suggested was garden-variety colic, Chrissy frantic with worry that the new pediatrician didn't know what he was talking about, and Jed and Stephen enjoying a pepperoni, mushroom, spinach, and extra garlic pizza—which didn't, as she had expected, keep either man from sleeping right through the night.

One baby crying is difficult to ignore, two even more difficult, but Susan had been making an effort to do so when there was a knock on the bedroom door. Jed's response was to move one leg a quarter of an inch closer to the edge of the bed and ratchet up the volume on his snoring. Susan got up, grabbed the robe she had left on a nearby chair and, gently nudging Clue out of her path, left the room, closing the door behind her. The hallway was deserted and she hurried to the nursery, praying nothing was seriously wrong.

Nothing, she discovered, was wrong with Ethan or Rosie. Both twins were drifting off to sleep, bottles of formula in their mouths. As Susan had planned, the matching rocking chairs were being used by Shannon and Chrissy. But nothing else in the room looked as she had planned it. The wastebasket was on its side, tissues spilling onto the floor. The diaper pail lay nearby; fortunately Susan had purchased one with a tight top. Receiving blankets were tossed around the room as though someone had been playing a game with them. Dirty baby clothing overflowed the pretty wicker hamper and CDs had not been returned to their spots on the shelves. In fact, Susan wondered if someone had misplaced all the CDs as the music coming from the high-tech speakers sounded more appropriate to a college dorm room than a baby nursery. "Someone knocked on our door. Do you need me for something?" she asked.

"We thought we needed someone to help heat more formula, but I think they're going to sleep now." Shannon could hardly be heard over the base beat of the music.

"Then I'll go back to bed," Susan said and started to do just that.

"Mom."

Susan, recognized the exhaustion in her daughter's voice and turned around at once. "What?"

"I have a sore throat."

Susan started into the room and would have been at her daughter's side immediately if she hadn't stepped on a large stuffed animal. "Oh . . . What in the world is this?" she asked, bending down and picking up a large black-and-white stuffed animal. "Some sort of zebra?"

"Oh, Mother, it's not a zebra! It's a polar bear! Those aren't stripes—they're letters. If Ethan and Rosie are exposed to letters right from the start, they're more likely to read at an early age."

"Couldn't you just wrap them up in yesterday's *New York Times*?" Susan muttered, feeling a bit cranky. It was, she thought, awfully late for educational lectures. But back to the business at hand. "If you're not feeling well, I can give Rosie the last of the bottle and you can go back to bed."

"Ethan. Not Rosie. And I don't want you to take care of him. I want you to bring me a cup of peppermint tea. You know the kind you used to make me when I didn't feel well?" Chrissy added plaintively.

Susan had no idea whether that brand of peppermint tea—which she herself thought absolutely disgusting—was still made, but she'd grow the herb and dry it herself before she refused this request. "I'll just run down to the kitchen and see what I can find. Would you like some, Shannon?"

"Once the babies are settled, I'll make myself some tea. Thank you, though. "

Shannon sounded even more exhausted than her daughter, and Susan went down to the kitchen determined to find a snack as well as those tea bags.

Fifteen minutes later she was back in the nursery carrying a tray loaded with a plate of blondies, mugs of tea, cream, sugar, and a hastily assembled bowl of fruit salad. Everyone in the room was asleep. The twins had been placed together in one crib, all the dirty clothing and bedding tossed into the other, and, apparently too tired to drag themselves the few feet to their own bedrooms, Chrissy and Shannon were dozing in the rocking chairs. Susan smiled and returned to her kitchen with the snack.

She had put the envelope from the real estate agency in her desk drawer and now, after making herself a cup of decaf, she sat down to examine the papers. The Christmas card list was long and must have included everyone who had ever known the Baineses—or else Nadine and Donald were more popular than Susan had ever imagined. She counted.

Three hundred and nineteen names. No wonder Nadine had thought sending the cards out was such a chore.

The list was alphabetical and it took Susan a while to weed out the people who had lived in the same town as Nadine and Donald before their move to Hancock. But she finally came up with thirty-nine names and addresses. She would, of course, wait until daytime to call, but operators (and their computer equivalents) worked all night, so she spent some time collecting phone numbers. Thirty-nine information-only calls later, she had thirty-two numbers. She then turned her attention to Donald's phone message list.

The messages from his mother interested her the most so she saved them for last.

There were five messages of condolence and Susan cross-checked them with the list of former neighbors. Two matched and she decided she would call them first in the morning . . . well, later this morning. Three messages were from clients, one seeming to think that the murder might bring down the price of real estate in Hancock. There was a message from someone called Daria, who suggested that dinner at her town house just might assuage his grief. A brief "call me ASAP" from someone named Connie. And those puzzling messages from his mother.

Susan read through the list:

> *11:45 AM—Your mother called and asked that you call her as soon as possible.*
> *1:00 PM—Your mother called again. Says it's important that she talk with you today.*
> *4:00 PM—Your mother says it is urgent that you call.*

Susan stared down at the paper and wondered again why Donald's mother would call him at his office rather than his home. Of course, they might have kept their personal lives and professional lives separate by calling at the office concerning business affairs and at home when the topic was personal. But such a division seemed awkward and these three messages, all variations on the "call me" theme, sounded more personal than business.

But if the calls had been business related, why hadn't she mentioned it? Explained that Blaine Baines Executive Homes and Estates was about to buy a house or sell one or something similar and that the deal rested on something that must be done right away?

On the other hand, if the calls were personal, why call the office at all? Why not call his home or his cell phone? Or had she tried that and Donald hadn't answered or responded? Well, without access to his home answering machine or his cell, she had no way of knowing any of this. Susan picked up a slice of pineapple from the tray she had fixed, then munched and thought.

She was still thinking and munching—in fact, the plate was almost empty—when she heard footsteps on the stairs and Shannon appeared in the doorway.

"Hi."

Susan swallowed the raspberry she was eating before responding. "Are the babies still asleep?"

"Yes. And Chrissy has gone to bed, too. I have this"—Shannon pointed to a baby monitor tucked into the pocket of her robe—"in case the situation changes."

"Would you like a cookie? I'm afraid I've eaten most of the fruit."

"Yes, I'm starving. And I'm going to make some tea, but I need to talk to you as well."

"Now is as good a time as any," Susan said.

"Good." Shannon turned and filled the kettle with water.

"I spoke with Mike this evening," she said, placing the kettle on a burner and flipping on the gas.

"He called you!"

"Actually, I called him. I've been leaving messages in his mailbox for days, but he hasn't answered. Tonight he picked up."

"And?"

"We had a long talk. Mrs. Henshaw, I'm afraid Mike may not be as innocent as I thought he was."

"What do you mean? What did he tell you?"

"He may have been . . . well, he says he was . . . he says that he helped someone die."

"I don't understand," Susan said.

"He said it was assisted suicide, that she wanted to die."

"Who?"

"Mrs. Hershman."

"The woman you found. The woman who was pushed off the roof."

"Yes. But Mike said that she wasn't pushed. That she jumped. He . . . he unlocked the door to the roof for her. That's what he says."

"When you told me about the murders, you lied to me about that one, didn't you?"

Shannon looked astonished. "No, I didn't! I had no idea that Mike might have had anything to do with Mrs. Hershman's death! I don't tell lies!"

"You told me that you went outside to cool off, but you also said you were wearing a sweater. It didn't make any sense at the time. I don't think it does now. I'm not accusing you of anything. I thought maybe you were protecting your cousin."

Shannon sat down at the table and considered the suggestion. "I was," she answered slowly. "But not because I ever thought he might be involved in killing anybody. I thought he might be using drugs again. I was worried."

"So what happened that night? You didn't go outside because you were hot . . ."

"No, I went out to find my cousin. I was on the day shift—nine to five—and Mike usually worked evenings five to one."

"Why? Did you choose your own shifts?" Susan asked. She had no idea if this was important information, but she was curious.

"I did. I prefer working during the day. Not just because it's easier to stay on schedule, but because there is more interaction with the residents. And Mike was hired to work the night shift. He was the only male aide and there was only one male nurse at P.I.C.C. Many of the male residents preferred the help of people of the same sex with some of the more personal aspects of their care—bathing, dressing and undressing—and most of that took place during the night shift."

"So he was hired for that shift."

"Yes. And sometimes I stayed late and ate dinner with him. Which is what I was planning to do that night."

"Because you were worried about him."

Shannon sighed and dipped her tea bag in and out of her mug. "Yes."

"Because he had been involved in drugs before and you were worried that he was again."

"Yes." She picked up the bag, wrung it out and placed it on the edge of the empty fruit plate. "He really screwed up his high school years. Mike is very artistic, but shy and a little lost. He went from a small junior high to a huge urban high school and, unfortunately, found himself with a gang of kids who expressed themselves doing various illegal things—recreational drugs and graffiti mostly. But Mike was never a lucky kid. He was with the group painting the underpass when the police caught them. And he was the one who became addicted to drugs."

"Not an unusual story," Susan said. For years she had watched children from one of the most affluent communities in the country grow up and make bad decisions about their lives.

"No, but Mike had changed. He was lucky enough to get a good probation officer and he cleaned up his act. Went into drug treatment, started going to NA meetings, got a job."

"At P.I.C.C."

"Yes. And things had been going well for months. Then he started acting . . . well, acting weird."

"How?"

"It's hard to explain. Mike smokes so he was always out behind the kitchen on his breaks. It's the designated smoking place for staff. But suddenly he wasn't there and I couldn't find out where he was. That was what I first noticed. And then, when we were together, he talked about how being around so many old people bothered him. I can understand that. Working with the elderly isn't for everybody, but it hadn't bothered Mike when he started. I didn't know why it would bother him all of a sudden. Of course, I didn't know what was going on at the time then."

"And what was that?"

"That's what Mike told me this evening. He says he was getting upset because Mrs. Hershman had asked him to help her kill herself."

"Did he say more than that?"

"Not much. I didn't even know that she and Mike had developed any sort of special relationship, but he says they had. That . . . well, that she was having trouble sleeping and . . . well, he said he had scored her some extra sleeping pills."

"Not quite within the rules of P.I.C.C."

"No, of course not. But Mike never was good at following the rules. Anyway, he had a lot of sympathy for her and spent a lot of time talking to her late at night when the pills didn't work. He said she asked him to help her kill herself. If he had worked there longer, he would have known that this isn't an unusual request. A number of our residents are afraid of pain."

"Don't they get medication for that?"

"Of course they do. P.I.C.C. is an enlightened place. There is no reason for anyone with a terminal illness to suffer needlessly. But apparently Mrs. Hershman was ready to die. At least that's what she told Mike. She said she was lonely, unhappy. I don't remember everything. Just that she asked him to help her die. It upset him a lot and he says that's why he was acting so strangely the week I thought he had started using drugs again. Anyway, he told her he couldn't do it and she told him that she understood. He asked her if there was anything he could do and she said she was tired of being cooped up at night and asked if he could get the key to the roof so she could go up there and look at the sky."

"And he did."

"Yes and then she was killed."

"Did he know who might have killed her?"

"He says no."

"Does he think she might have asked someone else to end her life and set this whole thing up?'

"I don't know."

"Do you think he would talk to me?"

"I don't know that either."

NINETEEN

Despite her interrupted night's sleep, Susan was on the road by ten the next morning. She had gotten up early and, after making a dozen phone calls, had found three people who were willing to "contribute" to the eulogy she claimed to be writing. Among those three were two women who were the Baineses' former next-door neighbors. She was going to see them first.

Sheets of paper printed from MapQuest's Web site had slipped from the passenger's seat to the floor when she braked suddenly to avoid a large purple tractor trailer that had swerved into her lane, but she was fairly sure of her route. Before moving to Hancock the Baines had lived near the border that Connecticut shared with Westchester County, New York. It was a rural area and Susan was enjoying the meandering roads when she spied a familiar name on a street sign. Brampton Lane. She turned right onto a narrow road. On her left, a stream twinkled in the midday light, the first wild greens of spring lining its banks. On the right, walls of stone and wooden fences protected homes worth millions of dollars. Many of the homes bore elegant names; some displayed street numbers as well. She was looking for number twenty-three. One hundred and nine . . . Ninety-nine . . .

Eighty-seven . . . A long row of houses without apparent numbers . . . Thirty-three . . . Thirteen . . . Susan slammed on the brakes. She'd missed it!

A loud blast came from the green BMW behind her and she reluctantly put her foot on the accelerator. Brampton Lane was too narrow for a U-turn. She drove slowly and wasn't surprised when the car zoomed around her, honking loudly. She ignored the driver's incredibly rude gesture and searched for a driveway to turn around in.

Brampton Lane ended abruptly and Susan found herself facing a stone mansion and the choice of turning either right or left onto Fern Lane. She frowned, glanced in her rearview mirror, and made an illegal U-turn. She watched for number thirteen and saw that there was a long driveway after the white colonial that carried that unlucky number and before number thirty-three. She turned, discovered what she had mistaken for a driveway was actually a private road leading to four large homes. It appeared to be some sort of development. All the houses were colonial style, all were brick with white trim, all had been built within the last few years, and all were massive with wings extending in numerous directions and four- or five-car garages peeking out from behind. And, happily, they all had mailboxes on the street—numbered mailboxes! She realized she was about to pass number twenty-three, made a sharp right between tall brick pillars, and drove up a wide brick driveway. Two chocolate labs appeared around the corner of the house and dashed across the lawn, barking happily. A tall redheaded woman wearing black wool slacks spattered with soil and a bright Dale of Norway ski sweater followed the dogs.

"Don't worry. They're friendly," she called out as Susan pulled her car over and stopped.

Susan took her at her word and got out to greet the animals and their owner.

"You must be Daria Woods."

"And you must be Susan Henshaw. Come into the house. I'm dying for some coffee . . . unless you would prefer tea?"

Susan followed her hostess up the brick steps and into a large two-story marble-floored foyer. One of the biggest crystal chandeliers she had ever seen dominated the space. The owner kicked her muddy shoes off and tossed them into a corner where a few similar pairs lay as the dogs slid around on the floor's slippery surface. She padded across the room in her socks. "Do you garden?" she asked.

Susan thought of the crew of men who appeared at her home weekly when the weather was good and trimmed, mowed, and filled her beds with annuals. "A little," she said, although she was in the position of directing rather than doing any actual tilling of the soil.

"I love it. In fact, the opportunity to have a big garden was the only reason I agreed to buy this hideous McMansion."

Susan looked around. "You don't like this house?"

"Hate it. It's too big, too pretentious, too formal, too . . . well, I could go on forever. But it's my husband's dream home and the grounds were exactly what I wanted. Tea or coffee?" she asked as they entered the kitchen.

"Coffee, please. This is amazing." The kitchen was exactly what Susan expected from the outside of the house—large, filled with the latest appliances set in the midst of hand-painted and glazed tiles, granite countertops, custom-made cabinets, designer lighting. The back wall had been removed and a sunroom, lined with metal shelves, had been added on to the house. It brought sunlight into the room and displayed an extensive collection of bonsai.

"We lived in an apartment in the city for twenty-seven years. This was my only garden during that time. Now I'm expanding a bit." She pointed outside and Susan realized that the backyard, easily two acres, was almost entirely cultivated. Hundreds of early small bulbs were blooming in the flower beds with the foliage from thousands of others pushing through the surface of the soil. Rose bushes had been cut to the ground to winter over and delicate shrubs were wrapped in burlap to protect them from the bitter Connecticut winter. Dried vines twined around rustic wood arbors and a knot garden was right outside the kitchen door.

"I'd love to see this in the summer," Susan said.

"Perhaps we'll get along this morning and I'll invite you back in a few months. Although I must warn you that if you and Nadine were good friends, I don't imagine we'll be particularly compatible." Daria was busy at the counter grinding coffee beans and Susan couldn't see her face.

"I gather you didn't like her," Susan said, examining an elegant tiny split leaf Japanese maple.

"She was my next-door neighbor. I was determined to get along with her—and I did—but, no, I didn't like her. She was too much like this house for my taste."

"I don't understand."

"Pretentious. It was all show with that woman. Nothing underneath the surface, no root system." She put a steaming coffeepot and mugs down on the table. "Have a seat. Cream?"

"No, black is fine." Susan sat down and decided to be honest. "I didn't like her either."

"So why are you giving a eulogy at her memorial service?"

"Two reasons: the first is not one I'm proud of—I'm one of those people who has trouble refusing any request. And the other reason is that I'm . . . uh, interested in finding out more about Nadine and this was an opportunity to talk with people who knew her."

"Why?

"She was my next-door neighbor too," Susan began.

"So I think you'd be glad to get rid of her. If I was looking for her killer, I'd look at the people who live nearby—unless she had changed a lot since leaving here."

"Why?"

"Oh, nothing horrible—unless you value your sanity and your privacy. The woman was an egocentric pest."

"Did she come over and sit in your kitchen all day long too?"

"No, but only because I don't sit in my kitchen all day long. When I'm home, I'm usually outside and the rest of the time I teach classes at various garden centers. But Nadine did seem to feel that I was just what she was looking for whenever I went out to work in my garden."

"What do you think she was looking for?"

"An audience. When we first moved out from the city I thought she was lonely and I put up with her constant dropping in."

"I did, too. I mean, when she moved to Hancock that's the way it was."

"And how long did it take for her to become irritating?" Daria asked.

Susan grimaced. "About a week."

"Then you're more tolerant than I am. I put up with it for three days and then told her I needed to be alone—sounded a bit too much like Greta Garbo to be believable—which might be the reason why she didn't believe me and just kept on coming over. I finally just stopped paying any attention to her and went on with what I was doing. It was rude, but I didn't think I had any alternative."

Susan nodded. "That's what I did, too. And then, when she died, I realized that I didn't really know very much about her even though she had talked and talked and talked about herself. I guess I wasn't listening."

"It may have had nothing to do with you. She didn't have much of a life."

"Do you really think so?"

"Well, what did she have?"

"A husband, a house, a—"

"And that's all they were for her—accessories. They weren't serious interests."

"You don't think she took her marriage seriously?"

"Oh, I think that's the one thing in her life that she took seriously. So seriously that when I read the article about her murder in the paper, I assumed Donald had killed her." Daria walked over to the window and bent a copper wire coiled branch on a tiny evergreen. "Can't say I would have blamed him if he had."

"Why?"

"She was holding him back."

Susan leaned forward. "Really?"

"Yes. He could have been one of the most successful businessmen in this state, but she quite simply was not up to the task of being the wife of someone like that."

"Really?" Susan repeated.

"Absolutely."

"Did he tell you this?" Susan was thinking that it sounded like something that might come from the inflated ego of Donald Baines.

"No, his mother did. She's a remarkable woman. Do you know her?"

"We knew each other a bit years ago."

"Well, I think she's wonderful. A self-made woman. She's smart and funny, a real people person. Not something anyone would say about her daughter-in-law."

"Nor her son," Susan added. "I mean, he does try, but there's no warmth there, is there?"

"Well, Blaine is remarkable. Her husband left her when Donald was just a baby and she went to work as a secretary for some little real estate agency somewhere. She got her license at night and worked during the day, accepting the free rent of an apartment above the office as part of the payment for her job. She bought that agency less than two years after she got her license. That's how well she did. She opened a branch office in a better community less than a year later and began Blaine Baines Executive Homes and Estates before Donald was ten years old! She was completely focused. They lived in that small apartment until Blaine Baines Executive Homes and Estates was making money—big-time."

"You like her a lot."

"I admire her drive, her determination, her energy. And Nadine possessed none of those qualities."

Susan sipped her coffee and didn't say anything. She was thinking about a woman who could move up from poverty and create a successful statewide business in less than ten years—and leave her son living in a tiny apartment the entire time. Maybe it wasn't so surprising that Donald had married a woman with less ambition.

"She's also interested in gardening. Of course, she doesn't have lots of time now, but when she retires, she's planning on creating a vegetable-flower garden at her house—very Rosalind Creasy."

"So she's seen this?" Susan looked out the window and

wondered if, perhaps, there was room for a rustic pergola in her backyard.

"Not yet, but she was in on the planning. She's always saying she'll stop by, but she's a very busy woman and it's difficult to get together. We keep in touch, but mostly by phone."

Susan was reminded of the phone messages Donald's mother had left for him. "Do you have any idea how she felt about Nadine?"

"She was much too diplomatic to make disparaging remarks in public but, as I said before, she thought Nadine was holding Donald back. The truth is, I got the impression that she wasn't particularly impressed by her son's choice of wife."

"Did Nadine like her?"

Daria looked up and seemed to consider this question. "You, know, I'm not so sure. She never said anything negative about her mother-in-law per se—although she used to blame her for Donald's many late nights of work. I always thought that was a bit odd."

"Why?"

"Well, in the first place, all real estate agents work strange hours showing people homes. She should have known that when they got married, or at least adjusted to it over the years. And, to tell you the truth, I figured that Donald was happy to be working away from home. That way he didn't have to waste his entire life listening to Nadine babble on and on." Daria stood up. "I hate to be rude, but I'm teaching a class on bonsai at the New York Horticultural Society in a few hours and I need to shower and get into the city."

Susan took the hint. "Of course. Thank you so much for taking the time to talk to me. I should leave anyway. I have other people to speak to—including your neighbor at number twenty-seven. I think her name is Sophie Kincaid. Will I find her house if I keep going on up this road?"

Daria laughed. "Oh, you'll find her up the road, all right. But take everything she tells you with a big grain of salt."

"Why?"

"I don't listen to a whole lot of gossip, but it was hard to live in this town a few years ago without knowing that Sophie and Donald were a hot item."

TWENTY

Susan had no trouble finding her next stop: It was less than a half mile away. She had spent the short drive contemplating how to bring up Donald's name since ostensibly her purpose was to find out about Nadine. But nothing appropriate had come to her, and now she was here.

The Kincaid home was built in the same style as the one she had just left, but the white trim had been painted a dusky green and the foundation was planted with common evergreens. Susan parked, walked up the steps, and knocked on the front door.

It was opened so quickly that she couldn't help but wonder if Sophie Kincaid had been waiting nearby, anticipating her approach.

"Hi," Susan began.

"You must be Susan Henshaw. I'm Sophie Kincaid. Please come in and tell me how dear Donald is doing. I can't tell you how worried I've been."

Susan smiled and followed Sophie through the foyer and into her living room where a small plasma screen television had been hung in the place of honor over the formal fireplace. They continued on through what Susan assumed would be called the library (shelves and books lined the walls and a television was set upon a walnut console), to the media room (massive plasma screen television on one wall, a complicated looking music system on the other, CDs and DVDs everywhere), through the media room and into a playroom (toys of all shapes and sizes shared the room with a big screen television and a cabinet filled with more videotapes than she had ever seen collected in one place outside of Blockbuster Video), through the playroom and into a sunroom where a tiny white television was tucked on a shelf beneath a wrought iron table draped with a brightly striped tablecloth. Each room had been opulently decorated. She probably wouldn't even have noticed the televisions if they hadn't all been turned on.

Sophie Kincaid sat down on a couch upholstered in a brilliant tropical print and Susan perched on a chair nearby, a surfeit of pillows making it impossible for her to lean back comfortably.

"This is a huge house," Susan said.

"Yes, six bedrooms, seven full baths."

"Really? How many children do you have?"

"One. But he won't bother us. He's away at boarding school."

Before Susan had an opportunity to comment on this, Sophia asked a question. "How is dear Donald holding up?"

"He seems to be fine." The image of him jogging down the street popped into Susan's mind.

"I've called and left messages, but he hasn't called me back. I don't blame him. I know he must be devastated, losing Nadine like that and now the police investigation into her death. It's just too much for a sensitive man."

"I'm sure it's difficult—," Susan began, but Sophie Kincaid raised one hand to shush her and reached for the remote control lying on the coffee table with the other.

"I have to watch this," she said and turned up the volume.

Susan looked over her shoulder at the small television screen where a press conference was being held. A short dark-haired man leaned on a podium and answered questions about an international monetary fund for about three minutes until the shot changed to one of a perky anchorperson explaining that two of the most beautiful actors in Hollywood were getting a divorce and that interviews with both would be coming up momentarily.

"My husband," Sophie stated, picking up the remote and turning it off.

Out of the corner of her eye, Susan saw the screen on the television in the playroom flicker and turn black. "Does that control two televisions?"

"Eleven. All the TVs in the house. It's some sort of whole house system," Sophie explained rather vaguely.

"And that was your husband?"

"Yes. He's in Bruges . . . or maybe Zurich . . . or possibly Munich today. I can't always keep up with his schedule."

"What does he do?"

"He's involved in international relations—banking. He works all over the world." Sophie waved her hands in the air, perhaps to indicate her husband's all encompassing job. "Right now he's working for our government . . . I think . . . You know how it is—after you've been married for a while, you just don't listen as closely as you once did."

Susan nodded. She did know, although this woman's ignorance seemed to be remarkably complete. "Does he travel a lot?" she asked.

"Constantly. I used to go with him, but sitting around in rooms in four-star hotels is so boring, don't you think?"

Susan, who was here to get along with this woman, merely nodded. "And you don't find it lonely to stay here alone?"

"I do now. Things were different before Donald moved, of course."

Susan, who had been assuming Sophie would be reluctant to discuss her affair, was stunned. "You and he . . . you two spent a lot of time together?"

"Naturally. Donald always said he couldn't get along without me."

Susan couldn't help asking the next question. "How did your husband feel about that?"

"I just told you. He travels a lot."

Susan wondered if her eyes could possibly open any wider. "So he didn't know about you and Donald?"

"I told him, of course, but it's like we were just saying— after a while, you don't listen as well as you used to. When I first started with Donald, I got the impression that my husband was relieved. He knows I like to keep busy."

"Your husband must be very . . . unselfish . . . generous . . ." Susan wasn't sure what word to use.

"Oh, he is. He bought this house from Donald for me."

Susan was speechless; fortunately Sophie decided to expand her explanation. "And even though I was working for Donald at that time, my husband didn't even ask for a discount on the price. That's how generous he is."

"You sell real estate?"

"Oh, no. You have to go to classes and be licensed for that. I was what Donald called 'a finder.' "

"What exactly did you find?"

"Houses. Building lots. Whatever Donald was looking for."

"So your relationship was professional."

"Well, Donald didn't pay me anything but he gave me lovely gifts." She looked around the room as though expecting to find an example of Donald Baines's generosity hanging on the wall.

"You said your husband bought this house for you—from Donald Baines, right?"

"Yes."

"So you knew him before you moved here, before he became your neighbor."

"Oh, yes. Donald and I have known each other for years and years."

"Before you were next-door neighbors?" Susan asked, trying to clarify something.

"Oh, yes."

"How did you meet?"

"My older brother was his roommate in college. I don't think they were very close, but they did like to do the same things so they spent a few vacations together. I remember my mother being upset when Howard, my brother, went home with Donald for Thanksgiving his freshman year. She thought he should come home, but Howard was intrigued by the fact that Donald had grown up on an island and wanted to see it. You see, we're from the Midwest and Perry Island sounded very exotic to my brother—and to me when he told me about it."

Bingo! Susan hoped she didn't look as excited as she felt. "I didn't know Donald grew up on Perry Island." She spoke slowly.

"Oh, yes. His mother didn't have any money at the time. I don't know all the details but I know she worked in a small real estate office on the island when he was young. Perry Island is a nice place now. At least in the summer months it is. I mean, there's a small summer colony that has some interesting people who stay there, but when Donald was growing up it was pretty rural. But his mother bought property there and that's where the family celebrated holidays. My brother loved it. He's now a national park ranger in Montana. The more rural the better as far as he is concerned."

"What about Donald?"

"Oh, Donald was just happy to have someone around his own age during vacations. Apparently his mother invited colleagues or potential customers for what she liked to call old-fashioned family holidays. They weren't, of course. And Donald was lonely there as a kid and teenager. The main business on the island back then was this old old-folks home."

"Are things so different now?" Susan asked, remembering her drive the previous day.

"Probably not, but they would be if Blaine Baines had had her way."

"What do you mean?"

"She's been planning for decades to build a development of executive homes out on the point where the old-folks home is."

"Are you sure?"

"Absolutely. Donald and I've talked about it a lot over the years. I keep hoping to find something comparable for him to develop. He's always been a bit competitive with his mother and that would be quite a coup for him."

This new connection between the Blaineses and Perry Island stunned Susan. But Sophie had more to tell. "About a year ago, Donald told me he had a plan, a way to put that old-folks home out of business."

"How?"

"He didn't tell me that, but he said he was sure it would work."

"And then his mother could buy the property and build houses on it?"

"That was her idea, but Donald said it was old-fashioned. He thinks a multiple-use development would make more sense. Private homes, of course, but also a big hotel, a conference center, maybe a private golf course, a spa."

"Sounds like a lot of development for a small island."

"Oh, it is. It would change the island completely. Every single home owner would benefit. That's why Donald's been buying up every property he can find for the past decade or so."

"Really?"

"Yes. Nadine was very upset about it. She said they were land poor. She really didn't understand him."

Susan, who had learned more than she could possibly have imagined, decided to bring up Donald and Nadine's relationship. "Did you get the impression that they had a good marriage?"

"What is a good marriage? They weren't headed for divorce court or anything. At least not that I knew about."

"Did you ever get the impression that Nadine resented the time you spent with her husband?"

"Probably. But not because she was the jealous type or anything like that. She resented all the time he spent working. You would think any smart woman would know better than to criticize a man's work. After all, how did she think Donald provided the lifestyle that she liked so much?" Sophie looked around her room with a satisfied expression on her face and Susan realized that this was a woman who wouldn't make that particular mistake.

"When you called here, you said you were going to give a speech of some sort at Nadine's funeral," Sophie said.

"A eulogy at her memorial service," Susan corrected.

"But we've been talking about Donald, not Nadine."

"I know, but you—"

"You're going to say that I brought up his name, aren't you?"

"You did actually."

"I know. I suppose you can tell that I'm nuts about him, can't you?"

"I had sort of guessed that."

"Yeah, I got a crush on him the moment we met. Unfortunately it was at his wedding to Nadine. My brother's date dumped him and he asked me to fill in." She shrugged. "Oh well, I met my husband a few months later and I think I've done okay for myself."

"I can see that," Susan agreed.

"Yes. I don't believe a woman should be completely dependent on a man. My work for Donald gives me some outside interests and, of course, there are fringe benefits." She smirked.

"You are having an affair with Donald."

"Perhaps, but that's not your business and I can't imagine that that has anything to do with Nadine's eulogy."

"No, I can't either," Susan admitted. "But you might be careful about who you tell. After all, Nadine was murdered. Some people just might consider you to be a viable suspect."

Sophie stood up. "Ignorant people might, but anyone who knows me would tell you that I know on which side my bread is buttered. And an international authority on almost anything is much more reliable than someone who speculates on real estate—and works for his mother."

"I guess I'd better be going," Susan said, getting up immediately. "Perhaps I'll see you at Nadine's memorial service."

"Not me. I don't go to memorial services for people I'd rather forget."

TWENTY-ONE

SUSAN SOON REALIZED HOW LUCKY SHE HAD BEEN THAT HER
first two interviews had been located on the same street.

Immediately after leaving Brampton Lane she became
thoroughly lost. She thought she could call for directions,
but discovered that she couldn't get service in this part of the
state. Positive she was heading east, she drove into New York
State. Turning around, she ended up repeating the route she
had just traveled. It was simply dumb luck that she made
enough wrong turns to arrive at her intended destination—
the home of Edith Kraus, a woman who sounded almost
eager to speak with her on the phone.

She was over an hour late. And starving. The scent of baking
bread drifting out of the open window of the house before
her made her mouth water. She parked her car on the edge of
the white pebble driveway and considered her options. She
had passed a McDonald's earlier today. Perhaps she should try
to find it and eat before continuing. Perhaps she shouldn't
even continue. She'd learned a lot—the connection between
the Perry Island Care Center and the Baineses must be significant. Maybe she should just go home, get something to
eat, play with her grandchildren, and consider what she had
learned.

Or maybe she would greet the woman who had just opened the front door and beg for something to eat.

Edith Kraus approached the car, both hands extended in welcome. "Susan Henshaw. I've always wanted to meet you." In jeans and a cotton turtleneck with a well-worn cashmere sweater tied around her shoulders and the type of exotic earrings that Susan sometimes bought but was too self-conscious to wear, the woman was smiling.

"I . . . Really?"

"Heavens yes. I've read about you for years and I've often wondered how you do what you do. And why."

Susan, fortunately, didn't have to answer.

"But it's chilly out here. Please come inside. I was just fixing myself some lunch and I was hoping for company. You'll join me?"

"Do I smell homemade bread?"

"And chowder, walnut and orange salad, and my very best lemon pound cake for dessert."

"Sounds like heaven," Susan said, smiling widely.

"Good. Come on in."

She followed her hostess up the path to the front door of a gleaming white Cape Cod cottage. They entered a compact living room dominated by a brick fireplace in which a small fire crackled. Sun streamed through multipaned windows onto wide chestnut floorboards and worn silky Oriental prayer rugs. The furniture was old and looked as though it had been chosen for comfort rather than style. Bowls of blooming blue muscari were a reminder that spring was on the way. "This is wonderful," Susan exclaimed.

"Thank you. I've lived in many places over the years and this one suits me best. Sit down and I'll get our lunch."

"May I help?" Susan offered, hoping for a glimpse of the rest of the house.

"Of course. The kitchen is this way."

Susan and her hostess passed through a narrow hallway into a tiny old-fashioned kitchen. Cupboards covered with many layers of paint hung on the walls. Blue and white Delft tiles formed the backsplash. Two loaves of bread were cooling on a stained Formica counter and steam was rising from a cast iron soup pot simmering on an old gas stove. "I just have to finish up the salad," Edith said. "You can wash the lettuce." She pulled a head of Boston Bibb from the hydrator.

"Okay. Do you have a salad spinner?"

"I'm the old-fashioned type. I use dishtowels." She pulled out a linen cloth, soft from years of wear, and handed it to Susan.

With both women working, the meal was ready in minutes. At Edith's suggestion they set up a drop leaf table in the living room and sat down in front of the fire to eat.

"This is absolutely delicious," Susan said when she had wolfed down about half of her meal.

"You were hungry."

"I was starving. And you're a wonderful cook."

"It's fun to cook for someone other than myself. And I've never had a famous detective visit before."

"I'm not famous—or a real detective either," Susan protested.

"Newspaper stories about the crimes you've solved have been amusing me for years. I assume you're looking into who killed Nadine Baines now?"

"Yes," Susan said. "I know I told you that I was here collecting information about Nadine's life for the speech I'm giving at her memorial service . . ."

Edith put down her butter knife and nodded. "But it's just an excuse."

"Yes. Although I do have to think of something to say at the service."

"Say she was a fine neighbor and a good friend and be done with it. Most people will probably attend out of curiosity rather than an honest desire to honor her memory—poor woman." Edith bit into another slice of bread.

"Why do you call her that? Did you like her?"

"No, but I felt sorry for her. She had no resources, no interests, and that made her vulnerable. And boring, of course."

"How did you know her?" Susan asked.

"She and Donald used to own this house. I rented it from them—at an exorbitant price, I must add—for years until they decided to finally allow me to buy it."

"They owned this house?" Susan looked around. "It's not at all like their home in Hancock."

"It's not at all like the home they lived in here. And it wasn't like this when I moved in. They had the whole place tarted up—gingham curtains, statues of roosters scattered about, and all sorts of fake colonial touches. They didn't touch the basic structure though—for which I'm grateful. I don't imagine this house suited them very well. They were much more comfortable in the big place they built over there." She nodded toward the window and Susan spied a large mansion through the trees.

"That looks like the houses I was in this morning," Susan said.

"That's not surprising. It's the first house built in Donald's first development. You see, he bought this house for the land and then, after getting the town's approval—and I'll never know just how that happened—he built seven houses on the property. When you called, you said you were talking to former neighbors. I've been wondering who—besides me, of course—agreed to speak with you."

Susan was still puzzling over what she was hearing. "The people I spoke with live on Brampton Lane."

"That's the house at the top of Brampton. Donald had his own built first and then the rest of them were constructed, starting at his house and then going right down to the road."

"Brampton Lane? I talked to Sophie Kincaid and Daria Woods. Is that really the same Brampton Lane?"

"Yes."

"Then why did it take me over an hour to travel from there to here?"

"You went by car. On foot you would have made it in less than five minutes."

Susan shook her head. "I knew I was lost, but I had no idea how lost."

"The roads around here aren't well marked."

"I guess. How long have you lived here?"

"Almost ten years. I moved in right after my divorce. I rented for six years and this place has been mine for the last four."

"Whose idea was it for you to buy this place? Donald's or yours?"

"I wanted to buy it as soon as I saw it, but Donald wasn't interested in selling. I knew he was developing other homes in the area, and just hoped that eventually he would lose interest in this place and sell it to me and that's the way it worked out."

"Did you get the impression that he needed the cash?"

Edith thought about that for a minute or two. "Probably. He came over here one Saturday afternoon and told me he was interested in selling and named an outrageously high price. And I paid it. In cash."

"Why?"

"I love this house and I could afford to pay what he was

asking. And it was worth it—not just to get the house, but to be relieved of the worry that Donald would turn me out once my lease was up, tear this place down and replace it with one of those pretentious houses he's so fond of."

"Do you like Donald?" Susan asked, although she was fairly sure she knew the answer.

"Can't stand him. He knew how I felt about this house and he never once renewed my lease until the last minute. Every single year I had weeks of worry. I spoke to him about it more than once, but he said that's the way he preferred to run his business. I was so thrilled the day he and Nadine moved to Hancock, I could have danced naked on the roof." She grinned. "Not that I did. But I could have.

"You know, ever since you called this morning, I've been thinking that it's interesting that they bought the house next to yours," Edith continued.

"Because Nadine ended up murdered and I've investigated murders?"

"Exactly."

"But there's no way anyone could have known Nadine was going to be killed when they picked out that house."

"Except—possibly—for the person who killed her," Edith suggested.

Susan thought about this for a moment. "That's an interesting idea. And it would limit the possible suspects . . ."

"To those who knew they were going to move and found them the house next door to you!" Edith continued enthusiastically. "How many people might fall into that group?"

Susan shook her head. "I have no idea. But unless we're sure that there's a connection between Nadine's murder and the move to Hancock, it really doesn't eliminate anyone from the list of suspects."

"Now, see, that's why you're so successful when you set

out to solve a crime!" Edith said enthusiastically. "I would have gone off in the wrong direction and made all sorts of mistakes. You stay on point, don't you?"

"I try," Susan admitted, not mentioning that she had gotten involved in this investigation because she didn't want it to come closer to her home or anyone living with her at present.

"I assume you've eliminated both Donald and his mother."

"The police eliminated them immediately. They were together when Nadine was killed."

"Blaine Baines is probably busy celebrating. She and Nadine didn't get along at all."

"I've heard that she wanted him to marry someone with more drive."

"Sophie Kincaid told you that, right?"

Susan nodded.

"Don't believe her. Sophie doesn't like to think she's not the most important person in Donald's life."

"Daria said they'd had an affair and Sophie sure didn't bother to deny it."

Edith shook her head. "They may have, but I doubt if it was important to them. I mean, it's not like they were in love with each other or it was going to break up their marriages. They're both such self-centered people. I can't imagine either doing anything that might jeopardize something they value."

"So you think Donald's marriage did matter to him."

"Yes. Donald appreciated that his marriage brought him stability and a certain place in the community. And a place in the community meant a lot to Donald."

"Really?"

"I gather you've never dealt with him professionally."

"You mean bought or sold a house. No."

"Part of his shtick was I live here and love it so you'll live here and love it. He mentions that he's been married for years and years. He talks about how he and his wife belong to this club and that, and go see plays at the local theater, and walk in the nature center, and that sort of thing. It's a fictional sort of 1950s view of the suburbs—completely untrue, of course, but it must work. His business is thriving."

Susan thought about that for a moment. "That's not how his mother works, is it? I mean, she was a single mother struggling to make a living from what I understand."

"No, Blaine's big on snob appeal. But I'll bet Donald learned the value of image from his mother. They may not project the same image, but they do project images. Hers as a rich single professional is as effective as his as a happily married man. People might think they're completely different, but, believe me, they're as alike as two people can be."

"Maybe it's time I spoke to Blaine Baines," Susan said. "I don't suppose I could tell her that I'm looking for information about her daughter-in-law."

"You have the perfect excuse. Tell her you're going to put your house on the market, that you don't want to live next door to a house where a murder took place."

"Considering my reputation, I doubt if she would believe that. But I wonder if she might have a very small inexpensive luxury estate on her list. Something suitable for a young couple with twins."

TWENTY-TWO

SUSAN DROVE HOME WITH ONLY HALF HER ATTENTION ON the road. She had learned a lot this morning and she spent some time mulling it over, trying to put the pieces together. The connection between the Baines family and Perry Island must be significant and might be useful if the police began to think that Shannon was the only person in Hancock with connections to Perry Island. But, less than an hour after bragging to Edith about her ability to stay "on point," she found the idea of locating a home nearby for her Chrissy and the twins (and Stephen too, she amended hastily) very distracting. Chrissy hadn't mentioned moving to the city since the day she arrived. Perhaps she now realized how helpful having family nearby could be. And the twins kept her so busy. Certainly if Susan found the perfect place—like one of the cute carriage houses that had been converted to single family homes in the older part of Hancock—Chrissy might review her options. Besides, it was time for Susan to find out just how Blaine Baines was reacting to the murder of her daughter-in-law.

Her cell phone was still searching for a signal, so she decided to go home. She would call Blaine from there and maybe play with her grandchildren for a few minutes. She might even find an opportunity to sound out her daughter on a possible move to Hancock.

But she knew the patrol car parked in her driveway indicated a change in her plans. She pulled into the garage and hurried into the house.

It was strangely quiet. Even Clue, after greeting her enthusiastically, returned to her nap on the kitchen floor. The mastiffs seemed to think greeting anyone without a dog biscuit in each hand was a waste of their time. Someone had made a trip to the local warehouse store and left two cases of Pampers on the table along with a giant bag of jelly beans. She was heading for the living room when she heard voices from behind the closed door to Jed's study. She knocked and, when no one answered, opened the door just enough to peek in.

Brett Fortesque was leaning against Jed's desk, arms crossed, staring down at the Oriental rug with a frown on his face. An officer she didn't recognize perched on the arm of one of two matching wing chairs that faced the desk. Donald Baines sat in the other chair, his arms propped up on his knees, his head in his hands. The policemen looked up as Susan entered the room.

"Brett? Has something happened . . . Chrissy . . ."

"Chrissy and the babies are fine. The baby nurse has driven them all to the museum. Apparently your charming daughter thinks three weeks is old enough to be introduced to art."

Susan smiled. That sounded like her daughter.

"But something has happened," he continued. "Blaine Baines has been murdered."

"Blaine . . ." Susan looked at Donald. "Your mother?"

"My mother," he confirmed without looking up. "Someone has killed my mother and my wife."

Susan glanced at Brett. She didn't know what to say.

"Perhaps you could make some coffee for us," Brett said.

She nodded and hurried back to the kitchen. She was pouring water into the pot when Brett entered the room. "Do you want something with your coffee?" she asked, having no idea what to offer when the bag on the table caught her eye. "Jelly beans maybe?"

He grinned and reached out for the candy. "Actually, they do look good. Do you always buy such large bags of sweets?" He ripped open the top.

Susan reached into an overhead cupboard and passed him a large crystal bowl. "No, but it's hard to resist a bargain sometimes. Dump them in here. That way everyone can pick out their favorite color." Brett did as she suggested while she ground coffee beans. When the water was dripping through the grounds, she joined him at the table. "Why are you all here?" she asked, selecting one bean of each color, and popping a green one in her mouth.

"Sorry, I should have explained right away. I was driving by your house. We're patrolling this neighborhood more than usual since the first murder. Some of your neighbors are a little nervous. Anyway, I was driving by and Chrissy and Shannon were putting the babies in the back of the car. I stopped to say hello and see if I could help out in any way when a call came into the station that there had been another body found next door to you."

"What?"

"Blaine Baines was found in her son's house," he explained, popping a handful of mixed jelly beans in his mouth.

"Where?"

"In the kitchen."

"How was she killed?"

"She was stabbed."

"Just like Nadine."

Brett nodded.

"And Donald found her."

"Yes. He obviously couldn't stay in the house, and Chrissy said she was going out and offered your home as a . . . a refuge for him."

Susan sat down at the table and grabbed a handful of candy. "I don't know what to say. It seems, I don't know, impossible."

"That's pretty much what Donald has been saying. It's almost as though he's in shock—or thinking hard about something else. That's one of the reasons I suggested the coffee."

"What's the other reason?"

"I wanted to talk to you for a minute, to let you know what's going on."

Susan began collecting cups and saucers and placing them on a tray. "And?"

"To ask you if Donald could stay here while we're working next door. We'll get the job done as quickly as possible, but it will be at least an hour before we get his mother's body out of there."

Susan considered his request. She didn't want Donald to run into Shannon again, but how could she turn Brett down? She was still trying to figure that one out when the other police officer entered the room.

"Mr. Baines wants to go to his mother's office and tell her staff what has happened. I didn't know what to say," the young officer explained.

"We need to ask him some questions. . . ." Brett began.

"I could drive him to his mother's office," Susan said, seeing a way out of her problem. "He probably shouldn't be driving—or alone. And I could take him down to the police station when he's done there."

"That's not a bad idea," Brett said slowly. "I can understand if you want your house free of this when Chrissy comes home with her babies," he said to Susan. Then he turned to the officer. "Tell Mr. Baines that Mrs. Henshaw will drive him to the office and then to the police station. And that he is not to speak to anyone on his mother's staff—or anyone else—alone. If he agrees with that, we'll let him go.

"Keep an eye on him," he continued to Susan when they were alone again. "I don't want him running off and talking privately to God-knows-who unless I know about it."

"I'll try to keep track, but—"

"Just do the best you can. And keep in touch. Let me give you my cell phone number. If anything unusual happens, if you even feel uncomfortable about anything he does, call me immediately."

"I will, but he might not even want to go with me . . ." she was starting to say when the officer returned.

"Mr. Baines says fine, but can you leave immediately."

Susan looked at Brett. "Isn't this urge to dash down to his mother's office a little unusual?"

Brett frowned. "I can't say I disagree. Susan, maybe you shouldn't do this. One of my officers can take him down to the station and he can wait until we're done."

Susan saw a possible opportunity to learn something begin to slip through her fingers. "I really don't mind doing this, Brett."

He looked over at her and frowned. "Okay. But you and I had better spend a little time together soon. At this point, an exchange of information might be beneficial."

"Great." Susan got up. She didn't want to tell Brett about Shannon or Perry Island, and she realized he was going to find out for himself if she didn't get him out of here before Chrissy and the twins returned. As much as she admired Chrissy's determination to start her children's education early, she doubted if the babies would find art enthralling and suspected they could be home any time now. "I'll just collect Donald and we'll be on our way."

"And you'll call if—"

"I'll call if anything at all happens, is unusual, or . . . or anything," she promised him.

Donald's entrance prevented more conversation on this particular subject. After assuring Brett that they would let him know when they arrived at the police station, Susan led her neighbor through the connecting door to the garage.

"I'm very sorry about all this," she said, realizing the inadequacy of her words as soon as they were out of her mouth.

"I was very close to my mother. She brought me up alone, you know."

They were settled in the car and Susan pressed the garage door opener and backed out. The scene had changed since she arrived less than half an hour before. Police cars lined the street, lights flashing. Vans from the local television station were in the process of setting up. Susan glanced over at Donald. He was scrunched down in his seat, collar up, staring straight ahead. She accelerated and they managed to make their escape without attracting undue attention.

Donald remained silent until Susan was turning into the parking lot behind his mother's office. "You don't have to go in with me, you know."

No way, Susan thought. Not only had she promised Brett that she would keep an eye on him, but she had every intention of finding out exactly why he had insisted on coming here. "But I do," she answered without thinking. "I . . . I have to use the bathroom." She settled on a reason she knew he couldn't refuse.

"Oh. Well, then I'll show you where to go," he offered rather ungraciously as he got out of the car and slammed the door behind him.

Susan reminded herself that this man had just lost his mother—surely a time when she shouldn't be critical of his manners, or lack thereof. She hurried after him into the building.

Donald's appearance in his mother's office in the middle of the afternoon didn't seem to be considered unusual. The well-groomed, well-dressed women sitting at their desks greeted him with smiling faces. Donald's grim response caused a few raised eyebrows, but no comments. "The bathrooms are down that hallway," he said to Susan, pointing, and continuing to the rear of the room without breaking his stride.

Susan had no choice but to start down the short corridor, but she had no intention of letting him out of her sight for long. She turned around almost immediately and, leaning against the wall, watched him walk to a desk at the back of the large room. He fiddled with some papers, moving a pile to the left and then to the right, straightened out a few silver-framed photos, then picked up a pen and gently tapped on the desktop. "I need everyone's attention up here."

He had had everyone's attention since his arrival, but now the women looked up at him with bright attentive expressions on their faces. Donald glanced at the front door. "Is anyone due back here with clients in the next fifteen minutes or so?"

"Millie is out showing the Abbot property, but she won't be back for at least an hour," a perky blond replied.

Donald nodded. "Good. I have some tragic news. My mother is dead. She was killed. This afternoon." He didn't look at his audience, but fiddled with items on the desktop. "I don't know much more. The police are, of course, involved and I think we can depend on them to figure out what is going on . . . and to find the killer. This does not concern

Blaine Baines Executive Homes and Estates. We have an obligation to our clients to provide them with continuing service of the high standard everyone has come to expect from us. When the time and date of the funeral is known, I will disseminate the information via e-mail—of course you all have your BlackBerries with you at all times—and the offices will be closed during that time out of respect for Mother. Naturally, all staff members are welcome to attend." Donald paused and looked up at his audience for the first time. Susan was surprised to see the hint of a smile on his face. "Mother was always proud of the business she created and I am determined to see that it continues . . . and even thrives. And I am depending on each and every one of you so see that this happens."

As soon as Donald finished speaking, he was surrounded. Almost as one the women had abandoned their desks and rushed to his side—to comfort, to reassure, to declare their loyalty to the company and to him. They were, of course, shocked by the news. Susan doubted if anyone other than herself noticed when Donald slipped a sheet of paper from the bottom of a pile on his mother's desk into his jacket pocket.

TWENTY-THREE

SUSAN WAS CONVINCED THAT DONALD'S DESIRE TO VISIT HIS mother's office had been driven by a need to obtain the paper he had slipped into his pocket, despite his statement to the contrary. After accepting condolences from his employees, he had wasted no time chatting, but found Susan (wiping her hands, pretending to have just left the restroom—an effort wasted on him) and pretty much demanded to be driven immediately to the police station. She was happy to oblige. And even happier to discover an officer smoking outside the station door who came out to the car to greet Donald and escort him inside.

Her responsibilities completed, Susan drove straight home. Her street was now more crowded than ever, with roadblocks set up at both ends. After identifying herself to the officer manning the barricade, steering around a reporter speaking earnestly into a camera in the middle of the macadam, and driving right over cables laid down by someone for something, she arrived home. Chrissy had parked in her mother's spot in the garage so she left her car in the driveway and went into the house. This time not even Clue was waiting for her in the kitchen. In her living room she discovered an impromptu party in progress. Erika Fortesque had brought her six-month-old daughter over to see the twins. Zoe Fortesque was, until a few weeks ago, Susan's favorite baby as well as her goddaughter. A miniature of her mother, Zoe had dark brown hair, big serious eyes, and a slow smile. Sitting on her mother's lap, she was flirting like crazy with Susan's grandson. Shannon was sitting on the couch, a twin in each arm, chatting with Erika. Chrissy was kneeling on the floor, unwrapping a bulky package with Kathleen Gordon's help.

"Zoe and I thought we'd stop in for a visit now that she's over her cold," Erika said. "Of course, I didn't expect to discover Brett and most of his department next door."

Susan nodded. "You know what happened over there, don't you?"

"Yes, I called his cell phone as soon as we arrived. Incredible, isn't it?"

"Yes, I—"

"Mother, look. Look what Erika and Brett gave the twins."

Susan looked. "Amazing. But what is it?"

"An antique sled. Probably made in Connecticut or Rhode Island between 1790 and 1810," Erika answered. "I was at an antiques fair over the weekend looking for things for the store, came across this, and couldn't resist. Look." She sat Zoe down on the floor and joined Chrissy. "It was made for two children to use at the same time." She pointed to the double C shape of the back support. "I know it's not terribly practical."

Chrissy hugged the bulky object. "I love it! Next winter Stephen and I will take Rosie and Ethan sledding in Central Park the very first snowstorm."

So much for moving to Hancock, Susan thought.

"Sounds like fun," Kathleen said, moving over to Susan. "My in-laws are in town for a few days . . . ," she began, lowering her voice.

"I didn't know they were coming."

"Well, things have been so hectic, which is why I'm here now. Jerry and Jed are going to meet us for dinner at the inn tonight. I called them right after hearing what had happened next door." She looked at her friend, a stern expression on her face. "You need a break."

"But the kids . . . ," Susan began to protest.

"My kids are probably already pigging out at Wendy's with Jer's parents and I'm sure Chrissy and Stephen can manage here."

"We can, Mom," Chrissy jumped in. "You and Dad go out. You've been looking exhausted."

"Well . . ."

"Come on. Run upstairs and change your clothes." Kathleen checked her watch. "We're due there in half an hour."

"But how will Stephen get home from the station?" Susan asked.

"Stephen is driving Jed's car home. You and I will drive over separately. I'll drive home in my car. Jerry will drive home in his and . . ."

"Jed and I will come back here in mine," Susan continued the pattern. "You've thought of everything, haven't you?"

"We've tried. Go get dressed."

"Go on, Mom. You don't want to be late." Chrissy sounded just like a mother.

Susan gave up. Why should she scrounge around in her kitchen for food, prepare a meal that would be eaten, not in the dining room while the family conversed about the day, but around the needs of the twins, then spend at least another hour in the kitchen cleaning up when she had been offered an opportunity to dress up and let someone else do all the work?

"Okay. Give me twenty minutes to change."

"I'll give you fifteen. If we get there early, we can have a quick glass of wine in the bar and catch up," Kathleen said.

Susan, who was dying to tell Kathleen about her day, took ten minutes to change, two to make sure all the dogs had done what they needed to do in the backyard, and five more saying good-bye to Erika and Zoe. It took less time to drive to the inn than to maneuver out of the driveway and around the mayhem in the street. But she and Kathleen entered the inn fifteen minutes before Jed and Jerry's train would arrive at the station.

The Hancock Inn was in full flower. Pots of spring bulbs lined the walls and sat on the tables. Massive glass urns full of flowering quince, forsythia, and pussy willows filled the deep windowsills of the old stone building, their vibrant colors reflected back into the room. Hundreds of votive candles in frosted glass holders augmented the brass chandeliers and electric wall sconces. The effect was warm, lush, and as different from the nightmare that was going on next door to the Henshaws' house as it was possible to get. Susan took a deep breath and felt herself relax.

Charles, maître d' and owner, dashed to the door to greet his guests. "Mrs. Henshaw. Mrs. Gordon. I was thrilled to see your names on the reservation list. It has been too long since we saw you."

"Three weeks, I think," Susan said, smiling at Charles's enthusiasm.

"Too long. Too long. And you must try the New Zealand cockles tonight. They're on the menu as an appetizer, but, of course, we can prepare them as an entrée. They are absolutely superb."

"Sounds sensational," Susan said. "Charles, Kathleen and I only have a few minutes before our husbands arrive. Do you think you could find us a private spot in the bar where we could chat?"

"Of course, girl talk. Follow me!"

Charles seated them in a booth at the back of the bar and hurried off, promising to send a waiter and two glasses of chilled Prosecco to their table immediately.

"So, tell me about your day!" Kathleen demanded.

"I don't know where to start."

"Did you speak to Nadine's neighbors?"

"Yes! Although I can't tell you how much trouble I had finding them."

"Well, save that for later. Tell me what they said."

Susan leaned across the table so her words could only be heard by her friend. "Donald grew up on Perry Island!"

"What?"

"But not in the family home we've heard about. He lived in an apartment over a real estate agency when he was a kid, before his mother bought the family home there."

"That's interesting."

"And she wanted to build a development out there."

"What?"

"Yes, on the point of land where Perry Island Care Center is located!"

"But—"

"And Donald told Sophie—"

"Sophie?"

"A neighbor at their old place. She and her husband live in one of the houses that Donald built on the land that he purchased along with Edith's cottage." She saw the mystified expression on her friend's face and backtracked a bit. "Sophie and Donald have known each other for years. And they had an affair."

"Susan . . ."

"Look, none of that is important. What is important is that Donald told her . . ."

". . . in a moment of passion?" Kathleen said, grinning.

"Possibly in a moment of passion, but more likely in a moment of bragging. He told her that he knew a way to put Perry Island Care Center out of business."

"What?"

"You heard me! He said he knew a way to put the care center out of business."

"So that the land would be available for his mother to develop."

"For someone to develop. Apparently there was a bit of competition between Donald and his mother and he had even bigger plans for Perry Island. Something about a multiple-use development—homes as well as a hotel and a conference center. You know the sort of thing."

"How was he going to do it?"

"I don't know exactly, but he has built developments before."

"That's not what I mean. How was he going to put Perry Island Care Center out of business?"

"I have no idea. Maybe he was going to arrange for some mysterious deaths." She stopped speaking as the waiter appeared with their wine.

Kathleen took a sip of the wine and smiled. "This is delicious. Thank you." She nodded and he left them alone.

"You know, Blaine Baines Executive Homes and Estates is the same business entity as Donald Baines Executive Homes." Susan took a sip from her flute.

"Really? Why would they have two different names if they are the same company?" Kathleen smiled over Susan's shoulder. "Private time has come to an end. Guess whose husbands are standing in the doorway?"

"Ours, I hope. I'm starving!"

The women got up and joined their spouses.

The two couples were seated in a small bay window in the

dining room. They chatted a bit then got down to the serious business of deciding what to order.

"I'll have the New Zealand cockles as a starter. And the grilled swordfish with cucumber lime salsa," Kathleen ordered.

The waiter looked over at Susan. "I'm not quite ready," she said. "Let the men order first."

Jed, who knew that his wife liked to hear what everyone else was having before she made up her mind, leapt into the breach. "I'll have the scallop brochette with spinach for an appetizer and the prime rib."

Jerry frowned at the menu. "Sounds good. I'll have the same appetizer and the duck."

"And madam?"

Susan looked up. "The New Zealand cockles and the roasted salmon filet. And can we get a bottle of the Prosecco, too?"

"Good idea," Jed agreed.

Now that their selections were made, Susan could return to a problem she had been grappling with all afternoon. She turned to her husband. "Jed, can you run a business and use different names for the same business?"

Jed looked at his wife and smiled. "You're going to have to explain your question a bit before I can answer."

Kathleen knew exactly what Susan was trying to say. "Susan and I were wondering about the Baineses and their real estate companies. They have a few offices that we know about. One is called Blaine Baines Executive Homes and Estates. Blaine Baines runs . . . ran . . . that one. And the office that Donald set up in town is called Donald Baines Executive Homes."

"And you're wondering if they are the same company," Jerry said.

"Actually, we know they are, but why would they use different names?" Susan said.

"There's an excellent reason for a company like that to use different names at different outlets," Jed said.

"Why?"

"Shelf space. Think about the soda beverage aisle in the grocery store," Jed continued when he saw the mystified expression on his wife's face. "There's a huge selection. Some shoppers buy Coke. Some buy bottled spring water. Some are looking for diet drinks. Most of those choices are created, bottled, marketed, and put on the shelves by a few big conglomerates. But they don't brag about the common ownership. Because the common ownership blurs each individual brand's image. That a drink made from sugar and chemicals with artificial colors added might come from the same purveyor as the water from the pristine stream in Montana doesn't help either product sell."

"You're saying that they might just be two different faces of the same company," Kathleen said as their appetizers arrived.

Susan stared down into her bowl of shellfish and wondered if she was imagining that this might be an important concept.

TWENTY-FOUR

Susan opened the front door to take Clue for her morning walk and found Brett Fortesque standing on the porch.

"We need to talk."

"I—"

"We need to talk right now."

"If we could do it while I walk Clue . . ."

"Fine."

". . . then you could walk Rock and Roll at the same time."

"I could, but I'm not going to. Susan, this isn't a social call."

"Then we'd better go before Clue has a nervous breakdown. Golden retrievers are not known for their patience."

"Neither are police officers," Brett said, starting down the walk.

Susan hurried to catch up. "You know about Perry Island." The words were out of her mouth before she could think about whether or not they were wise. Damn! She shouldn't even think of leaving the house until she'd taken the time to drink at least one cup of coffee.

Brett looked down at her. "I know about Perry Island and I know the woman who is taking care of your grandchildren right now was employed there when the murders happened."

Susan waited for more.

"And I know about Mike Armstrong and that he's her cousin."

"Oh." Susan stopped to allow Clue to sniff the corner of a neighbor's stone wall. "So why do you want to talk to me if you know everything."

"Susan . . ."

"Brett, you're not going to arrest Shannon!" Susan cried.

"I'm not going to arrest anyone. Now. But I may suggest that she come down to the station house so I can ask her some questions." He stopped, turned around, and faced Susan. "Two dead women have been found in the house next door to you, Susan. I have no reason to suspect anyone in your home is involved, but you know perfectly well that I can't ignore the connection."

"I know, Brett. But I'm sure Shannon didn't kill anyone. She was with Chrissy when Nadine was killed. Besides, she's a wonderful person and a sensational nurse." She wasn't sure, but she thought she heard him snort at this statement. "It's true, Brett. The police on Perry Island didn't arrest her, did they?"

"The police on Perry Island didn't arrest anyone. It's an ongoing investigation."

"And what reason would she have to kill Nadine—if she had the opportunity—or Blaine? She didn't even know them."

"Really? Donald recognized her."

Susan thought for a minute. "Yes, but the fact that Donald knew Shannon doesn't mean she would kill his wife. Think about it, Brett. What reason would she have to kill Nadine? If she was trying to hide her connection to Perry Island Care

Center, she would have needed to kill both Nadine and Donald."

"And Blaine Baines, too," he said.

"So have you ordered extra protection for Donald?" Susan asked. She realized she sounded sarcastic, but she had been caught unprepared. She had hoped she and Brett wouldn't have this talk until she had figured out who killed Nadine and Blaine and all those poor old people. Clue stopped and she was glad of the break. She couldn't do it. Too many murders over too long a time. She was never going to figure this one out. She looked up at Brett who was standing quietly by her side.

"I don't think she killed anyone, Brett," she said quietly. "And she *is* a wonderful nurse and I don't know what Chrissy and Stephen would do without her. But I can't figure out anything about all this. I've talked to so many people, but nothing I've learned leads in any particular direction. And, of course, now Blaine's dead."

Clue looked up impatiently and pulled on her leash. "We'd better walk. This poor dog's main exercise for the past week has been trying to keep Rock and Roll from stealing her dinner and barking at all the confusion next door."

"Not exactly the ideal dog's life," Brett said.

"Not exactly."

"Susan, you know I've grown to respect your investigative abilities."

"It took you long enough," Susan yanked on the leash to prevent Clue from flattening a gorgeous curbside display of crocus.

"You're probably right."

Susan blinked. Where was this conversation going? "But I thought you were angry at me for not telling you about Perry Island and Shannon and all."

"Not angry. It would make my job a lot easier if you shared what you know with me, yes. But sometimes you . . . well, sometimes your enthusiasm for what you think you know gets in the way of rational thinking."

"Brett, why are you here? I mean, you didn't show up on my doorstep at dawn just to chat, did you?"

"No. To be honest, I wanted to pick your brain. You usually have insight into the personal relationships of the people involved in any of my cases."

Well, he already knew what she had been trying to hide. Why not? "Okay. But I don't think I know anything. I mean, I've heard that Nadine and Donald were having marital problems, and that Donald and his mother were competitive, and that Nadine and her mother-in-law didn't get along. And, damn it, that's really all I've learned.

"Not much, is it?" she added when he didn't respond right away.

"Not much," he agreed. "Of course, you were investigating a single murder. Now things have changed. Two women have been killed."

"As well as those patients at Perry Island," Susan said.

"Perry Island is not, of course, the primary focus of my investigation, but I haven't forgotten them since Donald Baines told me about your baby nurse."

"Donald told you about Shannon! When?"

"Last night."

"Because he was trying to protect himself! You suspect that he killed his mother!"

"I certainly checked that out right away."

"And?"

"He has an alibi."

"That's not possible. Did you even know when she was killed last night? When was the autopsy completed?"

"Her personal secretary called the station right after she heard about the murder. Blaine Baines had lunch with a prospective client at the Hancock Inn at noon yesterday. I haven't spoken to the client yet, but I did speak to Charles who says she's one of his best lunchtime customers and he saw her there. My understanding is that the last time Blaine Baines appeared in public was around two-thirty when she walked the client to her Jaguar in the inn's parking lot."

"And Donald . . ."

"Was in the office of a lawyer in Darien closing on a house from around two until five when he drove home, walked into his kitchen, and discovered his mother on his kitchen floor."

"How do you know he didn't walk in the house and find his mother alive and kill her?"

"Because she wasn't killed in his kitchen."

"What?" It was a possibility Susan hadn't even considered.

"Definitely. She was killed someplace else and carried into the kitchen."

"You're sure?"

"No question about it. Not only was there no blood splattered around the room—"

"Like when Nadine was killed," Susan muttered, remembering the mess.

"Yes. But Blaine was carried into the kitchen in a throw, a small blanket, one of those cashmere things that people hang over their sofas in the winter. You know what I mean."

Susan nodded.

"It was still under the body when Donald found her," he explained. "It looked as if the killer tried to duplicate the first death."

"So where was she killed?"

"We have no idea. Yet."

Susan thought about all this as she strolled behind her pet. "Maybe she met Donald someplace else, he killed her, wrapped her in the throw, and . . . and . . ."

"And brought her home with him, claimed to find her in the kitchen and raised a hue and cry? It doesn't make any sense. And it's not possible. Donald was driven home from Darien by his client's lawyer."

"Isn't that unusual?"

"Apparently they're friends. Donald's car was scheduled for routine maintenance so they arranged to do this."

"Why didn't he take Nadine's car? It's not as though she's using it."

"No, but the battery is dead. That's what he told us and it was easy to check out. He's given us complete access to his home."

"So Donald has an alibi again."

"Yes."

"Doesn't that strike you as unlikely?"

"Unlikely?"

"Suspicious."

"You mean he arranged for his wife and mother to be killed and then made sure he was going to be someplace else while it was happening?"

"Exactly!"

"Possible, but a stretch. He's a very busy man, Susan. I think that may be the only explanation here."

They walked down the street in silence for a bit. "Why would anyone want to kill Donald's mother and his wife?"

"I was wondering if you had come up with any suggestions," Brett answered.

"Perhaps a future wife who doesn't want an interfering mother-in-law?"

Brett chuckled as she had meant him to. "Seems a bit drastic, but I'll take it under consideration."

The walked in silence a bit longer. "Do you think Donald knows something he's not telling you?" Susan asked.

"Damn right. I must admit I don't trust him."

"Why not?"

"He seems a bit detached from these murders, almost as though he has something else on his mind."

Susan chuckled. "Nadine would be more than a little irritated to hear that. She was always complaining that he didn't pay her enough attention when she was alive. She'd be furious if she knew his inattention continued after her death.

"But it's interesting that he's responding to his mother's death pretty much the same way he responded to his wife's," Susan went on.

"I'm giving him the benefit of the doubt and assuming that he might be in shock."

"That's possible. After all, it isn't every day that a man's family is wiped out . . ." Susan paused and turned to Brett. "Is it his whole family? Are there other relatives?"

"We're looking into that."

"And you'll let me know when you find out?"

Brett didn't answer immediately. In fact, he changed the subject. "Who did you talk to on Perry Island?"

"A few of the residents at the Perry Island Care Center, the admissions person there—Astrid something—and a woman who owns the island bookstore."

"And what excuse have you used?"

"Why do you think I need an excuse?"

"Because most people who work in a nursing home admissions office are hired to talk to people who are interested in admitting someone," Brett said.

"I'm telling everyone that I'm interested because I'm looking for someplace for my mother to live."

"Has she gone out with you?"

"No, my parents are in Europe."

"And you've been out there once?"

"Twice."

"Can you think of a reason to return?"

"I suppose. They asked me if I wanted to eat a meal there and I could say I was testing the food for Mom. Or I suppose I could bring something out to one of the residents I met the last time I was there."

"Good."

"You want me to go out there again."

"Yes."

"To find out something for you."

"To check out something for me. Yes."

"Why don't you just send one of your officers?"

"Because I hate outside interference in my local cases and the authorities out there might feel the same way. I'd like to avoid it if I can."

"And if I help you, you'll share what you learn with me?"

"When I can" was Brett's obscure promise.

Susan realized he had given her no guarantees, but she had been planning yet another visit to Perry Island anyway, although she saw no reason to admit this to Brett. "Tell me what you want to know" was all she said.

He did.

And many of Susan's neighbors were awakened that morning by her indignant cry of "He said what?!"

TWENTY-FIVE

GRANDPARENTS WHO ARE HAPPY TAKING CARE OF THEIR grandchildren are the best people on earth, Susan decided. She was watching Kathleen give final instructions to her father-in-law about helping her son with his homework. Finished, Kathleen picked up a large canvas boat bag and hurried down the driveway to the curb where Susan waited in her car. "That man is so sweet. He and Alex are making a volcano that actually explodes as a science project."

"I think the word is erupt," Susan said, remembering the mess the combination of baking soda and vinegar had left on her kitchen table back when her son was in elementary school. "Or maybe explode is more like it. Where's Jerry's mom?"

"Listening to NPR and hemming her granddaughter's Easter dress," Kathleen said, fastening her seat belt.

"The woman is a saint."

"You can say that again. She's also making lamb stew for dinner tonight. Jerry and I always gain a ton when his parents are here, but the extra pounds are worth it." Kathleen took a bright red Tupperware carton from her bag and pried off the top. She passed it to Susan. "Have a coconut cranberry oatmeal cookie."

"Thanks! Also your mother-in-law's work?"

"Yes."

"Hmm. They're delicious!"

"They are, aren't they? I brought a few dozen. I thought we might offer them to some of the residents."

"That's a great idea."

"You know, you didn't explain a whole lot when you called. Are we going to the nursing home first or are we going to look for the Baineses' house?"

"Depends which ferry we catch. We're due at Perry Island Care Center for dinner at noon."

"You mean lunch, don't you?"

"I think the main meal of the day is at noon in most nursing homes," Susan said.

"Well, since they think we're there to check out the food for your mother, they probably won't expect us to do more than taste everything."

"No, and we can use the time to talk to people."

"Do you think the residents know anything at all about who owns the place where they live?"

"I don't know. Some of the women I spoke with were really sharp," Susan answered. "Of course, even if Donald is right about who owns P.I.C.C., he might be lying about Shannon's cousin."

"That's what you're hoping, isn't it? You don't want him involved in this."

Susan kept her eyes on the road. "That's true."

"But you don't even know him. I know he's young, but he might be a truly bad person. He might be the killer."

"He might, but I don't think he is. Shannon's not the only person who believes in him. I told you about the resident I met there . . ."

"The one with the grandson at Yale," Kathleen said.

"Yes. She seemed like a very smart person. And she liked him, said he wasn't a person who would hurt anyone else."

"And you believe her."

"I do."

"So who do you think the murderer is?"

"I have no idea. Donald is the only person I know of who benefits from the deaths."

"But he lost his wife and his mother."

"And gained freedom and a whole lot of money."

"Are you sure about that?"

"Not really. Brett's seen Nadine's will and he said that Nadine and Donald had left everything to each other. So we know Donald didn't lose anything financially when she died, but Brett doesn't know whether Donald's mother owned the entire agency and left it to him or if they owned it jointly or what."

"Of course there's his mother's house. That's got to be worth a fortune."

"Her house?"

"Yes. Susan, you know where she lives, don't you?"

"I have no idea."

"Woodwinds."

"Woodwinds? When did she move in there? I had no idea!"

Kathleen considered the question. "Sometime last summer. The only reason I know about it is that there was talk of the garden club holding a benefit party on the grounds there last August, but after the sale went through we had to find another location."

"Really?"

"You sound surprised."

"I am. I never imagined that Blaine Baines had that kind of money."

"What kind of money?"

"Rich people's money. Kathleen, Woodwinds was on the

market for years. I'll bet I've seen over a dozen ads for it—in the *Times,* even the estates for sale section of *Architectural Digest*—and I know the price was well over ten million dollars!"

"What?"

"Ten million dollars!"

"Are you sure?"

"Absolutely. Jed always says that a rock and roll star would be the only person who could afford it."

"I can't imagine the Rolling Stones practicing guitar riffs in that music room," Kathleen commented.

"I remember you telling me it was one of the most beautiful rooms you had ever seen," Susan said. "I still regret not going on that tour."

Woodwinds was the name of one of the great Connecticut shore estates. Set in the middle of ten well-tended acres, it had been built in the thirties for a famous musician who loved to entertain. It was known for its three-story rotunda, sunken living room, massive music room, and formal dining room where guests, staying in one of the house's nine bedrooms, had cavorted for decades until the owner died. Kathleen had toured the public rooms years ago during a rare opening of the home to raise money for a local charity.

"You know, it's odd that Woodwinds was empty for so long," Kathleen said.

"Not as odd as Blaine Baines buying it. Why would a single woman need a home that large? Or a music room?"

"Status? It's a fabulous house on a fabulous property. The greenhouses alone—"

"There are greenhouses there?"

"Yes, they're huge. Right behind the pool house. That's where we wanted to hold the garden club benefit."

They drove along in silence for a while and then Susan spoke up. "I wonder if the property could be subdivided."

"And if Blaine Baines bought it planning to develop it," Kathleen continued, catching on immediately.

"Yeah. If she could build ten large homes on an acre each on the water, she could probably sell them and get her own home for free."

"It's possible," Kathleen said. "But two-acre zoning is standard in that part of town, isn't it?"

"I don't know, but that's easy to find out down at the municipal offices. . . . Oh, damn! I almost missed the turn-off!" Susan slammed on the brake and made a sharp right turn. The driver of the Lincoln Navigator behind her made his anger known with twin blasts on his horn and Susan flinched. "I hate it when people do that to me, too," she said. "It's only a few more miles to the ferry. We may make the early run."

"Great."

By staying a few miles over the speed limit, they arrived at the ferry landing as the boat began loading for the trip to the island. Almost without a pause, Susan guided her Cherokee into the center of the ship, switched off the engine, and turned to her friend. "Want to ride over in here or to get out?"

"It's warmer in here."

"Definitely."

"So let's stay . . ." The ferry lurched just as it began its trip and stopped Kathleen in midsentence. "This means we can find the Baineses' house before going to the nursing home, right?"

"It means we can try to find it. Brett gave me the address and I recognized the name of the road which, I think, is the one that circles the island. We'll just drive around and, if we come across it, we'll—"

"We'll what?"

"We'll look around to see if we find any evidence that Mike Armstrong was ever there."

"Do you believe Donald's story that he helped Mike Armstrong hide when the police were looking for him after the deaths on Perry Island were discovered to be murders?" Kathleen asked, remembering what Brett had told Susan this morning.

"I think it's weird that anyone would stay on the island if they were trying to avoid the police," Susan answered.

"The police may have set up some sort of roadblock at the ferry dock so that it was impossible to come and go without detection."

"Maybe, but lots of people on the island must own boats and might have helped Mike if he felt it was important to flee. And there are people on the mainland who could have traveled across the Sound, tied up at a private dock where no one was home, and helped Mike leave."

"That's possible. But it's also possible that the young man didn't have the right contacts to have access to a boat and was thrilled to stay at the Baineses' house until the investigation had cooled down a bit."

"True." She started the engine as the ferry bumped gently into the shore. "Well, maybe we'll know more in a bit."

"How are we going to learn anything without getting into the house?"

"Donald told Brett that there's a key hidden beneath a flowerpot near the back door."

"How convenient."

"Well, we'll find out if it's there if we find the house." Susan drove off the boat and turned at the first main road they came to. "This is the road. Brett said to turn right and continue on for three or four miles."

"What number are we looking for?" Kathleen asked, peering out the windshield.

"That's the problem. The island has a quaint tradition of naming properties rather than bothering with boring things like street numbers. We're looking for Windswept. Apparently it's painted on a board at the end of a dirt road that leads to their driveway."

"You're kidding. How do people get deliveries? Mail or FedEx or whatever?"

"I have no idea. Just keep looking on your side of the road for Windswept. It must be on the water, don't you think?"

"It may be, but that doesn't mean we'll find it," Kathleen replied, squinting to read a hand-painted sign that, as far as she could guess, said UBERHOLM.

They drove along slowly, but they didn't find what they were searching for. Susan was about to suggest giving up when she realized what she was looking for was right in front of her. "That's it! Windswept! It isn't on the water! It's right there. On the left. On my side!" She slammed on the brakes, turned down the road she had almost missed, and found herself on a narrow, bumpy dirt road through the woods. During the summer, it would be impossible to look through the woods, but now, with the leaves barely covering the branches on the trees, there could be little doubt that the house they were traveling toward had no near neighbors.

"Tell me again why Donald says he allowed Mike to live in this house," Kathleen demanded.

"He told Brett that Mike had trouble finding a place to stay on the island and, since he was working nights, didn't want to travel back and forth to the mainland. So Donald offered Mike a room in the caretaker's cottage on the property here in exchange for helping keep the driveway plowed in the winter."

"I don't understand how they even ended up in contact with each other."

"Well, Donald claims that Mike went to the real estate agency in town looking for a place. And the agent there, who knows that the Baineses rent out their place in the summer and were looking for someone to do some minor caretaking over the winter, put them in contact with each other."

"Makes sense."

"Yes, but there is one problem."

"What's that?"

"Shannon was doing laundry when I left and I ran down to the basement and asked her about all this and she says it's a lie. She says that when Mike couldn't get off the island for some reason, he sacked out in a storage room near the kitchen, that he never, ever stayed in any place owned by the Baineses."

"Interesting . . . Well, will you look at that?"

"Yes." Susan put her foot on the brake and both women stared at the sight before them. "Will you look at that?" Susan repeated Kathleen's words.

TWENTY-SIX

"IT LOOKS LIKE IT COULD USE A BIT OF CARETAKING," KATH-
leen said.

"It looks like it could star in an old Alfred Hitchcock
movie," Susan replied, getting out of the car without taking
her eyes off the house standing before them.

"This family invests in some incredible real estate, doesn't
it?"

"I'll say."

"Windswept. Woodwinds. Maybe they're just collecting
mansions with similar names." Kathleen was walking up the
pebble drive toward the house.

Susan followed her, still trying to absorb the sight in front
of them. Built in the shingle style so popular on the Connecticut and Long Island coasts in the early twentieth century, the house was immense and gloomy, rising out of the
land without benefit of landscaping. A four-car garage sat
off to one side and, as Kathleen made her way up onto the
deep porch that encircled the house's first floor, Susan wandered over to take a closer look. Windows on the floor above
the car ells were curtained and she suspected this was the
caretaker's apartment that Donald had mentioned. Piles of
plastic flowerpots leaned against the side of the building and
she went over to rummage around for the house key.

Spiders fled and a mouse scared her almost as much as she scared it, but she didn't find the key and was giving up her search when she heard Kathleen calling her name.

"It's open! Susan, it's open!" she was saying. Susan stood up and realized that her friend was standing in the doorway of the mansion. She ran over to join her. "How did you get the door open?"

"Turned the knob. Did you try the door out there?"

"It never even occurred to me." Susan walked into the house. "It's got to be ten degrees colder in here than it is outside."

"Probably feels wonderful in the middle of summer," Kathleen said, pulling her jacket closed.

"Yeah, I guess. Let's look around."

"Do you think Mike could have stayed here?"

"I suppose anyone could have." Despite the bedraggled grandeur of the outside of the house, the interior had been decorated in the fashion of many vacation homes with hand-me-downs and cheap upholstered pieces. Dust bunnies hugged the corners and mouse droppings dotted the worn area rugs. Susan and Kathleen had a wonderful time looking around. The kitchen pantry was bare except for a few cans of tomato soup and a musty box of Triscuits, but there were sheets on beds in two of the nine bedrooms upstairs and one had obviously been slept in. The electricity worked although space heaters seemed to be the only source of warmth.

"He might have stayed here for a bit," Susan said as she and Kathleen wandered into the last bedroom on the floor.

"Yeah, I guess." Kathleen walked over to the window. "You know, we may be on the highest spot on the island. The view is incredible from here."

Susan joined her. "You're right. Look, there's the Perry Island Care Center."

"Where?"

Susan pointed.

"Wow! That is some location. Right on that thin peninsula out on the Sound. Amazing!"

Susan stared out the window. "You're right. I didn't realize it when I was inside the building." She stood a while longer considering the scene before her and then turned to her friend. "I don't think there's anything else to be seen here. Obviously Mike Armstrong could have stayed here, but I don't see what that proves. Let's go out to Perry Island Care Center. Maybe we'll come up with something there."

Susan glanced down at her watch. "We still have about half an hour before we're expected there."

"Do you have another idea?"

"Yes. I'd like to see the real estate office where Blaine Baines got her start. It must be downtown."

"Are you just curious or are you thinking of buying a second home?" Kathleen asked as they made their way downstairs.

"I'm just curious, but that's not the story I'm going to tell anyone who asks." She looked around as Kathleen closed the door behind them. "I wonder just how much a place like this costs."

"Well, we're going to the right place to find out."

"You know, we've been in a lot of real estate offices in the past week, but this is the first one without the Baines name on the door," Kathleen said, as they paused outside Perry Island Realty.

"It's also the first one that didn't promise exclusive or executive homes," Susan pointed out.

"No, in fact, some of these homes seem to be anything but executive," Kathleen said, squinting at one of the photographs displayed on a wooden board outside of the office. "This one's not much more than a shack!"

"It's a rental property. Most seem to be."

"Maybe the sale listings are inside," Kathleen said.

"If you women are looking for something to buy on the island, you're not gonna have an easy time of it. Not much for sale this time of year."

Kathleen and Susan realized they had been joined by a short, elderly man with a florid complexion and brilliant blue eyes. He was beaming at them. "We're getting ready for a big summer rental season though, so if you're in the market for a nice quiet house on the beach, you've come to the right place."

"That's exactly what we're looking for," Kathleen lied.

"Although we were thinking of buying sometime in the future," Susan added, trying to cover all bases.

"Why don't you both come right in and I'll see if I can help you find everything you're looking for." He pulled a key chain from his pocket and unlocked the front door. "My name is Walter Heckman. Most people call me Walt," he added, as though this was an unusual idea. "We're pretty casual here on the island."

"Is this your agency?" Susan asked. She and Kathleen followed him into his modest office.

"I don't own it, but I run it and I'm the only agent here during the off-season. We don't get enough business to make it worthwhile employing anyone else most of the year. Of course, we're the only agency on the island and, in the summer, I'm swamped and I hire extra help.

"Just sit yourselves down on that couch right there and I'll bring our listing books over." He picked up two large looseleaf folders from a cluttered desk in the back of the room. "Let's see. You said rental and sales, right?"

"Yes," Susan answered.

"Houses for sale or undeveloped property or both?"

"Uh . . . both. I'm interested in buying and my friend is thinking of renting for the summer," Susan said.

"Someplace suitable for young children," Kathleen added, getting into the spirit of the charade.

"I'm sure I have what you're looking for right here then." Walter put a stuffed loose-leaf folder down on the coffee table before Kathleen. "And these are for you," he said, giving Susan two loose leafs with barely a dozen listings in each.

"That's quite a difference," Susan commented, opening the top folder.

"There was a time that we had a lot of properties for sale on the island, but things have changed a lot in the past few years."

"Really." Susan flipped through the sheets, remembering that Donald was supposed to have bought many properties on the island.

"Yes, I suspect it will be easier to help you find something to rent," Walter Heckman said to Kathleen, pulling a chair across the room and placing it across from the two women. Susan noticed that he had placed himself slightly closer to Kathleen and he immediately reached out and began to flip through the notebook, describing some of the properties and when they would be available. Susan silently studied the material he had given her.

There were twelve houses for sale. They seemed to be arranged in descending order according to price. Susan perused each one, from the large turn-of-the-century stone mansion built on a seawall overlooking the Atlantic to a tiny fifties ranch huddled in the woods, looking for anything that might be significant but finding nothing. She then turned to the undeveloped properties, but, with only black-and-white photographs and having little idea of what acres of land actually meant, she found herself listening in on Kathleen's conversation and wondering if her friend might actually be planning a summer vacation on Perry Island.

"I like these two, but they're not on the ocean side of the island, are they? My daughter is not a very strong swimmer and I'm a bit concerned that she won't be comfortable in large waves."

Walter Heckman's assurances that both of the properties in which Kathleen was professing an interest were on the Sound rang a bell. Susan examined the notebooks again and then gathered them up and wandered to the back of the room where a framed map of Perry Island hung on the wall.

"Can I get anything for you?"

"No, I was just wondering where . . . uh, where one of these houses is located."

"The rental properties are marked with red pins, those for sale with green."

Susan studied the map for about five seconds, idly listening to Kathleen and the real estate agent's conversation, before she recognized the pattern before her: the red pins were scattered all over Perry Island although most were within a short walk of the water; all the green pins were stuck into the map on the Atlantic side of the island. Susan squinted and walked a few steps closer.

Friends and families of residents of the Perry Island Care Center could find many places to rent close by, but if they wanted to buy a home, they would be forced to travel all the way across the island to visit their loved ones.

Susan was continuing to examine the map, considering what this might mean when Kathleen joined her.

"Walt is going to get some application forms for me. I hope we won't be late for lunch at P.I.C.C."

"Dinner," Susan corrected automatically.

Kathleen leaned closer to Susan. "You won't believe what I've learned," she said.

"Me, too." Susan stopped speaking and smiled as Walter hurried over to the women, his hands full of contracts.

"I understand you're in a hurry, but if you have any problems figuring these out, you will give me a call, won't you?"

Kathleen turned back to him with a wide smile on her face. "Of course. I just need to speak with my husband and then I'll get back to you."

"Excellent. Perhaps I should give you my home phone number and my cell phone."

"I can just leave a message on your phone here, can't I?" Kathleen asked.

"Yes. Of course. If that is what you would prefer to do."

"I would."

"And thank you for your time. This has been very interesting," Susan added as the women made for the door.

"Some of those homes are bargains, you know." He rushed to get to the door before them. "There are very few ocean side estates available in the Northeast."

"I'm afraid the places I'd like to own are slightly out of my price range," Susan explained, trying to sound disappointed.

"I could put you on our list of prospective buyers. To let you know if anything new comes on the market."

"That would be nice. I'm afraid we're in rather a hurry right now though. Perhaps I could also call and let you know."

The smile that had been fixed on Walter Heckman's face since meeting Kathleen and Susan outside of his office vanished. "That would be fine. Of course. Whatever works for you."

"You've really been very helpful," Kathleen assured him warmly. "And I really will call."

The smile returned to Walter's face as he swept the door open for the women and they thanked him politely, waiting until they were alone in Susan's car before saying any more.

"You won't believe this," Susan began. "There's not one property for sale anywhere near Perry Island Care Center! Only rentals. The sale properties are all on the ocean side of the island."

"And you won't believe this. The majority of the rentals on the island—on the Sound side—are owned by Donald Baines Executive Homes, and the others are owned by Blaine Baines Executive Homes and Estates!"

TWENTY-SEVEN

Dɪɴɴᴇʀ ᴀᴛ Pᴇʀʀʏ Iꜱʟᴀɴᴅ Cᴀʀᴇ Cᴇɴᴛᴇʀ ʀᴇᴍɪɴᴅᴇᴅ Sᴜꜱᴀɴ of meals in her college dorm—minus salt. But if the food was slightly bland, the company was not. Susan and Kathleen ate at Sally Worth's table. One of her tablemates subscribed to the *Hancock Herald* and began asking questions about the murders of Nadine and Blaine Baines as soon as Susan introduced herself. She ended up answering as many questions as she asked.

But once the subject of murder was introduced, it was easy to mention the deaths of the residents. Each of the three women at the table had her own opinion, and each was happy to share it with Susan. "After all, you're the expert," Sally said and her companions seemed to agree. They also agreed that Mike Armstrong either was the murderer or knew the identity of the murderer.

"I can't imagine why else he would have disappeared the way he did," said the woman sitting on Sally's right.

"Well, I agree with that," said the woman on Sally's left. "After all, he was so in love."

"You think so?"

"I certainly do. They were going to get married. She told me so herself."

"Oh, please. She was imagining things. Mike had no intention of getting married to anyone. He may have liked her. He may have enjoyed her company, if you know what I mean, but that young man wasn't going to marry anyone!"

Sally Worth put down her fork and spoke up. " 'Enjoyed her company.' Good Lord! Mrs. Henshaw and her friend are going to think they've slid right into the middle of a Jane Austen novel. They were sleeping together, having sex. And if Penny had fantasies of getting married to him, well, she wouldn't be the first young girl to justify her hormones with romantic thoughts."

"Penny?" Susan asked.

"Young girl?" Kathleen abandoned the rest of her chicken and rice and placed her fork down on her plate.

"Penny Bracken. You've probably met her, or at least spoken with her. She's the receptionist. She's usually sitting at the front desk."

"The pretty blond girl?" Susan asked.

"That describes her perfectly," Sally answered. "She's a charming child. Grew up here on the island and has been working at the center after school and during vacations for years. She graduated from high school last year and I had hoped she would go to college, but then Mike came into her life." Sally shrugged. "I miss that young man and I certainly think he was foolish to take off the way he did, but perhaps now I can convince Penny to start taking classes at the local community college. She needs more to occupy her mind."

"You believe he's out of her life then?"

Sally swung to her right to answer that question. "You don't?"

"Well, I heard that Mike Armstrong had been back to visit Penny—"

"Here?" Susan interrupted. "Mike Armstrong has been here?"

"I heard that he has. More than once."

Sally Worth leaned forward. "Who told you?"

"One of the night aides told me that she's seen him here. Waiting out in the parking lot to see Penny is what she said."

"We don't have enough to occupy our time, Mrs. Henshaw, so you might want to take anything we say with more salt than you'll find in our food. Gossip is rampant here—and not necessarily any more accurate than anyplace else, I'm afraid."

"He was here," her companion insisted.

"Perhaps, after we finish our dessert, we could find Penny and ask her ourselves."

"That would be great," Susan said.

"Do we need to wait for dessert?" Kathleen asked.

"It's chocolate cake with ice cream," the woman on Sally's right announced.

And that settled that.

They found Penny Bracken leaning on the admission office's doorjamb, chatting with one of the nurses.

"Penny, we were wondering if you had a minute to answer a few questions," Sally announced although the answer was pretty obvious.

"Of course, Mrs. Worth. I shouldn't leave my desk." Penny glanced down the hallway to her empty chair and blushed. "Well, I need to make sure no one enters without greeting them. So as long as I can see the door, I'm fine," she said.

"That's not a problem. We can chat at your desk," Sally continued.

"Okay." Penny spoke to the nurse and walked back to the entrance, followed by Susan and Kathleen. Sally Worth, moving more slowly, trailed behind.

"Do you need a chair?" Susan asked, surprised by Sally's sudden weakness.

"I would appreciate that." Sally leaned heavily against the wall.

"I'll get one from the living room," Penny said, trotting off down the hallway.

"It just occurred to me that Penny might not want to talk about Mike unless we explain that we're trying to help him," Sally said, perking up as soon as the women were alone.

"I could mention Shannon—," Susan began.

"Don't do that! I'm not sure Shannon and Penny got along all that well. I know Shannon didn't like Mike dating her."

"And if Penny knew that . . . ," Kathleen began.

". . . she wouldn't be inclined to answer our questions," Susan ended the thought. Penny was heading back toward them, a heavy oak chair held close to her chest.

"It might be best if I explain why we want to talk to her," Sally whispered.

Susan and Kathleen merely nodded as Sally draped herself against the wall again.

"Here you are," Penny said, setting the chair down close to Sally.

Sally dropped into its seat with possibly just a bit more enthusiasm than necessary and Penny got a concerned expression on her face. "Are you feeling okay? Should I call a nurse?"

"No, I'm fine. This is nothing. I didn't sleep well last night is all."

"You're sure?"

"I'm sure.

"Now, Penny, I should tell you that these women are here to help Mike Armstrong."

The expression on Penny's face made it perfectly clear

that, whatever she thought of this statement, she still cared for the young man. "Do you know where he is?" she asked Susan and Kathleen.

"No, but we're worried about him," Susan said.

"Oh, so am I! The police have questioned me about him over and over. And when I told him that . . ." Realizing she had just given herself away, she slapped her hand across her mouth.

"So you have seen him," Sally said quietly.

Penny hesitated before deciding to answer. "Yes, but I don't know where he is now."

"When did you see him last?" Sally asked.

"And where?" Susan added.

"Just a few days ago. He was here, but I don't know where he is now and I don't know how to get in touch with him."

"Doesn't he have a cell phone?" Kathleen asked.

"He does. But I don't know the number. I never knew the number. We saw each other here and . . . and I didn't ever think of phoning him."

All three of the older women knew she was lying, but only Sally spoke up. "Sometimes men get nervous when they think their . . . uh, their women can reach them at any time."

Penny nodded eagerly. "That's sort of what Mike said. He said he needed his freedom and that I should trust him and believe in him and . . . and let him be the one to contact me."

"So he refused to give you the number of his cell phone?" Sally came to the point.

"Yes . . . I . . . To tell the truth, I think he may have been seeing someone else while we were"—Penny paused before finishing the sentence—"together."

Sally didn't hold back. "He was two-timing you while he was working here. Is that it?"

"Maybe. Probably. Yes."

"Which is it?" Susan asked gently.

"He was. I knew he was. The other girl . . . woman . . . she gave him the cell phone as a gift. And that's why I didn't have the number." She looked down at the floor. "I suppose I shouldn't have put up with that. Should have told him that I wasn't willing to share him with another woman."

"Do you have any idea who this other woman is?" Susan asked.

"No. Someone rich."

"Why do you think she was rich?" Sally asked.

"He said that's why he liked her, that she could buy him anything he wanted and that he was making so little money here." Penny looked up from the floor. "He wasn't used to this you know. He had grown up with money and he always thought he would have money. Living on the pittance he was paid here was very difficult for him. And I love him so I understand." She jutted her chin up a bit.

Susan, who didn't think that a change in lifestyle justified taking up with any woman just for her money and suspected her companions would agree with her, tried to ask the next question without sounding judgmental. "Do you think he's with her, the other woman, now?"

"Oh, no, I'm sure he's not!"

"How do you know that?" Kathleen spoke up for the first time.

"She's . . . well, she's . . ."

"She's married, isn't she?" Kathleen continued.

"Yes. And Mike isn't the first . . . or the only . . . man she's been involved with! He said she's had lots of lovers, that she only stays with her husband because he's rich."

Susan was beginning to think this woman and Mike probably deserved each other when Sally asked another question.

"Then you do know where he is right now?"

"I know he spent some time on the island. There are lots of empty houses this time of the year and Mike liked to . . . to explore them. I know this sounds bad, but he didn't steal things or damage anything. He just liked to look around. But the police were looking for him and had started checking out some of the empty properties, so he left and I don't know where he is now. Really," she ended sadly.

"When was the last time you heard from him?"

"He was here and then that's the last time. I've been so worried. If something has happened, if he's been arrested or something, don't you think I would have heard?"

"I'm sure you would have," Susan said.

"Probably," Sally said more abruptly. "But you know there are other men in the world."

"Oh, not for me. I'll always love Mike," Penny protested. "We're going to get married!"

"If you hear from him, will you let me know?" Sally asked. "Ask him to talk to me if that would be easier for you. I don't believe he killed anyone, but he does need help. Running away wasn't a very smart thing for him to do, you know."

"I do. I do know that. I'll try to talk him into talking to you. Mike always said you were the best of the . . . of the residents. He likes you."

"I'm flattered."

Susan thought Penny missed the sarcasm in Sally's comment. "I think we'd better be going," she said to Kathleen. "We don't want to miss the ferry."

"And I'd better get back to work," Penny said. "The two o'clock ferry usually brings over some visitors. I need to get this chair back to the living room."

"And I have a date with a jigsaw puzzle," Sally said, standing up.

The four women parted. Penny picked up the chair and headed for the living room. Susan and Kathleen paused to say good-bye to Sally.

"Poor girl. She really loves him," Kathleen said, looking down the hallway.

"She's young. She'll get over it," Sally said.

"Are you surprised at what she said about Mike?" Susan asked.

"Not surprised. Sad, but not surprised. I'm afraid that young man has a tendency to get in over his head. I hope he grows up before he gets in serious trouble."

"This is my phone number." Susan handed a small slip of paper to Sally. "Will you call me if you hear anything else about him? If I'm not at home, you can always leave a message."

"Of course. And will you do the same? Of course, you won't have to leave a message. I'll be here. I'm always here," Sally ended with a rueful smile.

TWENTY-EIGHT

HE WAS SCREWED AND HE KNEW IT. THIS PLACE MADE Perry Island Care Center look like Canyon Ranch. The pay was rotten, the staff incompetent, the management only interested in making a profit. The residents . . . He couldn't help himself; he woke up in the middle of the night worrying about the residents. Not that they were worth it. Poor and old and boring. Maybe they'd be better off dead. He sure hoped he didn't end up like them, all alone in a rotten nursing home.

Susan stopped at Kathleen's house only long enough to say hello to Jerry's parents before heading straight home. Chrissy was walking out the door as she turned into the driveway.

"Have to run, Mom," her daughter called out without slowing down. "I'm meeting Erika and I'm fifteen minutes late!" She climbed into her car and had the key in the ignition before her mother could protest.

"Where are the twins? And Shannon?"

"The babies are in the nursery and Shannon is in the kitchen. Everything's fine." Chrissy waved out of the window of her car and backed down the driveway.

Susan parked her car in the garage and used the connecting door to enter the house. Shannon was, in fact, in the kitchen, skimming through one of Susan's favorite cookbooks as she ate her lunch. The baby monitor sat on the table next to an almost empty soup bowl.

Shannon looked up when Susan entered the room. "Hi. There's still some tomato soup left if you would like some."

"No, thanks. I've already eaten." Susan wasn't sure whether to mention P.I.C.C. or not.

"The babies are both bathed and are sleeping. Chrissy and I didn't know if you had any plans, but we thought I could make dinner tonight. I do a wonderful chicken and chickpea tagine that she and Stephen like. Except for couscous and chicken thighs, you had all the ingredients here. I dashed out earlier and got what I needed. I hope it's okay with you."

Susan smiled. "I don't know a single woman who wouldn't be thrilled to have someone cook dinner for her. Perhaps I could whip up something for dessert."

"Sounds great to me, but Chrissy is trying to lose weight."

"I'll do fruit in brandy. There's Ben & Jerry's vanilla in the freezer. Chrissy can skip the ice cream if she's worried about calories, and the men can have double scoops. You, too," she added glancing over at Shannon's slender figure.

"I've been thin since my first year of nursing school. You burn lots of calories being a nurse." Shannon got up to put her empty bowl in the dishwasher.

"Even in a nursing home?" Susan asked. She removed her jacket, draped it on a chair, opened the refrigerator, and began pulling fruit out and placing it on a nearby counter.

"Especially in a nursing home. When people are in wheelchairs someone else has to do their walking for them. When I was growing up, my mother used to say that taking care of people at the beginning and the end of their lives is some of the hardest work there is—as well as the most rewarding."

"And you've done both," Susan said, examining a quart of blueberries for any signs of mold. "Which do you prefer?"

Shannon seemed to consider the question seriously. "I'm not sure. Old people . . . well, I always planned on working with old people. But taking care of babies is wonderful."

"Rosie and Ethan are your second job with babies?" Susan asked, picking up a pineapple and breathing in its tangy scent.

"Yes. They're so adorable and this job is a dream—nice family, nice home. What more could anyone ask for."

"Cookies?" Susan muttered, opening a cupboard door.

Shannon looked startled. "Cookies?"

"They would go well with the fruit and ice cream and I know the men would love some. I was just wondering if I had some stashed away. But no. When I buy them, I eat them."

"I'm the same way," Shannon admitted. "But we could bake some. Brownies are quick."

"Good idea. I use the basic *Joy of Cooking* recipe and add a half teaspoon of almond extract."

"Yummy. My favorite brownie recipe has a layer of raspberry jam in the chocolate."

"That sounds wonderful."

"It might be interesting to combine recipes. You know, make the brownies with almond extract the way you usually do and then add a layer of raspberry jam. If you have jam."

Susan reached up and opened a cupboard high over her coffeepot. "I always have jam," she explained as about a half dozen jars were revealed. "I buy it, but no one in the family has time for breakfast these days, so it just hangs around." She pulled down a crock of French raspberry jam. "I think this will do."

Shannon nodded and the women got busy.

Susan had forgotten how comforting it was to share the kitchen with another person who enjoys cooking. They discussed ingredients, recipes, family favorites, nothing of any importance to anyone who didn't share their enthusiasm. Susan forgot her quandary over whether to tell Shannon of the morning spent at P.I.C.C. when the twins woke up and decided that nothing would do except for them to join their grandmother and nurse in the kitchen.

When Chrissy walked into the kitchen two hours later, the babies were perched on the table in their baby seats, surrounded by a tray of cooling brownies and a crystal bowl of fruit, sugared, brandied, and sprinkled with fresh mint leaves. (Rosie had grabbed a spray of mint and waved it around for a bit, much to the delight of the women.) An exotic combination of cinnamon, cardamom, cumin, coriander, and vanilla emanated from the oven where the chicken tagine was beginning its long, slow baking. Shannon was playing "this little piggy" with Ethan's toes, much to his sister's delight, and Susan was filling the dishwasher with dirty crockery.

"Mother, I thought you were going to go to that place on Perry Island today. Stephen said you told him you might be back late. That's why I thought Shannon could cook dinner for us all," Chrissy commented, brushing an imaginary lock of hair off her daughter's forehead.

Susan glanced over at Shannon who had stopped wiping strawberry pulp off the cutting board and was staring at her. "Actually I was there. Kathleen and I went over this morning," she admitted.

"Did you find what you wanted? Stephen said you told him that Kathleen was looking for a cottage to rent this summer vacation."

"Yes. She is."

Chrissy continued her questions, oblivious to the change of mood in the room. "Did she find a place?"

"She spoke with the real estate agent there and there are a few possibilities," Susan answered. Shannon had picked up the sponge again and was scrubbing with more energy than necessary to do the job.

"That's interesting. Oh, I think Ethan needs changing. I'll take him upstairs. Maybe you could bring up Rosie when you're done there, Shannon?"

"Of course. I should only be a few minutes."

Susan waited until her daughter's footsteps could no longer be heard on the stairs before turning to Shannon. "I was going to tell you," she began.

"Tell me what? You have every right to go out to Perry without letting me know about it."

"But I'm trying to help," Susan explained. "As long as the person who killed the residents of P.I.C.C. is at large, you and your cousin will be suspects."

"Are you trying to solve those murders? I thought you and your friend were helping the police figure out who killed your neighbor's family." Shannon picked tiny pieces off the edge of the sponge as she spoke.

"Yes, but I'm looking into both Nadine's and Blaine's lives and there is a connection to Perry Island. And, maybe even your cousin."

"Mike! That isn't possible. Mike worked at P.I.C.C., but that's all. He's not related to P.I.C.C."

"Contrary to what you think, he may have been staying in a house that the Baineses own on the island when he 'disappeared.' "

"Really?"

"Yes, really."

Shannon carefully placed the now mutilated sponge down

on the sink and turned to look at Susan. "If I could get Mike to talk to you—"

"That would be incredible! He may be the only person who can answer some of the questions I have."

"If I can get him to talk to you, will you have to tell your friend the police chief about it?"

"Do you think you could convince him to talk to me?"

"You didn't answer my question. Would you have to tell the police chief if you talk to Mike?"

"Ah . . . To tell you the truth, I should, but Brett . . ."

"Is a cop who is looking for a killer and who will probably be thrilled to have someone turn an ex-junkie over to him as a possible suspect."

"That's not true," Susan protested. "Brett isn't like that. He's fair and honest and caring and—"

"And investigating a double murder."

"Yes, but he's not going to arrest the first suspect he finds. If Mike is innocent, he doesn't have anything to worry about," Susan said.

"But he won't arrest Mike if he doesn't know about him," Shannon said reasonably. "And if he's only investigating the murders next door, he won't know anything at all about Mike."

Susan, who knew this wasn't true, didn't say anything immediately. Carefully covering the fruit salad with Saran Wrap, she placed it in the refrigerator and then turned back to Shannon. "I can't keep anything from Brett that might help him discover the identity of a murderer. It would be illegal." She wasn't really sure whether this was true or not. "But there are a lot of things about the situation out at P.I.C.C. that Mike might know—and no one else. Talking to him would be a real help."

Shannon stared down into the sink. "I'm not sure he'll even call me back if I leave a message on his phone."

"But you could try! You could tell him that it's important, that I'm trying to help."

"I know that, but . . . I don't know how to explain. . . ."

Susan waited quietly for Shannon to continue.

"I love my cousin," she began slowly. "I'm an only child and Mike is, too. He's younger than I am and we didn't have a whole lot in common when we were growing up. But when Mike was thirteen, his father died and his mother began to depend on my parents more and more. They spent time together and Mike and I did, too. We became close in some ways, but not in others."

"Sounds a little like my kids. Chrissy's brother is very different than she is, but they've become closer as they got older."

"He has the room she's painting in, right?"

"Yes."

"Where is he now?"

"At school. He's a senior at Cornell."

"Oh, well, Mike didn't have a lot of interest in school. He did a lot of stupid things after his dad died."

"But you said he had cleaned up his act."

"Yes, I think so, but . . ." She shrugged.

"You never really know, right?"

"Right. I worry about him. He's grown up so much, but still. . . . He's young and he's made a lot of mistakes, and he doesn't handle pressure well."

"But if all this could be cleared up. If I can figure out who killed Nadine and Blaine and what was going on at the Perry Island Care Center, it would take the pressure off him."

"That's true."

Susan was glad Shannon agreed rather than asking her just how she was going to perform this particular series of miracles.

TWENTY-NINE

SUSAN HAD NEVER EXPECTED TO FIND HERSELF A GUEST IN A home as prestigious as Woodwinds. She had a lovely home of her own and she had friends with homes even larger and more elegant, but Woodwinds was extraordinary. She loved houses and was thrilled to be here—despite the company.

The dinner Shannon had cooked last night was delicious and, amazingly enough, the entire family had enjoyed it seated in the dining room with the twins nearby happily hanging in their mechanical swings. Chrissy and Stephen had finally finished opening their gifts as Susan and Jed enjoyed an after-dinner brandy while examining the many advances in baby equipment, toys, and clothing since their own children were young. After walking the dogs, everyone went to bed early. Susan had slept well. If the twins cried, she hadn't heard them. When Jed had snored, she had ignored him.

At seven this morning, Donald Baines called and asked her to meet him at his mother's home. He claimed to need her help with something there. Not the most detailed explanation, but it was an invitation she couldn't resist.

So she found herself, a couple hours later, walking up wide and deep marble steps to the forged iron doors of Woodwinds. If there was a bell, it was hidden in the pattern of waves, fish, shells, stars, and moons decorating the entrance. Feeling a bit like a fool, she knocked on the metal, but the resulting sound couldn't possibly alert anyone to her presence.

Despite this, Donald appeared almost immediately, smiling like the most genial host. "Susan, I'm so glad you could make it." He held out his hands and she had no choice but to offer hers in return.

"I'm glad to be here. I've always been curious about this house," she said. "It's practically a legend in this part of Connecticut."

He smiled. "It is, isn't it? Mother and I have always loved it and I know how much you enjoy looking around homes like this one, so . . ." He held the door and waved Susan into the foyer.

Her mouth fell open. It was a mouth-dropping space. A mosaic marble floor abutted marble slab walls that connected to a frescoed dome three stories overhead. The only place she had ever seen that was even slightly similar to this was the Capitol building in Washington, D.C. "I had heard about this but, to tell the truth, it's more amazing than I imagined."

"It's been in *Architectural Digest* twice, *House and Garden* three times, and the *New York Times* six times. As well as *Elle Décor* and a few other publications."

"Wow." She had no idea what else to say.

Her brief reaction seemed to be all that was needed. "Would you like to see the rest of it?"

"Sure, I'd love to." She wondered what was going on. If he had invited her here as a prospective buyer, he was going to be disappointed. Jed had a good job and they were financially comfortable, but there was no way they could afford a home like this one even if they were in the market for a new place, which they weren't. And if Donald had invited her here to talk about the murders, he was certainly going about it in an extraordinarily roundabout manner.

On the other hand, what an opportunity—a private tour of Woodwinds by its new owner.

Donald happily pointed out the frescoes on the dome and the mosaic on the floor. "Shells, fish, and waves fashioned from Italian tiles beneath our feet and stars, planets, and clouds above us painted on the roof by one of the premier artists of the time."

"Incredible," Susan said honestly.

"But once you leave the foyer, the musical themes begin," Donald continued.

Their shoes clattered on the hard surface as Susan followed her host across the foyer and down a few steps into another, larger room.

"This is the living room," he explained, barely slowing down as their feet sank into dense wool carpets laid across walnut parquet floors.

Susan had only a few minutes to note the rich apricot-linen upholstered couches set up beneath massive abstract oil paintings and the fireplace fashioned from what appeared to be real jade over which hung a dozen or so brass and woodwind instruments before they were in another room. This, apparently, was the famous music room. The enormous room dwarfed the twin Steinway grand pianos that stood in the middle of the floor. Many different exotic woods had been fashioned into musical notations and then inlaid in the chestnut floor. A treble clef had been painted all around the room near the ceiling and, Susan assumed, someone sitting at one of the pianos could play the tune permanently on display there by spinning in a circle.

"Do you play?" Susan asked.

Donald looked at her for a moment as though he didn't understand the question.

"The piano." She pointed. "Do you play the piano?"

"Good Lord, no. I've never had time for that sort of thing. I believe Mother planned to hire pianists when she entertained."

Susan decided not to ask if he had similar plans. Donald was walking out of the room. She scurried after him and found herself in a large sunroom shaped like a crescent, floor-to-ceiling windows on all outside walls. The room was furnished with white-painted antique wicker. Cushions were covered with pink-and-white striped cotton. Old, rambling geraniums dotted the room placed on mismatched plant stands and tables. The effect was feminine and charming. Susan would have been happy to bring a favorite book, stretch out on one of the wicker chaise lounges, and spend the afternoon.

But apparently Donald felt that more than two minutes spent in any room was about a minute too much. He spun on his heel and headed back in the direction they had come, turning when they arrived in the foyer and starting off in another direction.

The dining room and kitchen were on this side of the house and Susan did everything but grab her host and wrestle him to the floor in her attempt to spend some time examining these rooms. The formal dining room was large enough to seat sixteen around the chestnut table placed there. The kitchen was equally large and twice as fascinating.

It appeared to have been furnished the year the house was built and, except for updating a few appliances and adding two microwave ovens, it had changed little since that time. Brick-colored sheet linoleum covered the floor and a well-worn butcher block took the place of more modern countertops. Gleaming white-and-black tiles covered the walls. Milk glass lamps hanging from the ceiling provided illumination and curtains fashioned from black-and-white check kettle cloth covered the windows. Susan loved it, but a quick glance was all she was allowed before she was whisked away again for the rest of Donald's tour.

They hurried back to the foyer and up the circular stairway to the bedrooms. It wasn't until they had dashed through the fourth bedroom and connecting bath at record speed that Susan realized Donald was looking for something—or someone. The first hint that it might be the latter came when she realized he was spending as much time looking out the windows as glancing through the rooms. And he seemed unusually interested in showing her the size of the various closets.

"Beautiful pool," Susan commented, walking up to Donald and looking out the window down onto a large patio. "Guitar shaped?"

"Violin shaped," he corrected her. "Now the bedrooms on the other side of the hallway look out over the Sound."

Susan followed him as he dashed across the wide hallway and straight to the window.

The view was magnificent. The Sound was calm and almost navy blue in the morning light. Spring was coming and patches of pale chartreuse green dotted the land to the east. "Long Island?" Susan nodded to the thin strip of green.

"Perry," Donald replied, glancing up at the scene before them before returning his attention to the driveway in front of the house.

"Perry Island? That's Perry Island?"

"That's what I said, isn't it?"

Susan decided there was no reason to point out that his one-word answer might be open to misinterpretation. "I'm surprised to see it. I'm not really familiar with this part of the coast."

Donald was still staring down at the driveway, a puzzled expression on his face.

"How many other bedrooms are there?" Susan asked when he seemed to forget that the tour still had many more rooms to go.

"Two more bedrooms on this floor. And there are lots of rooms for servants and such upstairs."

Susan was curious to discover what "and such" might indicate, but she didn't know how to ask.

"The third floor is closed up. If you're interested, why don't you look at the rest of the bedrooms here? I need to go downstairs and make a call on my cell phone."

"Great." It made no sense that he would get better reception on his phone on a lower level, but, thrilled to finally be allowed to snoop in peace, she decided not to mention this fact. "I'll be down as soon as I look around, okay?"

"Sure. There doesn't seem to be any reason to rush," he said and started down the hallway toward the stairs.

Susan frowned. Donald was acting very strangely. He hadn't even mentioned why he had asked her to meet him at Woodwinds. If he didn't come to the point soon, she decided, opening the door to the next bedroom, she would claim a prior engagement and leave. Just as soon as she looked around here.

She had come to the master bedroom and, she realized looking around, it seemed to be pretty much the only bedroom occupied at present. It was sensational. Susan walked around slowly, examining the inglenook around the fireplace, the huge walk-in closet, the updated bathroom with a Jacuzzi as well as a small sauna. But the most remarkable feature of the corner room was the view. Susan sat down on the large window seat and looked out. She could see the complete western coast of Perry Island now, north to south. In fact, the Perry Island Care Center was directly across from the spot where she was sitting.

And, of course, all the pieces fell in place. For a moment, she remained still, thinking, then she heard footsteps in the hallway and realized that staying where she was could be the stupidest—and last—thing she ever did. The footsteps were coming closer and Susan knew she had to keep Donald from suspecting that she was interested in anything other than Woodwinds.

"This must have been your mother's bedroom," she said, getting up from the seat and moving toward the middle of the room. She had no idea how she was going to get past him as long as he stood between her and the door.

"Yes, Mother loved this room," he said.

"And will you move in here now that your mother is dead? Into this room, I mean?"

"I don't plan to live here, if that's what you're asking me."

"Oh, you're going to put Woodwinds back on the market?" Susan edged an inch or two toward the doorway, but Donald stood his ground.

"No, I'm going to develop it. And I'm going to develop the land you were staring at across the Sound, and I'm going to be owner of the most profitable multiuse development in Connecticut."

"That's nice . . . uh, this has all been interesting, but I have to go," Susan said.

"It's been less than interesting for me, but I can assure you that you are not going to go, so you may as well stop inching toward the door. I may have only begun my new exercise regime, but I'm stronger than most women I've met. You included."

"You . . . You're a murderer," Susan said, trying to hide the panic she felt.

"No, I'm not. That is," he added with a nasty smile, "not yet."

"Not ever." The voice came from the hallway and Donald swung around as Brett Fortesque entered the room, gun drawn.

Susan's first thought was that after all the murders they had investigated together—or perhaps simultaneously was the more accurate word—she had never seen Brett with a gun in his hand. The sight, under these circumstances, brought her considerable relief.

Until she realized Brett wasn't the only armed person nearby. Sophie Kincaid was standing right behind him and she, too, was armed.

"Sophie, where the hell have you been?" Donald said, obviously furious. "I've been waiting for you for damn near half an hour!"

It was no way to talk to a lady, but even Susan was shocked when Sophie pulled the trigger and shot Donald Baines in the chest.

THIRTY

"ONLY THE GOOD DIE YOUNG."

"Donald is neither good nor young, and he is going to live."

"Would you like some more champagne?"

"I would love some more champagne." Susan offered her glass for her husband to fill.

"Mother, we don't drink alcoholic beverages in front of the babies!" Chrissy protested, apparently shocked by her family's behavior.

"Then perhaps you and Shannon should take them up to their nursery, honey, because your mother and I and our guests are planning on opening another bottle," Jed said gently.

"I . . . well, we'll do just that." Chrissy gathered her daughter to her breast as if to protect her from the sight of her grandparents' corruption and left the room.

Shannon picked up Ethan and started to leave, too. "I'd better take this little guy up as well."

"Once the babies are asleep, you could come back down and join us," Susan said.

Shannon smiled. "I might do that. I'm really curious to know what happened today," she added as she left the room.

"As are we," Kathleen spoke up.

Her husband and Jed nodded their agreement.

"Brett knows more than I do and he's going to be here in a bit," Susan said.

"Well, we have lots of champagne," Jed said. "And I'd like to thank Brett for saving your life."

"I'm not sure Sophie would have shot me—"

Jerry held up his hands. "Susan, I know you're going to think I'm dense and I swear that I hang on my wife's every word so I thought I'd been keeping up with your investigation into your neighbor's death, but, damn it, I can't remember anyone named Sophie." He glanced over at the pile of canines sprawled in front of the fireplace. "Unless she's one of Clue's new friends."

"The mastiffs are named Rock and Roll," Kathleen informed her husband.

"And Sophie is Sophie Kincaid. She was one of Donald and Nadine's neighbors before they moved to Hancock. She was also involved with Donald romantically . . . well, sexually. She didn't strike me as a very romantic person to tell you the truth." Susan paused to sip from her flute. "She was involved in his business as well as his personal life."

"She worked for him? What did she do?" Kathleen asked.

"Paid killer?" Jerry suggested.

"I don't think she was paid for anything she did. Not directly at least," Susan added, remembering Sophie's reference to gifts. "And she didn't have an official job, but she looked for properties for Donald to develop and, I suspect, one of the ways she benefited was by ending up with a premier property in those developments."

"So she had something do with Donald's Perry Island project?" Jed asked.

"No, she didn't. And I think that's the reason she came to Woodwinds with a gun. After all, she had killed Blaine Baines.

She probably thought she should benefit from her death at least as much as her son planned to do."

"You've lost me," Kathleen admitted.

"Me too, but we've been married so long that I'm used to it," Jed said.

Jerry just reached for the champagne, refilled his flute, and sat back to listen.

"Donald and his mother—" Susan began.

"You are starting at the beginning, aren't you?" Jed asked.

"Yes. So stop interrupting and I'll explain.

"As I was saying, Donald and his mother were in the same business—real estate. For Blaine it was a case of being in the right place at the right time. She started out selling homes on Perry Island in the winter and tapping into the lucrative rental market in the summer. Not that Perry Island is the Hamptons, but real estate has been an excellent investment for the past three decades and that's how long Blaine's been involved. She's probably made a very, very nice income and certainly has become one of the largest real estate agents in Connecticut. She was smart, hardworking, and ambitious, and her business expanded from Perry Island to some of the most expensive suburbs in the country."

"And Donald followed in her footsteps," Kathleen added.

"As much as she allowed him to," Susan said. "At least that's my guess."

"What do you mean?"

"Well, think about it. Donald always worked in a branch office in an area not quite as prestigious as where his mother's office was located. She kept the best properties, the most expensive properties, the most profitable properties for herself."

"That must have been hard on him," Jerry said.

"Emasculating," his wife suggested.

"Probably both, but Donald is his mother's son and he figured out a way to get some of the big money for himself. He kept selling houses, but he also began developing properties—buying up big chunks of land, subdividing, and then building lots of homes. He did it in the town he lived in before this and he was going to do it again on Perry Island."

"By shutting down the nursing home and building there, right?" Kathleen asked.

"Yes, but Blaine had her own plan for Perry Island," Susan said. "She was going to build matching developments on either side of the Sound, one where P.I.C.C. is located and one where Woodwinds is now. Which is where the problems began that led to all the murders. You see, Donald had his own plans for the same properties."

"So they were in competition," Jed said.

"I don't think they were at the beginning. I think they were in agreement when it came to shutting down P.I.C.C. and developing that plot of land. They probably both bear the guilt for the deaths out there."

"Which of them killed those elderly people?" Jed asked.

"Probably neither of them directly. But I'm sure they caused the deaths to happen. Let's ignore that for a moment because Brett will know more about it and he can tell us when he gets here."

"So go ahead," Jerry said.

"Well, Donald and Blaine didn't have the same vision. Blaine was interested in building large homes."

"Executive homes and estates, her ads call them."

Susan nodded to her husband. "Right. But Donald had done that and was interested in mixed-use developments—hotels and conference centers surrounded by those executive homes and estates."

"And then?"

"And then his mother bought Woodwinds. Donald, of course, saw immediately that its location made it perfect for an extension of their development on Perry Island. And that fact probably made him furious."

"Why?"

"She bought it in her own name and she was going to develop it her way. She had even drawn up plans for the project—plans Donald made sure no one would find after her death."

"How did he manage to do that?" Jerry asked.

"He went to her office after her body was found. He claimed to want to notify her staff in person, but, in fact, he was there to steal her plans. He took them right off her desk in front of all her employees and I was the only person in the room to notice. Donald," Susan concluded, "was not going to let his mother stand in the way of the plans he had made."

"So he killed her," Jerry said, sounding like a man who had just caught on.

"I don't think so actually," Susan answered. "Although he may have helped move her body."

"Then who?" Jed asked.

"Sophie," Kathleen guessed.

Susan nodded. "Yes. At least it makes sense."

"Sophie—this woman he was having an affair with and who helped him find properties to develop—she killed Nadine and his mother and shot Donald?" Jed asked.

"No. I mean yes, she did shoot at Donald and she probably killed his mother, but I think his mother killed Nadine," Susan answered.

"Susan, you tell the story any way you want to. I promise not to interrupt again, but please don't stop now," Jerry said.

"Okay. My guess is that Nadine was killed by Donald's mother. You see, they had moved and Nadine had been forced to pay a bit more attention to Donald and his business and his mother's business than she had before. In fact, she told me as much although I wasn't really listening at the time. Blaine Baines wasn't going to let anyone, not even her daughter-in-law, interfere in a big business deal so—and this is just a guess—she went over to their house to explain this to Nadine and ended up killing her."

"Did Donald know?" Jed asked.

"He must have. He provided his mother with an alibi. At the time I thought it was the other way around, that she was lying to protect him. But Donald was lying to protect his mother. And to protect the many real estate deals that they had together. And I doubt if he really cared about Nadine. Their marriage had become one of convenience. She managed to convey the image of a happy wife to the world, which was important to him, but they certainly were no longer close. In fact, his work made it impossible for them to be together a lot."

Susan paused for a minute. "I didn't like her, but what a terrible way to die."

"You said it yourself—Blaine Baines was ruthless," Kathleen said.

"Yes, she was. But not quite as ruthless as her son turned out to be." A deep male voice came from the doorway and everyone in the room turned to find Brett Fortesque standing there. "I knocked, but apparently no one heard me so I let myself in. I can't say much for your security system." He walked into the room and looked down at the pile of canines lying on the floor. "You must have the three laziest dogs in the world living with you."

"You should see them when they're awake," Susan said.

Jed poured another glass of champagne and passed it to Brett.

"I'm still on duty, but, just this once I'm going to ignore that fact," Brett said, saluting them and then taking a sip.

"Did Sophie Kincaid confess?" Susan asked.

"No. She claims to be completely innocent. And her husband has hired one of the hottest defense attorneys in the country. But it's going to be real hard not to get a conviction. After all, you and I both saw her shoot Donald Baines. And he's not exactly feeling kindly toward her at the moment so I think he'll be happy to make a statement to the police about just who killed his mother."

"She did do it, then," Susan said.

"She did indeed. Donald lost a lot of blood and he's not feeling too well, but he did manage to tell us that much. And he also claimed that Sophie thought it would be a good idea if his mother was found dead in the same place his wife was. So he helped her to move the body from her car into his house."

"Good Lord. He is a cold-blooded bastard," Jerry said.

"And a great real estate agent. He said discovering a body in a house would bring down its resale value and there was no reason to devalue two properties," Brett explained.

"I don't understand. Why did this Sophie kill Blaine Baines?" Jed asked.

"She helped Donald get what he wanted and he wanted the land that Woodwinds is on, but I think it may be more than that. I think Sophie probably isn't as independent a woman as she claims to be. Her husband may have found the best defense team money can buy, but he was never around. Her only child is at boarding school. She needed something in her life. Developing property probably became that something."

"Sounds like Donald was involved with some pretty sleazy women," Jerry said.

"Please, no one is as manipulative and directed as Donald

himself," Susan said. "He's been jerking me around like a puppet ever since Nadine was killed. He said he wanted me to speak at Nadine's memorial service so that I would go to his office. Then he left the messages from his mother on his desk knowing I would see them."

"Why?"

"They weren't real. I'll bet his mother was already dead at that point. He was setting up his own alibi."

"But you used that as an opportunity to check out their old neighbors," Kathleen said. "You wouldn't have even met Sophie Kincaid if he hadn't asked you to do that."

"That's true," Susan said. "And that turned out to be his big mistake."

"That and moving next door to you," Jed said. "Anyone who is planning to be involved in committing a murder should avoid living near Susan Henshaw."

"That's an interesting point," Brett said with a gleam in his eye. "I was going to mention one other thing. Donald told one of my officers that he got a bargain on his house because you were involved in investigating so many murders. Seems living next door to someone who stumbles over dead bodies is not exactly a selling point for a home in a nice neighborhood."

THIRTY-ONE

KATHLEEN AND JERRY WERE DUE HOME FOR DINNER AND left right after Susan promised to call Kathleen first thing in the morning and share all the details of their discussion. Jed got up to let the dogs out into the backyard and Susan and Brett were alone together.

"I'm going to have to talk to the baby nurse," he said.

"Shannon. Her name is Shannon Tapley," Susan said. "But why? You know who killed Nadine and Blaine."

"Three people were murdered out at the Perry Island Care Center. It isn't my case, but I wouldn't be surprised if Donald or his mother hired someone to kill them. And, if that's true, I'm sure Sophie will tell us all about them. In the position she's in, helping the police with unsolved crimes is always a good idea."

"So why bother Shannon?"

"Because she's involved in Perry Island Care Center in more ways than one." He looked at her. "That doesn't surprise you, does it?"

"To tell you the truth, I had wondered—"

"What had you wondered?" Shannon appeared in the doorway. "Perhaps it's time I cleared up all your questions. I think I knew I'd have to eventually when I returned to Connecticut."

"Would you like some champagne? I can get another glass," Susan offered.

"Thanks, but I'll pass. I don't think Ethan and Rosie are settled for the night. And I should run a load or two of laundry before I go to bed as well." She sat down on the couch and crossed her arms across her chest. "I don't know where to start."

"You grew up on Perry Island, didn't you?" Susan asked.

"Yes. Who told you that?"

"No one. But Donald grew up there and he refers to the island as Perry. Not Perry Island, just Perry. And you do, too," Susan explained her reasoning.

"Yes, I grew up there. In fact, I grew up hanging out at P.I.C.C."

"You and your cousin are the heirs to the center, aren't you?" Susan asked.

"Just me. My father inherited it from his parents and he married my mother who was a nurse there. I'm an only child. I grew up knowing that P.I.C.C. would be mine someday. That's probably the reason I'm a nurse." She smiled. "My father was a doctor, but he always said that it was the nurses who were the real workers in the health care system. I never even considered going to med school. I wanted to take care of people and I knew nursing was the field for me."

"But Mike?"

"Mike is my mother's sister's son. There's no connection to P.I.C.C."

"Except that you could help get him a job there," Susan suggested.

Shannon sighed. "That's true. But the patients come first. I was sure—well, as sure as I could be—that Mike had cleaned up his act when I helped him get hired there. And P.I.C.C. was in many ways the perfect place for him to work.

Mike is a people person and he's not put off by old people. He was a real asset to the center."

"Then why didn't he stay around?" Susan asked since Brett seemed to be letting her ask all the questions.

"Death scared him. Well, it scares us all, but Mike was spooked when people started dying and then . . ." She glanced over at Brett.

"You can tell Brett about Mike's fear that he caused one of the deaths," Susan said. "He'll find out eventually and Brett is capable of understanding the difference between a mistake and murder."

"Mike was asked by Mrs. Hershman to leave the door to the roof open for her. And then she fell—or was pushed— off the roof, and he panicked and took off. But he liked Mrs. Hershman. He would never have killed her."

Brett nodded slowly. "I don't know all the details of the P.I.C.C. investigation, but now that we have connected Donald and his mother with a desire to close down P.I.C.C., I know the police will be looking in some other directions."

"You think Mike should talk to the police in charge of the case?" Shannon asked.

"And he should talk to Brett," Susan suggested.

"I have nothing to do with what happened on Perry Island," Brett said.

"But I think Donald manipulated Mike the same way he manipulated everyone else. He suggested that Mike get out of P.I.C.C. as fast as possible—and that focused attention on Mike that might better have been placed on other suspects," Susan said.

"That may be true," Shannon agreed slowly. "And . . . well, Mike will probably tell you this himself . . ."

"He was involved with Sophie Kincaid, too, wasn't he?" Brett suggested.

"You're kidding! Sophie Kincaid is the older woman that what's her name—the receptionist—told Kathleen and me about?"

"I think that's the name of the woman," Shannon said. "I told Mike he was being used, but he has this adolescent male ego. He thought she liked him because he was 'hot.' "

"He's not the first male who let his ego blind him to the truth," Susan pointed out. "And many are a whole lot older than your cousin."

"I guess."

Susan changed the subject. "P.I.C.C. is a wonderful place, but its open-door policy for visitors means that pretty much anyone can get in and see—or harm—the residents."

Shannon frowned and was silent for a moment. "It's important—vital—that relatives and friends of the residents have twenty-four hour access to them. And because we're located on an island where there's very little crime, we never considered it important to keep track of the comings and goings of visitors. There isn't even a receptionist on duty at night. That," she added firmly, "will have to change."

Brett nodded. "It's sad, but it's better not to trust everyone than to end up with a tragedy."

"That's true," Shannon agreed.

Susan had a horrible thought. "Oh, no! You're going to leave Chrissy and the babies, aren't you?"

Shannon smiled. "I keep telling your daughter that I'm hanging around until Ethan and Rosie go to college," she answered. "But I suspect Chrissy and her husband won't need me that long. After this job, I'll go back to P.I.C.C., but not until this job is over. Working with babies has been a lovely change. And I've been thinking that it might be nice to start a day care center on Perry, one that's connected to P.I.C.C. Our residents would love to be around babies and small children on a regular basis, and I'll bet there are lots of parents on Perry who would be thrilled to have some professional care for their children."

"Sounds like a good idea," Susan agreed.

The back door opened and there was a commotion as the dogs dashed through the kitchen and into the hallway. Rock and Roll bounded up to the second floor and Susan shuddered as the newel post at the bottom of the stairway shook. Clue, more sedate than the younger dogs, walked slowly into the living room, over to Shannon, and rested her big golden head on the nurse's lap. Shannon scratched the dog and frowned. "I was afraid to take this job. I didn't want to come back to Connecticut. Those last few months at P.I.C.C. were horrible. My parents would have been devastated by the deaths there. I just wanted to get away and forget it all."

"So why did you take the job?" Susan asked. "Didn't you know Chrissy and Stephen might end up living here?"

"Yes. But, to tell you the truth, I knew Mike was still in the area and I wanted to help him if I could and . . . well, Stephen's parents told me about you."

"And you thought I might help your cousin," Susan guessed.

Shannon looked over at Brett then at Susan and then back down to the dog. "Stephen's mother said you were friends with the police in Hancock, and I was hoping you might influence them to . . . well, to overlook Mike's involvement out at P.I.C.C."

"It sounds to me as though your cousin doesn't need that type of interference," Brett said.

Shannon looked up and smiled at him. "I don't think so either. I . . . oh, I'd better get up to the nursery," she said as the twins' nighttime duet began.

"Call me if you need my help," Susan said.

"And I'd better get going. Mr. Kincaid's lawyer is probably still making a fuss, and I want to check in with the officer I left with Donald Baines at the hospital, and Erika has left a half dozen messages on my phone. She says she has fabulous news for me."

"Maybe she's pregnant again," Susan said, standing up to see her guest to the door.

Brett glanced up toward the stairway where the twins' wails had become even louder. "I doubt it. I think one baby at a time is all we can deal with."

"Maybe," Susan agreed, opening the door for him. "Unless, of course, they're both as wonderful as my amazing grandchildren. Or . . ." She glanced over at Shannon. "Or you're lucky enough to find the perfect baby nurse."

THIRTY-TWO

It was too much to ask that Ethan and Rosie would allow their grandparents to sleep through the night two days in a row. At five-thirty the next morning, Susan and Jed were sitting at their kitchen table waiting for the first drop of coffee to fall through the filter. Clue was still upstairs, probably sprawled on her back in the middle of their bed. The mastiffs had been put in the backyard a few hours earlier. Chrissy and Stephen had last been seen at four AM trudging a well-worn path between their bedroom and the nursery, yawning and exhausted. The sound of the washer being turned on in the basement proved that Shannon was busy down there.

No one expected the phone to ring.

"Who the hell would be calling at this hour?" Jed asked, reaching for the phone. "Susan, if this call has anything at all to do with another murder, I want you to promise me that you'll ignore it."

"Don't let Chrissy hear you talking like that in the same house as your grandchildren," Susan warned, moving over to the coffeepot and pouring out her first cup of the day as Jed answered the phone.

"Hi . . . Hey, I thought you were walking around England. . . . Last night? Really? Well, it's been a little busy around here. . . . They're wonderful and growing right before our eyes. When are you coming to see them? Anytime. Oh, of course . . . but I think I'd better let Susan explain . . ." Jed passed the phone to his wife. "Your mother."

"Hi, Mom," Susan began, prepared to extol the many virtues of her grandchildren for as long as her mother wanted. But she was rudely interrupted by a great-grandmother who had more on her mind than the future generation. Susan listened for a few minutes and then began her explanation. "I know you're not . . . I have no intention . . . Of course, I don't think . . . Never, I promise you . . . Never. You don't have to worry about that . . . I . . . Mom? . . . Mom? . . . Mom?" She pressed the OFF button and handed the phone to her husband. "She hung up on me. I can't believe it. She hung up on me!"

"It's probably a little disturbing to come home after a long vacation and find letters in your mail saying that your daughter is trying to have you admitted to a nursing home," Jed suggested.

"I didn't realize P.I.C.C. would contact her," Susan said. "They're up awfully early."

"Hon, it's almost noon in London. They're probably a little jet-lagged as well as acclimated to living in another time zone. Your mom will calm down as soon as she's seen her great-grandchildren."

"I forgot to ask her when they're coming to visit."

"Today. They'll be here around dinnertime. At least that's what I think she said," he added, yawning. "Lord, company tonight. Do you think we'll have time for a nap this afternoon?"

"A nap? Jed, my parents are coming. I have to clean and cook and . . ." Her list was interrupted as she imitated her husband's action, yawning for so long that her eyes began to water.

"They're coming to see Ethan and Rosie, not to check

under the bed for dust or make sure you're cooking gourmet meals these days."

"You're right. And we'll go out to dinner. I wonder if the small party room at the inn is free. That way the twins won't bother anyone else. Let's see. How many of us are there?"

"Eight."

"We could invite Jerry and Kathleen and their kids," Susan said.

"Twelve."

"And Brett and Erika and Zoe. Jed, isn't it wonderful that they're buying a new house and letting Chrissy and Stephen rent their place for a year?"

"Fifteen," Jed said, still counting. "And it is wonderful. But, remember, Brett and Erika said their place was too small for them, so I doubt that a four-person family—with two humongous dogs—is going to be happy there for long."

"But it gives me . . . us . . . them time to find something bigger in the area," Susan said happily. "How many is that?"

"Fifteen," he repeated. "Actually, sixteen. I assume you're going to include Shannon?"

"Of course. She's going to see Mike, but I'm sure she'll be back for dinner."

"Is this the Mike that I've heard so much about in the past twenty-four hours?"

"Yes, she's meeting him for breakfast. He called last night and agreed to speak to Brett. Of course, if he had talked to the police as soon as the deaths out at P.I.C.C. were discovered to be murder, everything would have been much easier."

"Why do you say that?" Jed said, looking a bit more awake now that he'd had some coffee.

"Mike leaving P.I.C.C. confused everything. The police assumed he was involved in the murders and didn't investigate such things as who would benefit if multiple deaths caused P.I.C.C. to shut down. Of course, Donald knew that would happen when he encouraged Mike to take off. What Donald didn't know is that Mike was involved with a young woman who works there and wasn't about to go very far. And he probably didn't know that Mike was having an affair with Sophie Kincaid as well."

"Sounds like a very busy young man."

"You can say that again. But he told Shannon he'd been working in a nursing home upstate—apparently not a very good one either—and he was thinking of returning to Perry Island, if they would have him."

"And will they?"

"I don't know, but Shannon is part owner of the place. If she wants Mike to have another chance, I suspect he'll get it . . . What is that?"

"Sounds like Clue barking. What would get her so excited at this time of the morning?" Jed stood up and looked out the kitchen window as, simultaneously, the back door opened and their son appeared, with at least a week's growth of beard on his face, his hair about three inches longer than the last time his parents had seen him, and a bulging duffle bag slung over his shoulder. Clue, pushing into the room from the opposite direction, had no difficulty recognizing the love of her life. She flung all ninety pounds of her furry self into Chad's arms, knocking him to the floor where the two of them wrestled happily.

Susan looked over at her husband and smiled. "How many is that?"

"Seventeen. Or maybe eighteen," he said, as a young woman appeared in the doorway behind their son. Nervously slipping a lock of her silky long brown hair behind one ear, she licked her pale lips and smiled apprehensively. "Hi."

"Oh, shit . . . sorry . . . Mom. Dad. This is Jennifer. She's . . . we're . . . well, I thought . . . I wanted you to meet her."

"We're always happy to meet friends of Chad's," Jed said, pulling his robe more tightly across his chest before getting up to shake hands.

"Although they don't always arrive in the middle of the night," Susan said, hoping her smile looked warm rather than surprised. "Would you like some coffee? Or maybe a glass of orange juice?"

"I'm fine, thank you," Jennifer answered shyly, looking down at Chad and Clue.

"Look," Chad began, getting up off the floor. "We've been camping for the past two weeks and we're filthy and everything we own is dirty. Do you think we could just shower and do some laundry before we worry about breakfast?"

"The showers will be fine, but I think Shannon is using the washing machine," his mother answered, still trying to adjust to the fact that her son had finally brought home a girl to meet them.

"Who's Shannon?"

"Chrissy's baby nurse," his mother explained.

"Please excuse my mother's syntax—I think she's trying to tell us that this unknown person named Shannon is the baby nurse of my nephew and niece, Ethan and Rosie, my sister Chrissy's twins," Chad explained to Jennifer.

"I know exactly what your mother meant, Chad. And we're both dying to meet the twins," Jennifer said, looking at Susan.

"They are remarkable babies and we'll be happy to show them to you as soon as they wake up," Jed said.

"Which is now," Susan added as a familiar wail wafted down the stairway, through the hall, and into the kitchen.

"Listen to the lungs on those guys," Chad said.

"Do you think we could go see them?" Jennifer asked. "I love babies."

"Go on up," Susan said.

"Your mother turned the guest room into a nursery," Jed explained.

"And . . . ," Susan began, but Chad and Jennifer, closely followed by Clue, had already started up the stairs. She turned to her husband. "He brought a girl home."

"Don't make too much of this."

"But he's never brought a girl home."

"Susan—"

"And she loves babies."

"Susan—"

"Do you think they'll get married? Have children? Bring their kids here?"

"Susan—"

"Jed," his wife interrupted him with his name. "Do you think we'll ever be alone in this house again?"

And her husband reached over, put his arm around her shoulder and pulled her close. "I don't know about you, but I'm banking on it."